CAMBRIDGE DAYS

CAMBRIDGE DAYS

Teodros Kiros

THE RED SEA PRESS

TRENTON | LONDON | NEW DELHI | CAPE TOWN | NAIROBI | ADDIS ABABA | ASMARA | IBADAN

THE RED SEA PRESS
541 West Ingham Avenue | Suite B
Trenton, New Jersey 08638

Book design: Dawid Kahts
Cover design: Ashraful Haque

Cataloging-in-Publication Data may be obtained from the Library of Congress.

ISBNs: 9781569025482 HB
       9781569025499 PB

DEDICATION:

I dedicate this novel to my wife Metshet Gebremedhin and
Caleb Teodros, Rowan Teodros, Solonia Teodros and Mahlet Desta,
May the Transcendent bless them all.

ACKNOWLEDGEMENT

My greatest thanks goes to the quiet and intelligent publisher of Africa World Press, Mr. Kassahun Checole, who has published five of my books so far, and the Transcendent willing, more to come.

Thanks also to Janet Kenney, my copy editor, and John Short my brilliant student who proofread the work, amidst his busy schedule.

Special thanks to Dr. Ghelawdewos Araia, Julie Rold and Chika Unigwe, who read and endorsed the novel.

I thank Girma Demeke for his editorial assistance.

I am totally responsible for all the flaws in this novel, eight years in the making, and hardly perfect.

I am not sure who suggested we go to the beach so late in the afternoon. The earth is on fire. Some would say the blazing tropical sun is in full bloom. I say everything feels and looks hot. It is supposed to be winter, when the rain comes and cools everything. There are hundreds of bodies at the beach today. I take up my spot on the faded wooden chair near the water. The brilliant turquoise of the Indian Ocean dances at my toes. Neil has folded his body onto a towel. Despite the gathering clouds he is ready to begin his afternoon baking ritual. He will face the sun from all directions. First he will confront it head on, then he will turn to the left and then to the right; he will lay on his side, his back, his stomach and then he will move back up to a sitting position and face the glare without blinking his eyes. He never seems satisfied after he is cooked through. I tell him he has grown black enough. He has been in Tanzania with me now for one year and I fear he will grow cancer if he does not take greater care. He is too busy arranging all his belongings to note this warning today.

Neil has placed everything he might need over the next hours within an arm's reach of any position he may take. The most important of these items today is Heidi's book, *The Invisible Black Woman*. He places this open near his shoulder. When Neil sun-bakes the backs of his arms from his stomach, he will turn his neck, rest his cheek on one page of the open book and read the other sideways. I think he has even perfected a way to turn the page without using his arms. Neil has also placed his tepid, nearly empty cool drink bottle near the top of the towel, his unopened sunscreen bottle at the foot and a pair of sunglasses on his knees. He will not use any of these things in the next hours.

'You are growing black,' I say to him after he had moved to his stomach. He seems not to hear me.

Neil's concentration is so focused on reading *The Invisible Black Woman* book because he is making up for lost time. The book is the one thing spanning the twenty years that Heidi and Neil spent apart. She will be flying into Dar Es Salaam in just three weeks and then returning here with Neil. I am not sure that they will marry this time around, but I wonder. She is fifty now and he is even older. Perhaps Neil's spurned proposal nearly twenty years ago in our old home in Cambridge turned him off to marriage, or maybe, they are too old to worry about either. I clear my throat and, when he looks up at me, I see that his eyes are glittery.

'The book may be true but so is this,' I say, sunscreen in my hand, 'you are becoming baked nicely.' His eyes gleam. 'But love will not stop you from burning. The sun does not get weaker at this time of day, Neil. It becomes stronger.'

I pass him the sunscreen. He fingers the tube of 50+ UVB sun protection as though he took it from me by mistake. Neil seems to liken my gesture to being handed a tube of toothpaste right before eating a long awaited meal. He sets the tube down politely beside him and goes back to his book.

I try to look at his skin disapprovingly but Neil is so proud. He thrusts out one olive tanned arm without looking up as though to prove this point and then he proceeds to admire its slowly changing hue. He surveys me approvingly. My color is already a deep red-brick .

'I use protection too,' I say, doffing my straw hat and tapping my round sunglasses down to show him the sockets of my eyes, clear and unlined by the veiny red streaks that crisscross his. I pull the sunglasses back up and adjust my hat. Neil just grins toothily at me so I settle back into my chair, if even I know it is momentarily . The cloud heads are gathered and looking fiercer by the second. Today there will be a big storm. Neil eases himself onto his back, pretending not to wince at the way his terry cloth towel rubs at his chafed skin. Round number two, I think to myself. The sun does feel good, but it is unbearably hot and the air is dense as the storm approaches. A few more minutes of time before we will have to get up. I let the water soothe my feet and savor the moment. I feel supremely content. For once, I do not remember I am an ex-professor from Cambridge, that my home country of Tanzania is plagued by problems or that Neil and I must begin to plan the gala event of the season, the second year anniversary of the school we opened. In this moment, I am only aware that we live, ready. We are two handsomely aging men ready to live for as long as we are given time.

**

Neil has fallen asleep and the storm is upon us. Swollen waves crash to the shore in a caravan of lines escorted by thundershowers threatening from what could be merely moments. The sky darkens and the gentle sea breeze begins to whip itself into foam. The bubbles turn to a wild froth that spray us both and makes Neil jolt upright and grope for his eyes. 'What have I been missing?' he demands as he gently brushes off the book he overturned into the sand. White sand sprays out over his knees. He sits up cross-legged, a hand on each kneecap, every sinew in his body alert, waiting.

While everyone else around us begins moving in haste, Neil and I gather speed more slowly. We are weighted down by the moist scent and heaving pregnant clouds, the heady scent of wet mangroves fills our noses. We can smell where the storm has been before it arrives at us. The mist coats us first, and then the thunder rolls out wide to open the way for the rain. We hear it pound at the sand before we realize the storm is right on top of us.

'Let's go, Nyerere!' Neil yelps. He is smiling, excited by the commotion. A young couple dash past, blankets thrown around their shoulders, cool drinks clinking in the cooler bag, shiny pink and silver crisp wrappers fluttering behind them like celestial butterflies. We are captured by the frenzy and follow suit to pack our meager things and move out toward some shelter. Haphazardly we run, laughing like children again and tripping ourselves on the sand, covering space quickly. We move toward the first ledge of trees marking the slow ascent into what the tourists call the foothills of the Eastern Arc Coastal Mountain Range. We finally arrive at the trees just as the rain releases. We huddle, separately but together, and we slant our eyes. The young palm fronds dip to catch the rain and, unable to hold it all at once, flatten themselves into balding, peeling stumps.

3

The cashew trees and old baobabs slow the rain and create pockets of silence. But our own bodies pulse. Rain must feel marvelous, I think, entranced by the way it glistens, graceful in its suspension between sky and earth.

I step out in to the open and Neil pushes himself forward with his nose out first, he follows my back, craving the rain. It is too perfectly cool and fresh to worry about being rational. We are greedy for the water, aching for it to enter our pores, our mouths, even our noses, to free us even (albeit) briefly from the heat. What can we do but surrender ourselves? Neil and I give over our bodies, and in return, the rain pours in. We cannot get enough and long for it to bombard us even harder. It does not last nearly long enough. After a brief respite, the sun reclaims its domain and sets our faces aflame again. We find ourselves blinking into the glare, strangers in an involuntary blindness. When my eyes refocus, I do not see Neil anywhere.

'Found it!' I hear from down on the beach and somewhere to my right where the coastal grove has thinned out into a near a small enclave of round rock, sedge and sand.

I peer through shaded hands, searching for Neil. There are not many people on the beach now.

'Over here, Nyerere! I've found us a great spot!' It is the voice again, but I cannot see the (its) owner. I move toward the rocks and, as I near, a long red arm and high-flying purple towel flap into the air. It is Neil. I find myself slipping up and then down again on the rocks as I try to mount them, but they are still slick with vanishing rain. At the top I look down to see Neil in the sand arranging his towel. I feel tall and free, though I know I could jump down easily if I tried.

'Great spot, isn't it?' he says cheerfully, waving up at me. The rocks cast a shadow over him and his burnt skin looks a slightly darker shade of purple than his towel.

'Find a seat, Nyerere! You don't even need a chair the way the rocks are shaped!' He smooths the edges of his towel in the motionless air and then begins to fold himself down again into the sand.

'I am going to stay down here in the shadow if you do not mind, he calls up, 'I think the blisters might be coming back.'

I peer at his shoulders. Translucent little volcanoes filled with clear liquid have burst up under the cracked and peeling shell of his skin. Neil has so many mottled layers of skin he will never become black; I chuckle to myself.

'OK. I will see you a bit later then,' I say and turn back toward the ocean.

The rock I stand atop is smooth and curved out like a belly on one side and bends in like an hourglass on the other. It is bone colored. I see an indented notch on the side of one of the rocks across from me; it looks as though it could mirror the curvature of my back and suddenly a burbling fatigue overtakes me. But a roving desire mounts in my blood as I maneuver myself into the chair of rock. I am in a mood for love. My hands itch, my feet sweat. I close my eyes in peace, thinking I am completely out of sight of anyone on the beach. Then, I sense a movement on the other side of the rocks. I hear Neil.

'Just look at you, sassy beauty!' I hear followed by a throaty whistle. 'What a fine piece you are!'

I can hear the appreciation, can almost hear Neil's lips smacking. So he is in a mood for love, too. Maybe Heidi's picture is on the back of the book, I think to myself, stifling a smile, settling deeper into the sand. It is warm, the rock cool. I long for sleep. But then I see the *hoopoe*. My breath catches and even if I had tried, I cannot move. She (It) appears from behind the rocks on short legs, her ruddy pink chest held high, her head cocked to one side. She walks like a princess, feeling good, basking in praise. I realize she is what Neil had been whistling at. The crest on her head fans up then out into a plume, her long black and white tail swishes right, then left, bobbing as she walks past me with gem eyes. Her beak is long and thin, like a hooked needle. I have heard about the *hoopo*e. She appears in much folklore, from Egypt to India but I did not know she came south to Tanzania. I shake my head at the wonder of my country and then, suddenly too worn out to do anything else, I dare to sleep.

But sleep does not come so easily. Adowa appears in front of me radiating that rare smile. I think it is a smile that can penetrate a soul and glue a person to the power of beauty. My hands reach out but her smile begins to fade the more I reach until finally, she relieves me by taking my elbow and steering me toward the door of her apartment. Through the doorway we go, up the short stairs, through the kitchen and towards the big burnt oak table. Many papers are spread out on its surface and at first I think it is a chapter of her dissertation. I know she is at the tail end of finishing her last brilliant chapter on the "African Biological Self." She will soon begin the laborious process of editing. She has less than two months until her dissertation defense in July. But when Adowa pulls out her chair to sit, I realize the papers have nothing to do with her dissertation.

There are exactly six different items placed in two perfectly aligned rows. On the top row are three sets of paper. The first two look to be letters, the last is a deck of blank sheets. Underneath are three envelopes. One has a US postmark. May 2008. Another has a red and white airmail border and is marked from Ghana. That postmark reads April 2008. My eyes wander to the final items, two blank envelopes with stamps at the corners, one with a small airmail label and the other without. I am curious and so I lean closer but Adowa blocks my vision as she also leans down in an uncharacteristic bent. She picks up an empty sheet of paper with one hand and reaches toward the first letter with her other. I notice her forehead is wrinkled, her hand shaking. My own hand lurches out to her and finds itself in her hair, cut short to fit her finely built forehead. It is a forehead built for thinking, for looking at things deeply. I move my hands to her strong shoulders and they are hard, reminding me of the thick braided ropes the coastal fishermen pull taut to bring in their boats. Something is gravely wrong. I wave off a fleeting guilt that warns I am invading a too private moment. Adowa has a strength of character that does not belie doubt to anyone, not even to me. As I begin to rub her scalp, her temples, I ask her what is wrong and pull at her ears, easing the lobes down from the cartilage. She has never pierced them like most women I know, carrying her beauty instead in the grace of her walk, the length of her posture. The black gleam of her skin, the seriousness of her disposition, her insistence. Adowa ignites fires in my being I cannot control and nor do I try I rub harder into her shoulders.

Adowa takes no note of me; she picks up her pen and begins writing. I long to hear her words as my fingers work to soften her muscles. Her words are always chosen slowly and carefully, with the precision of a scientist and the controlled passion of a writer. 'They are delicious, always,' our friend Elias says, 'as a ripe pear.' Adowa writes so determinedly. I realize she is not aware of me at all. I withdraw my hands from her and try to contain my curiosity. But it insists like a small child wanting milk. I crane to see what Adowa spells, but the words blur the closer I move. Unable to resist, I push my head through the triangle between her torso and her arm and then I rest my head at her breast so that I am nearly eye level with her pen. I am surprised to find that the characters are messy and unlike her perfect script. Still, I think I can see my name in the text. Maybe she is writing to me. I open my hands to see my fingers and then I count them, one by one, until I reach fourteen. That is the number of days since I have last spoken to her.

'It is too long,' I say aloud to her.

Adowa has finished the letter and begins to fold it.

'But I understand…'

Her back straightens as she picks up the first envelope, places the letter inside.

'You must be so very busy now…'

Adowa begins to write her return address in the left corner of the envelope.

'…but you are almost finished. The dissertation is nearly complete.' I strain to sound comforting, but my voice seems to bounce off the table and back into my mouth.

'I will wait for as long as it takes to finish…Adowa.' She sneezes, pauses, and then she moves her hand to the center of the envelope.

'Finish what you must there in America,' I say and grasp her hand as she writes, moving with the script as the letters appear, 'and then come home, to Tanzania.' We had agreed that she would arrive at the end of her summer, the beginning of our spring here.

I look down to what we have written and coil back in surprise.

Rosa. At 183 Morningside Road.

Rosa. The name rings bells and brings to me a smell. Sweet, then sour, but I cannot place a face.

183 Morningside Road, Somerville. Not in Cambridge. Rather, in Somerville, the town adjacent to it. An industrial town I rarely go

to. Yet, the address is familiar. Why?

Finished, Adowa sets the envelope aside and looks out her open window. The rustle of maple leaves and the cool breeze beckons me to follow Adowa's gaze. We stare out the window together. Waiting. The breeze tempts me, seducing me with the same sweet and sour smell until I agree to let it take me where it wants. I drift outside.

As I walk toward Harvard Square, I pass streets I know. The small shops shine fuzzy lights onto the narrow streets, past the little brick houses on Brattle Street, through the crowded sidewalks. A group of street musicians jam on a corner. Cambridge has an intoxicating beauty that can dazzle any passer-by. The breeze releases me for just a moment to enjoy the scene. It nudges me on, not too long after, and I find myself at a bus stop. I get on a bus that indicates it passes Morningside and we head north. To the other side of Cambridge then Somerville. The journey seems to take only seconds, and then I am at Morningside Road walking toward Rosa's yellow door at the end of the street. Before I have even walked through number 183 I can taste the sweet and sour on my tongue. I soon find myself in the kitchen, at a table. There is the pitcher, the glasses. There is the pink rose petals floating on the surface of the light green liquid. I cannot wait for the cool limeade, and so I help myself. It trickles down my throat as I listen. There is the light tinkle of a wind chime hung somewhere unseen. There is the rustle of maple leaves again. Then, there is Rosa.

She stands at the cupboard wearing a red and white flowered apron. Her hair is gathered up near the crown of her head. She has cocoa eyes that still glint with gold slivers. A string of small pearls adorns a young neck. Hands cross over a soft breastbone. I marvel for a moment at her honey colored hands. They lived through the death of two husbands, countless cats, and most recently, the brutal chopping of the ancient weeping willow tree in her front yard. The city said it was a nuisance.

Rosa. The only woman who can make such divine limeade. I take another swill from my glass and a rose petal gets caught on my teeth. As I peel it away I wonder again, how did she manage to find roses in the middle of winter? Of course her kitchen is filled with plants. They swing from baskets, from sills, from corners. Plants

8

everywhere, but I do not see any roses. Maybe because it is winter, I think, suddenly, looking to the frost on the open window pane. I look to the calendar on the wall. It is open to the year 2005, December. I am confused, but only for a moment. Elias walks into the kitchen and I have to laugh out loud. Somehow, I have fallen asleep at Adowa's house and found myself in a memory. It is December 2005. The year I decided to quit teaching and move home to Tanzania. The month after I met Adowa. The first and only time I ever saw Rosa. The last chance I had to see Elias before moving to Tanzania in May of the New Year. I do not have time to muse on this point because Elias is talking loudly, trying to get my attention. He is trying to explain to me about Rosa. He shivers at the open window.

'It is not only that she has a green thumb in winter, but that the ring she wears on it is magic.' I notice that Rosa does have a ring on her thumb, and on each finger. Rosa talks to her plants as though they are grown up adults and she cleans their leaves as though they are children's limbs.

'It helps with my arthritis,' she tells us, massaging her knuckles and sighing over the fact that she will soon be seventy. We settle at the table together.

'I do not feel old,' she says, filling our glasses for the third time, 'every part and every aging organ has its own aesthetic.'

We can appreciate this truth as we look at her. Rosa is stunning.

'Each organ has its own calling of beauty, its own markers, and its own destiny. Each have their own rules of beauty, of uniqueness,' she continues, her cheeks warming to a deep rose blush, 'but there are other markers of beauty, just as important.'

'It is true,' Elias says thoughtfully over his limeade, 'the beautiful person is the person with a good character. Her beauty is revealed in the morality of her actions.'

Rosa helps herself to the empty glass on the table and fills it just halfway with limeade. 'Here, there is more for you, Nyerere,' she says, pushing the pitcher toward me. 'Do not be embarrassed,' she adds, seeing the way I hold back. It would be my fourth glass.

'Suit yourself,' she says, turning back toward Elias, 'there is more in the refrigerator.'

Rosa clasps the glass in front of her and I pour myself a fourth glass. The pitcher is nearly empty and the rose petals lump together in the leftover liquid.

'Yes, for ancient African thinkers a person is loved for her ageless moral action,' Rosa continues, 'these outlive her organs. Her biological self. African civilizations had an extraordinary understanding of aging.' She looks at her ringed fingers, blue veined but energetic. 'They understood aging as a source of beauty, beauty as a biological and ethical form of humanity.'

She looks pointedly at each of us in turn. I feel suddenly like a teenage boy being reminded about the responsibility of manhood.

'For ancient African cultures, biological beauty and ethical beauty were inseparable.'

'We have to recover those insights of wisdom, do you think?' asks Elias, 'I mean, the wisdom of beauty.'

'Absolutely. We need to learn its properties.' Rosa nods to Elias, and leans back to set the timer on the oven to warm the casserole for dinner.

'If we can learn to adapt to the ongoing laws of beauty, we can begin to accept that beauty does not stand still. Beauty, as a biological form, is always evolving.'

Her words sound deceptively simple and in them, I recognize currents of Adowa's project on the "African Biological Self." I run over her relation to each of us in my mind. I know Adowa has been friends with Elias for a long time, and Rosa is Elias's mother. Adowa has known me for just a short time. In fact, we have seen each other only twice. Yet all of us at the table, I realize, are so enamored with her ideas that we speak about them as if they are our own.

'The moral ethical self hides the aging biological self,' I blurt out, interrupting them. My hands fly toward my glass. I had not meant to be so abrupt. Rosa is caught off guard for a moment and looks quizzically to Elias. I continue.

'But moral actions live forever, long after the biological self dies. Just like physical objects outlive us, the moral self lives forever. It leaves traces and lives again in other people.' I pause. 'Or, at least, that is how I understand this matter.'

My words sound formal, as though I am in front of a classroom again. My friend Makau often tells me it is OK to speak casually when I am not in front of the classroom and though I am convinced he always knows what is my most current philosophizing, he often yawns. He does not have patience for academic script and so cannot appreciate how difficult it is to speak casually. Especially after so many years of working to master the nuances of speaking formally.

'He knows Adowa, too,' Elias interjects to his mother in order to explain how I caught on so quickly to their conversation. Rosa puts her front fingers into a steeple and looks hard at me. With the glint growing large in her eyes she asks, 'And what are the attributes of the moral self, Nyerere?' I do not skip a beat. 'Decency, kindness, love are precisely the attributes of the moral self. To strive for these is the challenge to all of us.' I quote Adowa word for word.

The tiniest hint of a frown appears in between her brows, but then the timer on the oven interrupts us and Rosa jumps up, her motions directed now in full toward the dish she pulls steaming from the heat. Throughout our meal, I watch Elias and his mother, pleasantly amused by their mutual adoration of each other. They have reverence for each other's words. They seem to share a mind and link ideas together in a string. As they talk about things I do not know, my mind wanders to tomorrow's class. I need to prepare for my lecture. I realize I am tired and want to go home. Lately I have been taking great care to polish every element of my character in front of the classroom. I labor in the evenings to perfect my presentations. It is tiring but students can be so demanding, and so unforgiving of a professor's humanity. I have lectured at universities in Cambridge for ten years without promotion, lived in the poorest quarters of town, and yet there is always a new demand for perfection.

As Rosa and Elias talk about the universal kinds of challenges we face, I think about the specific. Being a professor has not made me transcend being black. The swings of judgment have often made my life unbearable. Excessive admiration about how lucky blacks are to have ageless black skin, veracious sexuality, and happy-go-lucky attitudes toward life often ended with a note about how lazy, sluggish, not ambitious, whining, and loose blacks are. One day, praise. The next day, contempt and derision. One day, kindness. The next day, cruelty. And, all blacks—professors or not—are supposed to go in and out on white people. One should know the codes to come in and have the tact to go out. From forgiveness to resentment, from love and then to hate, black people must know how to handle all of them.

Elias and Rosa have now finished their conversation and look satisfied. I determine I will share these thoughts of mine with them later. When we begin putting things away to go, Rosa stops suddenly and looks me directly in the eyes. She holds a spatula and looks grandmotherly for the first time since the evening began.

'One person can change the course of our destiny, Nyerere,' she says, her voice grave, 'but there is only one ability worth having in the face of destiny. That is the ability to recognize, in every circumstance, the power of beauty. Beauty is not owned by any one person. When you believe yourself to be in possession of beauty, it will surely die.'

Rosa puts down the spatula. I see that it is her time to lecture now. 'You may see the features of beauty to wither,' she says, motioning my gaze to a Christmas cactus at the counter, its shocking pink flowers turning crisp and black at the ends where they curl under. The cactus flowers are near the end of their season.

'You think that this death is a slow process,' she continues, plucking the dying flower from its base, 'but there is a struggle to live that occurs below the surface.' She begins to peel open the petal with her fingernails and the white, moist interior shines brightly.

'I chose to end this petal's life early,' she chuckles, placing it into the base of the pitcher, now empty of liquid, 'but I have noticed that if you can cover this variety of flower with something milky soon enough after it has been picked, the petal will not shrivel for days.' She pauses and looks toward the refrigerator, thinking.

'Apple milk is the best anecdote for this petal. Seems just the right alchemy somehow. It also is delicious to drink.'

'Apple milk,' Elias fills in, seeing my shocked look at the drink's name, 'Apples, sugar, milk and rosewater.'

'Next time you come, Nyerere, you must taste it. It is lovely, really.' Their voices come to me in unison.

The apple milk sounds delightful but I have begun thinking about Rosa's comments on beauty. My mind is busy, comparing our ways of understanding the law of beauty. One of the laws of beauty says that beauty is always illusory. The petal she showed us looked nearly dead on the outside but, in fact, when opened up, it was thriving. I wonder with some sadness how many years in Cambridge I spent trying to create my outside to look good while the inside died. As Elias walks me toward the door to leave, he asks me if I have seen Adowa lately. I find his question curious but Elias is a curious character so I cannot take much mind. Of course I have seen her lately, I want to say, but still my tongue. I can have no harsh words for this man. Elias had been the one to help me locate Adowa when I thought I had lost her the first time. It was Elias who had saved me from jumping into the Boston Harbor after her. He was the one I finally heard through the din of voices that tried to tell me I had gone crazy.

'Nyerere!'

The voice makes me jump but my mind clings to the memory of that day I thought I had lost Adowa. I can see the grey water, the cold rails, the New England sky. I remember how hard I had searched for her, how nearly I had jumped, and how funny everyone around me seemed to think it all was when I found her again, nowhere near Boston Harbor.

'Nyerere!'

The voice seems as though it were coming from inside the house. I realize I am on Rosa's doorstep, Elias having just bid me goodnight and shut the door. I listen in the street, but hear no sound. Tiny white flakes have begun to fall from the sky. I cross my arms over my chest. I am cold and have no coat. I had left Adowa's so quickly, taken by the breeze. I cup my ear to the door, hear nothing and start down the steps.

'Nyerere!' It seems to be coming on the wind, I decide, from down south. From Cambridge? I realize suddenly it is Adowa's voice I hear. I had left her sitting at the table, letters in hand. I did not realize how long I had been gone. Careening into the night, over streets covered in fresh snow I make my way toward the voice. I find myself on the bus, bumping past the elegant street lamps, the cobbled streets, and the musicians and, in no time, I am at Adowa's apartment again. The sun is shining brightly at her house and I notice the maples outside her window have began their slow change to

13

autumn red. Past the trees I go, through the door I go, up the short stairs, to the table. I am at the table, sitting down with the letters and envelopes spread out before me before I realize Adowa is nowhere to be seen. I am sitting in her chair but I do not see her. That is, until I see her long slender arms extend in front of me. I turn to face her, embrace from the front, but my own arms seem to *have disappeared*.The slender arms move and pick up a letter on the table. As Adowa's voice begins reading the letter, I hear my name again. It repeats, over and over but I cannot figure out from where it emerges. It seems to be coming from my own mouth.

'Nyerere!'

I am a man with ears and heart but no sight. It is as though they both grew so big they covered up my eyes. I want to know who is calling my name but I want to hear Adowa's letter more. Like an eavesdropper straddling a fence between two neighbors, I want to know two sides at once. Suddenly something warm splashes onto my face. I splutter, startled. A breeze cools the wetness and I reach to it.

'Hey! Nyerere! Are you awake?' Laughter. A swelling embarrassment. Hot breath on my nose. I still cannot see.

'My friend. Hey! You are talking to yourself. Wake up.' More water. It drips onto my collar. I am irritated as it begins to itch.

I am confused. I can see that it is Neil in front of me now, he is so close I can see the pores on his chin. But my lids cover my eyeballs. I wrench them, open them, and stare at Neil, a deep purple man, his back to the sun.

'You were in such a deep sleep,' he says with what seems a hint of concern. His towel is rolled up under his arm, an empty water bottle in his hand, and his shirt hanging from the waistband of his shorts.

'It's getting on night. Should we go to our spot now?' He is referring to the spot we like to sit at in the evenings. It is there that we relax, talk, reminisce and develop the script of the play we are creating.

I nod at him dizzily, not yet sure where I am, where I have just come from. I cling to Adowa's voice reading from the page but it retreats out into the evening air. A slow trickle of limeade moistens my throat, and then it too fades, the sweet and sour taste leaving just a trace of memory on my tongue. I rub my eyes again and wriggle my toes, debating whether to tell Neil about my vision of Adowa. But he is all movement, ready to go back toward the water, ready for some company, ready for a drink and possibly, a cigar. We have been at the rocks long enough that the late evening light has brought in a blue grey horizon. The stars will appear soon. I decide to keep the vision to myself.

'Sure, Neil,' I say. 'Shall we go now?'

'Yes, of course.' Neil picks up my sunglasses and offers me a hand.

'I have thought of a new beginning,' he says enthusiastically, pulling me up and already walking forward before I have stood. We are always thinking of new beginnings for our play. We have been working on it for some time, every evening in fact, but we still cannot decide where to start.

We walk side-by-side back to the ocean's edge. Me slowly, trying to fit the pieces of my dreaming together and Neil, bounding and basking in the newfound energy of his love for Heidi. Her book bounces against his thigh as he strides forward and each time he slaps it down it makes a louder noise, like a punctured tire popping suddenly while moving fast on the freeway. With each pop, the more convinced I become that Rosa, Elias and Adowa have something important to tell me. I am unsure I can join Neil in his delight. As we walk toward the water again, I look back at the rocks, half hoping to see Adowa there, letter in hand, answering questions. But all I see is a rock, curved in like an hourglass, and an indentation of where my body had been pressed sleeping in the sand.

**

Because I joined Neil I did not get to hear what Adowa read into the empty room of her apartment. If I had been able to hear what the first and second letters said and what she replied to them, things might all look different now. For one, I would not be worrying about why it has been fourteen days since we have spoken.

Adowa's voice is calm though the paper jerks up, and then down, as she fights to stay in control of her emotions.

"...All things are meant to be, Adowa,' the letter from Ghana

15

begins. 'They happen to all families. We are born, because we are fated to die, and along the way, we are struck with illness, and so it is now your brother's turn to undergo the pain of the killer virus. He just turned positive. Adowa, I know how much your only brother means to you. Bear it, girl. At least he is alive, for now, and let us simply enjoy his remaining days. After all, you are a scientist, a doctor of the human body. Look at his plight professionally."

The letter continues along the path of controlled grief until the end, where her mother signs it with love, the usual tender words of affection and declarations that the family misses her terribly. Adowa does not focus on these elements. She only wants to see her brother, to feel his pain, to see his face. As emotions try to form, Adowa struggles to organize her thoughts. We Africans are too poorly informed about our bodies, she thinks. HIV is taking too many people. An anger takes shape, she breathes through it, but her brain aches. Shame, disappointment and hurt take form. Africans are failing to protect themselves, she thinks aloud. She sees this as a failure to correct. They must learn to value their bodies, she says. We have always done this before. We must strive to do it now. Her tone is convinced and solid, daring away the shame.

Adowa does not know how her brother contracted HIV but it does not matter. He has been suffering without her. Her fingers trace her brother, then her mother on the paper. She caresses each syllable on the page. My book on the biology of the human body will not be just another academic text, she tells her family. It will be accessible. It will be available. It will be African. She begins to go through all the reasons the book must be published. We will learn how to protect ourselves better. We must learn to understand ourselves as contingent on each other. We are contingent bodies, she thinks, straightening out her face. We must learn to talk to each other again. To share knowledge about our condition. To stop hiding away the painful and face it. In the years that have separated Adowa from her family she has never stopped talking to them. Somehow, it almost seems, she has begun to understand them more the longer she has been away. She reflects on the past five years of her life. The years have been guided by a passion and a commitment to her project on the "African Biological Self." She has never questioned the seriousness with which she takes her work. Her book and her project face the painful. Shares her knowledge. Makes apparent what others cannot see. Adowa's project is the medium through which she talks. It is indispensable to her being. A guidebook that grows longer and more detailed with Time. Adowa has been gone for too long. The clock reads 5:48 AM. She stares at it for a long time then it blurs and she looks through the walls, out through the trees, directly into her mother's eyes. The dissertation will have to wait, she tells her. Her mother looks concerned, then nods.

Adowa realizes she is still clutching her mother's letter. She puts it down. Standing up from the table and swinging her arms over her head, she starts to move through what she will need to do. She stretches high toward the ceiling. The dissertation committee at Harvard will need to be notified that she is suspending her program. They will not understand, so close to the end. She will tell her supervisors tonight by email. The plane ticket needs to be booked, clothes packed. She would like to go to the gym, gifts need to be purchased for people at home. This will take time. Mother will protest she is suspending her studies so close to the end she knows, but she will be happy. Adowa is going home and nothing can change her mind.

She releases her arms from above her head. The colors in her apartment have taken on a sharp, hard line in the morning light; each thing is distinct from the other. Her eyes land on the phone. It is evening in Tanzania. She thinks of Nyerere and picks it up to call him, ashamed she has not answered its ring in nearly two weeks. First the grief of her mother's letter then just days ago, on the first of May, the letter from Rosa arrived. She is weary of the grief over the past two weeks. It made her careless with Time. She never forgets it this way. She grits her teeth, then relaxes her jaw, and forces her mind onwards.

I must call him, she thinks, fingers hovering over the buttons. But then she remembers what day it is. She looks to the clock again. Exactly 6:00 AM, Monday morning, Cambridge time. This means it is Sunday night in Tanzania now. Tomorrow will be Monday, their first day back to school after the first term holiday. He and Neil will be busy teaching and planning for the big second year anniversary event at the school. 'Our school is in the loveliest spot, outside of the

17

capital on huge acres of land,' she hears him telling her, the phone lines crackling between them. 'The place has fertile vegetation, lush. Plenty of water. It sits underneath a mountain with a clear view of the bright blue sky. She dares not believe him entirely, it sounds too perfect to be true. She asks him to tell her more. 'Nearby there is a convent, a church, a mosque not too far....convenient for the moral education of kids who chose the religious path,' he adds. 'The Best Values Must Be Chosen,' he tells her, is the motto. It was hung at the entrance to the gate. In the first year, so many families chose the school there is more demand than space. Nyerere already has plans to build another school. Time moves only forward; he always tells her.

'It may be longer than expected until I arrive to you,' she says to Nyerere into the receiver. She has not dialed the number yet. The words sounded much too sentimental. She wants to put the phone down but instead she stands there with it in her hand, trying to decide the best thing to do. She wishes to move on, to begin packing. She glances at the clock again. 6:09 AM Cambridge, 10:09 PM Tanzania. Nyerere will be at home preparing his lessons for tomorrow, she thinks. He likes to prepare the night before. Neil will be unable to contain himself; maybe he is even walking at the beach, planning the anniversary event. Nyerere tells her he loves the beach the most in Tanzania and that he is good at throwing events after all the years of fundraising in Cambridge. She is happy they are there now together. Nyerere 's decision to invite him to teach could not have been more appropriate. They will make it the monumental event of the year, she is sure. People will come from all over the country. It is as though both of them have become young again, she thinks, picturing Nyerere 's lean stomach, clean deep skin, the way his eyes look as though they have just been wiped with polish. She remembers how amazed she had been at Nyerere 's single-mindedness about going back to Tanzania to settle and to build the school. Telephone sales at night; cashier at a parking lot during the day; and waiting on tables on the weekend. Eighty hours a week he worked, pulling $4000 a month. It was triple what he ever made as a professor. In three years he managed to save over $400,000 and was ready for the move. Then, before he had even invested all the money, gathered all

18

the supplies and hired the people who would be a part of getting this school ready, the school became nationally famous. He held the first anniversary before the doors opened for students around the pile of fresh baked bricks that would build the toilets, in an of itself a cause for celebration. The school opened the following term and within months, journalists began calling it one of the premiere 'emerging African education centers.' It had everything. A new curriculum, creative teaching and scholarships.

A great rumbling shakes Adowa's mind back into her apartment. The garbage collectors have arrived. Of course, Adowa thinks, noting the time on the clock for the third time, the school also received so much publicity because of its founder. The beep beep beep of the garbage trucks outside is followed by the sound of laughter, a clatter, the crunch of the garbage inside the truck as it packs it down. Adowa listens to them for a moment, not wanting to pull herself from thoughts of Nyerere. Her suitcase sits upstairs, in the top shelf of her closet. Adowa brushes the image aside. Instead she imagines the people in his hometown celebrating his return. Nyerere, a long gone son of the soil, an ex-professor, a man who knew how to steer the money come home at last. They all traveled to help, arranging, sorting, managing all that needed doing, contacting the right people, concentrating on the details, preparing food for long meetings when they could sit and talk about what they had done, what could come next.

Her apartment is now very silent. She hears the first sounds of people on the sidewalk downstairs, on their way already to work. She looks down at the phone in her hand, she has not put it down. Not wanting to look at the clock again but not knowing how long she has been standing there, she puts the phone down. She cannot tell him the news about her brother or the news contained in the letter from Rosa. There is time for everything, she decides. It might march forward, but it is endless. I have promised to marry this man, she thinks as she kneels to pray, but it does not mean one must show everything. A sudden pang makes her reach for her throat. A feeling of tears grows hot behind her eyes. She wants to be careful with this love. Carefully, before any tears are spilled, she places his image in the cushion of her heart and then she promises she will call when she arrives home in Ghana. She concentrates on her prayer. On her knees, she wraps the silence around her tightly like a bandage, forcing herself to stillness until finally, she is satisfied that she will be able manage the next hours. Before she moves to begin packing, however, Adowa stops at the table. She picks up the letter she wrote back to Rosa. Sympathy rises to her chest and she grasps it more firmly, away from her body, away from her own heart. The fertile green images of Nyerere's Tanzania see-saw back and forth with the deep pain she sees etched on the face of her brother. He is now a part of all those suffering from the killer virus back home. Elias floats above it all, a shy look on his face, not wanting to touch, just wanting to look. He was perpetually curious about people, about the human body, but also terminally fearful of revealing his desires to be close to them. In her mind, Adowa cannot see his body as it floats, only his head roves, his eyes wide. She peers closer and then snaps herself out of the scene, in shock at what she sees. Red mixed with purple mixed with black. Eyes wide open, seeing nothing. She cannot look at him. Not now. Adowa shakes her head to free the images, closes her eyes, opens them again. She thinks about the suitcase upstairs. It might be big enough but there are many gifts to buy. She will grieve for Elias with Rosa later. She will tell Nyerere about him later as well. For now, she must concentrate on remembering the important things about going home to Ghana.

She walks to the hall, stops in front of a picture. It is a painting, from Nyerere's friend Conrad.

'We must accept beauty,' someone says to her, the painting is of the form of a human but its ears are very large and touch the ground. Adowa turns from it, feels grief rising, sensing Rosa's presence. Her words are soothing.

'Beauty surrounds us every day,' Rosa says, 'even in the worst times. We can only see it if we do not impose our own limits on it.'

As complicated a fellow as Elias was, no one could deny he sought beauty. 'Anyone can seek beauty,' she hears Rosa say as she walks into her room and turns on the radio down low, 'but it is only the rare person who will not seek to possess it.' Sober, hands placed one on top of the other, sneaking longing looks at each person that walked by. That was Elias.

She turns to her packing. Adowa begins sorting through her clothes, wondering what to take to Ghana. Her eyes fall on a flowery apron with ruffles at the hem. A gift from Rosa, something Adowa has never worn and would never have the interest to. She does not enjoy cooking, she prefers uncooked foods, and she is convinced that no one could possibly look as startlingly beautiful in an apron as Rosa. Adowa fingers the starched material until a disturbing question begins to grow. She wants to stop it, to turn it off even, to step on it but it feeds on her grief and grows too large in her mind to ignore.

'Anyone can seek beauty,' she hears Rosa tell her again, 'but if you try to possess that beauty, death will always follow.'

Adowa cannot stop her question before it flies into her mind. She wants to ask it. It is a question begging to be asked, begging to be put to rest. She ignores it. It grows louder. Adowa packs faster. But she cannot escape it, the question mocks her. As she pulls more clothes from the drawers, puts them onto the bed, some spill onto the floor. Adowa is not a careless person. She leaves them there all on the floor anyway, steps on a favorite blouse on purpose and then walks over to her bed. She is not herself now, she puts her palms to her temples, willing herself toward her tasks at hand. She surveys the mess she has made. Heaps of clothes, none of them the things she wants to take, glare at her. I must remember to buy myself a few new clothes before I go home, Adowa decides. She has never been one to fuss over clothes and the colors on the bed seem suddenly so lifeless.

If one tries to possess beauty, death will always follow. This plays over and over in her mind. It is an answer to something, she feels, but Adowa has not yet asked her question. She pushes her question away. If one tries to possess beauty, death will always follow. It is an answer, but to what she is not sure. Suddenly, she hears laughter. Loud and boisterous, laughter peels out into the room. It makes so much noise in her brain that Adowa sweats. The laughter is directed at her. Adowa has never been laughed at before. She has always tended to the answers, been careful not to make any mistakes. She is self-reliant. Her mother gave her her name because it fits her personality. The laughter grows louder, as though it is silly to have tended to the answers so well. She sought them and stored them and wrote them down in long page after long page of her dissertation. She is good with answers, so why the laughter? She begins folding clothes on the bed. The laughter does not stop. It seems to her that the answers have turned against her. The answer and laughter bully her, growing louder the more she folds.

Adowa finally puts the clothes down. Her patience is thin. She feels like running, but not in the measured strides she uses on the treadmill at the gym every morning. She wants to flee. Desperation comes on slowly, Adowa resists. She folds more evenly, lines up the corners perfectly. She does not run, she walks evenly, straight, calm. But like a wall of noise, the answer and laughter block her and in a flash of frustration, she hurls what is in her hand across the room as hard as she can. It lands. Without noise, the scarf crumples onto the floor. Adowa watches it fall, disappointed, but she feels herself stand a little taller. Laughter has no place in my heart, she says to the scarf as though it were alive. But Adowa does not get any lasting satisfaction. She does not realize her fear has become so apparent. But the answer does. Stilling the laughter, it begins to flaunt itself. Slow and confident, it sashays back and forth in her minds' eye. Adowa is exhausted.

Then the beginning of something new begins to form. The smallest tear squeezes itself out into the corner of her eye, and then it grows and grows and grows until her eye is so full she cannot move her lids. It begins to pain but still she holds on to it, willing the water back. She has much to do in the next months and the water will just make everything messy. The pain increases until Adowa feels a scream, rising with the taste of bile from her stomach, up to her chest, to the bottom of her throat. The water expands, the bile rises. Adowa cannot contain the water in her eyes anymore. She cannot see for the water, cannot move lest it spill, and cannot breathe in case the bile rise up higher. But Adowa can hear.

If one tries to possess beauty, death will always follow.

It is not her question it is an answer. An answer for many questions. An answer not intended for just one. Adowa's question prods her once more. It does not beg this time or plead to be released. Adowa feels the water begin to slip over and as she finds her voice, the water rushes down, soaking her face, making everything messy. Her cheeks feel the cool and thank her.

If one tries to possess beauty, death will always follow.

Adowa's voice is clear when she finally asks the question.

'If Elias had known this,' Adowa asks aloud, 'could things have turned out differently?'

Adowa turns to Rosa for the answer, wanting to hear it now, ready to embrace whatever is the answer but Rosa is now gone.

Adowa is stumped. Not triumphant like her name. Just stumped. May you finally rest Elias, Adowa says quietly. She has no energy for anything more. She looks at the mess in her room. Then, she begins picking it up.

**

The air after storms is always eerie. On our way back from the rocks, another storm had suddenly blown in, caught us off guard, soaked us through and cooled us down. Neil and I are at ocean's edge again. We have settled into our chairs. I like that we have spent the entire day at the beach and weathered two storms. The storm seemed to take away my concerns over the earlier vision. Adowa will call me when she is ready, I decide as we relax.

Usually, Neil and I come to the beach twice a day; in the evenings we work on our play, in the mornings we follow our own routines and come separately. Mornings are important for both of us. Neil likes to eat breakfast, throw on his clothes and meander to the beach. For Neil, work is play. He prepares his daily lesson while at the beach and it is not surprising to see him suddenly kick off his shoes, roll up his cuffs and wade calf deep into the ocean with his arm outstretched like propellers on either side of his torso. He plays with the gentle morning waves, he smiles at the squabbling birds and when he sees them, he admires the women who have slipped down to the beach from the big houses where they work as maids.

On weekdays I like to walk briskly for thirty minutes on the unmarked sand at dawn and then I go home to prepare for the day of teaching at the new school. I try not to think when I am walking and let the fresh air refresh me. Yet every day, as I am finishing my walk, the children arrive in cut off faded jeans and tee shirts with necks so wide the cloth falls over their slender shoulders. The fishermen are just pulling in and these young boys will help pull in the nets. They work their faces into stone like the teenage men who group together and drag in the boats. The fisherman will jump out before they have reached shore and join the group, hauling in the nets, bringing in fish, docking the boats on the sand and debating the merits of the morning.

I watch them all and wrestle with the whole of the African continent at dawn. I have to fight despair over the facts. Many things do not work in Africa because there is not enough money for everyone. It is a huge continent with millions of people and a bountiful wealth of resources. There are diamonds in the west, oil in the east, and copper in the south and the green fields and lush life of the north. When people wake up in the morning, they are told that there is no water, hot or cold. Too much of the population bathes and drinks from contaminated lakes and rivers. People without money find themselves begging, and people with money do not have any to spare. If one dared to casually stroll on the narrow streets, one hundred people would obstruct the way, begging for anything. The begging people receive what they do not need—pennies, nickels, cigarette butts and tattered cloth. Many people are filled with despair, but it is difficult to help them. A person might go to work with others who have been drinking their pains away the night before. Some sleep on the job. Some are caught vomiting at the bathroom. Others spread themselves on dirty grass in the back. They tell stories about their daughters who are mothers and even grandmothers at sixteen. Some wish to save those kids but do not know how. But I know desire cannot save Africa. Maybe, only God can.

Neil coughs. I reel myself in out of the wandering thoughts. We will talk about Africa later, I remind myself. We must begin with Cambridge though I am not sure if Cambridge was a beginning or an ending. He looks ready to begin scripting our play. Every evening, we always start the same way. First we prepare for it by sitting in absolute quiet, sometimes with a drink, other times with a cigar; often, with just ourselves. I like to think about the beautiful things of the day, like the generosity and perfect intelligence given to the birds. Tonight I think about what I see at dawn when I turn from the fishermen to go. I see the littlest boy's swollen knees knock together. He never flinches even though I think he is hungry because he is thin and working the nets hard enough to sweat. I know that if he is able to go to school he will arrive after a long walk and a very empty stomach. I wonder if he will not notice so much because he will be excited that he got to do two of his most favorite things in one day. He is becoming a man at the ocean, a bright future for his family at school. He will work as hard as he can for as long as there is money for him.

My thoughts wander to what Neil said to me just as we arrived to the oceanfront. I had been talking to him about the children who live too far from school and have no transport to come. They will not ever see our school and this makes me sad. He said, 'Our school is trying to make a difference. It is a drop in the bucket, but it is a big drop,' he reminds me. I told him the cycle never ends, the suffering circles round and round and round in the convoluted desire to be free. He said Time moves only forward and then reminds me I told him that as well. As I look at Neil now, a small smile playing at his lips, I am irritated by his brightness. I have to ward off old ugly thoughts before they reach me. I have to remember the reason Neil is such a good friend. In all our years together in Cambridge, I cherished his honesty, his refusal to succumb to hypocrisy and political correction. I love "correction. It is true that we agree on very few things. We do not see eye-to-eye on the causes of poverty, racism, why there are poor people, how to create a better world. Neil is a white man. He is an artist of sorts. He is prone to depression, dresses sloppily and he does not separate work from play.

But I invited him here and I cannot forget the past, the late parties at fund raising events Neil sponsored; the poetry jams at café's, the painting exhibitions, the walks, the talks about love. I cannot doubt the future either.

'One school now,' he says, 'Hundreds a few years from now.' He reminds me that I wrote those words to him when I invited him to Tanzania.

'Ready?' Neil says now. It is his signal to begin. We have done our contemplation as usual, now we begin. There is only one problem we must solve in the next hours, or maybe more. Neil and I cannot agree on how the play will begin. The script keeps changing. The play is supposed to be about our past in Cambridge. It is about all the people we knew, how our lives intersected, what happened to them, what brought us here now to ocean's edge. It seemed simple enough when we began. Neil is keen to freeze the beginning and build the other scenes from it. I am not sure this is possible. We are both somewhat baffled by just how childish memory can be. It never rests, never stands still, it pleads constantly for us to follow. We cannot catch it long enough to make it do what we want. This is not to say that we do not often use the same strategy. We often structure our conversations like interviews, for example. But the memory finds other memories and they run around in circles, jump between time zones, they are superhuman children. Neil and I cannot seem to complete any one scene. This is not to say we do not enjoy our attempts immensely. The reminiscing, even though it can be painful, is good for us.

I look back to Neil, and say, 'ready.' He has begun moving rapidly. Puffing out his chest. Inhaling through his nostrils loudly. Pressing down his hair so that it looks like a toupee. Licking his teeth loud enough to hear his saliva moving around in his mouth. Tonight Neil will be a Boston Globe editor, I guess. I want to ask him if my guess is correct, but I decide to wait and see. I do know that tonight we will have two interviews. We have Neil, a reporter. We have me, a columnist with the Boston Herald. The only thing Neil needs now is a different haircut. He has improvised the perfect reporters' costume with nothing more than a piece of driftwood and some very talented facial contortions. His puffed out posture and his voice, in an exaggerated American accent, is perfect.

'When did you arrive, Nyerere?' He holds the driftwood mic to my mouth.

'1982.' I speak directly into the mic, something I could never do at public lectures.

'You were...?'

'I was not even thirty.'

'A young, dynamic man, I am sure,' quips Neil.

'I was a pleasantly naïve young man.'

'It is the tumultuous years of the early 1980's...' drones Neil, 'when the world was just waking up to the existence of many ethnicities and cultures...' He pulls the mic close to his chin, leaning over

26

it like he is conspiring something.

'In the seat of the United States' cultural and academic hub, the search for self never ends. Cambridge, the city of illusions, taunts all those who seek...'

'And who said that?' I laugh, creating a break in our script.

'Oh, the Boston Globe editor,' he says nonchalantly.

'It is true. Cambridge is rich, attracts an international population, and provides all searchers with the best academic, cultured, and coffee filled environment.'

'So you came as a searcher?' Neil bends forward in exaggerated surprise. He is merciless with the script.

'We all came as searchers, thank you. And I came to America for a specific search. I was chosen for that task as a matter of fact. I was the best student in my high school and so I came to the USA on a scholarship. I believed in overcoming my condition through achievement and I wanted to rise to the top in America. I dreamt that in Cambridge, I would turn my life around for good.'

I am warming up now, enjoying the way I can now condense many details into paragraphs.

'What did you want to do in Cambridge?' Neil asks.

'I came to Cambridge to find work after the PhD was finished.'

'What did you think when you arrived? That first day, what was it like for you?'

I look out at the ocean, then to Neil. 'It was love at first sight. Especially Harvard Square. Oh, I had an insatiable curiosity about the many moods and manners of Harvard Square.'

I sink back in my chair, savoring the memory. Depending on where and when one looked, Harvard Square could form for a person any number of impressions. On an early fall Saturday afternoon, the Square appeared luminous. Café Au Bon Pain's patio teemed with a happy crowd - laughter written on the contours of peoples' faces as they listened to a Central American *mestizo* band singing melodies of joy and love. Customers filled the little boutiques. Mothers strolled their young children while the older ones walked alongside licking their ice cream cones. Lovers walked hand-in-hand. Nearby, Harvard professors composed their latest articles from the comfort of their offices overlooking the Square.

'People were cheerful in the earliest morning, terrible in the afternoon and much too perfectly happy in the evening, if I remember,' Neil says.

'Absolutely agreed,' I say.

We sink into memory about weekend afternoons in Cambridge. The sun would wane and the afternoon set in, moods would shift to oppose those of the first half of the day. The illusory law of beauty made it so that the perfect images always dissolved and produced others. The afternoon atmosphere could become suddenly aggressive in Cambridge, like a bull. The tourists had seen it all in the afternoons. They witnessed the hustle and the bustle of the bright morning change into something else, something not as easy to name. Some people sat and stared at the wall. Others seemed unsure of what to do next. They had eaten, taken pictures, drunk, and shopped to death. Inscribed on their faces remained the question of what they desired to do next. A customer scolded a cashier for being too slow. Someone returned a greeting with a rude stare. A mother took offense because her cute child attracted the attention of a passerby with the wrong looks. A woman chided a man for smiling at her. She made sure that everyone in close proximity heard and saw her embarrass the foreigner who was merely flirting with her. Impatience breezed in the air. Tolerance went on a holiday.

There was a certain beggar on the corner of Harvard Square who always asked for anything to be thrown his way. There were always homeless people in the Square—some sleeping on benches, others eating leftovers. An old black man persistently clowned to the crowd to make people buy newspapers. A woman with two children begged nearby. But the certain beggar on the corner could provoke outrage. He never left. Many found him repulsive—perhaps because he was overweight and black—and felt offended by his presence. The city had tried to put in zoning laws and then it passed a law forbidding any member of the public to sit idly on a bench for longer than an hour. It seemed to help cut down the presence of the homeless in the white quarters for a little while. This big black homeless man was an affront to people who thought they had been very clear about where people like him should not have dared to enter.

Others were oblivious to the politics of space and race. With

28

gummy smiles, tourists crowded out the homeless and gathered themselves around the statue of John Harvard to wait for the camera to flash. One, two and then ten pictures later they would rub their hands together in an uncontained disbelief that they were finally there, realizing their dream of visiting Harvard College.

Whenever the subway train dropped its tourist passengers into the square too early in the evening, elitist Cambridge dwellers gritted their teeth and steeled themselves. They hated them and their cameras.

'The Japanese are the worst,' one local remarks, a knowing look on her face.

'Yeah, at least the Europeans are quiet, less anxious,' says another.

'It's simple, really,' a woman with chic thick-framed glasses butts in. Her colleague who is glaring rather openly at the cameras makes her uneasy.

'They have a particular kind of passion for Harvard yard,' she insists to her friend. She wants her to stop grimacing at them. 'I wonder if there is something about their culture which permits such unabashed delight?'

Her friend forgives her for the chiding because what she is saying is interesting. 'Hmmm…interesting,' she says slowly, collecting her thoughts. 'Perhaps it is the young generations' form of resistance to the pervasive anti-Western sentiment common among the older generations who wish to preserve cultural homogeneity in the face of consumerism and globalization.'

The friend's voice quickens. 'Of course, after the terrible events…' her words linger, and she does not move back to her original thought.

'…perhaps they wish to just move on, to de-traditionalize the traditional stoicism of Japanese character.'

Their eyes cloud into theory and they fall silent. Though they might deny they are so extreme as to hold the Japanese as objects of contempt, I think they both are glad they still know some good neighborhoods none of the cameras and tourists has found yet. In those neighborhoods I know that beautiful bored young women like her sit inside expensive restaurants. With resolve, they stare at gourmet dishes they could not finish although they would have liked to if they and their men did not place so much value on the appearance of their figures.

'The intrusive city of juxtapositions...' Neil interrupts suddenly. We look at each other, aware suddenly that we had fallen silent and left our script.

'Who are you now?' I inquire. Neil can be very funny when he imitates reporters. He now has a larger piece of wood and he has placed onto it a bunch of seaweed. It looks like the giant furry-headed microphones the CBS reporters use at presidential conferences.

'A certain columnist from the Christian Science Monitor, of course,' he says briskly.

'Oh yes, well, of course.' I sense Neil wants me to resume the script.

'Some of the kindest people I have ever met lived in Cambridge, Neil. I must not forget to mention that. Americans are good at surmounting class distinctions. All Americans, when mood inclines them, can eat at the same place, shop at the same place, thanks to the equalizing power of the credit card. You are after all, an American.'

I do not just say this. Neil might be a transplant from Idaho farmland but he does not fit the stereotype. Also, Neil is my best friend.

'And you, Neil? What did you think of Harvard Square? Love at first sight as well?'

I am not as brilliant at switching into new character. My voice is flat. Neil does not mind and his eyes prick up. He stretches out his legs in front of him, admires them, scratches his calf, returns himself to the interview.

'Well?' Neil seems reluctant to answer any questions tonight. After clearing his throat for what seems interminably long, he answers.

'I wanted to believe I had arrived at he center of the world's mind when I came to Cambridge. But Harvard Square. Let me see. That was more like a feeling of...well, I'm not sure to be honest. But not love. No, I do not think I ever felt love for Harvard Square...I wanted to escape my life in Idaho, so I came to Cambridge. Harvard Square just happened to be there.'

I knew Neil did not spend much time in Harvard Square. He preferred the solitude of places like The Coffee Connection, the coffee shop I met him in. The women there thought he was on drugs he slept so little and spent so much time there. I persist anyway.

'But is that not what love is?' Neil raises his brows at me. 'What is love? Is that what you are asking?'

'It depends,' I reply. 'What I mean to say is that to most people love is escape...'

'Escape!' Neil is sarcastic. 'For me love has a been more like a prison.'

I smile. My mother has often commented Neil is fearful of love.

'Neil. I always thought you were fearful of love. Even my mother said.' He shifts his weight away from me. Flicks at something on his arm.

'Isn't everyone?'

'Perhaps. But I am being unfair. You are ready to embrace love now. Many people harden their hearts after they are hurt and then never soften them again.'

'It took a long time, Nyerere.'

'Yes, but how many people did we know that sealed their hearts into stone so tightly that no one could pry them open. How many people...?'

Neil does not allow me to finish. 'How many people died because of it?'

He sounds bitter. His sudden venom takes me aback. It is unlike him. We cannot escape the memory of Conrad. With the mention of death, it looms large.

'Yes, some did die.' I shake my head, fragments of memory rub at me.

Conrad. My painter friend. He had manic depression. Sexual exploits he plunged without limit. A sudden death took him. When he closed his eyes for the last time he asked God for forgiveness for his mistakes. He had been reading Tolstoy's *The Death Of Ivan Illich*.

The moon winks. I decide it is time to move on.

'Neil.'

'Yes, Nyerere?' He sounds weary. I feel weary as well.

'Let us keep going.'

31

'With the script?'
'Yes. You can ask the questions this time.'

**

'I do not have the energy to sugar coat memory any more tonight.'
Neil is not speaking. His character is. Neil is a roving reporter
this time around. He has a video camera on his shoulder. He looks
war torn, unsure how to begin his questions. He turns the soggy
cardboard box on his shoulder toward me.
'I do not either,' I say to the camera, 'we have to deal with sadness somehow. Cambridge was lethal at times. Monday mornings
were killers, for example.' The joke is crass. I know this. I am trying
to rouse something from us. Detachment is always the coping strategy of intellectuals. But it is a lost cause. Neil does not say anything.
My joke is not funny.
Conrad died on a Monday morning. When everyone was going
to work. Except the homeless man, that is, who sticks out his tongue
out at a busy passerby holding a coffee mug in one hand and a cell
phone in the other. My jest may not have been funny but it motioned to a truth. Monday mornings are a thing to see in Cambridge.
Streams of people cross each other on Massachusetts Avenue on
Monday mornings. Many onlookers found the scene hilarious. The
man was cool. He did not give it more than a moment of attention.
He laughed it off, huddled closer into his cell phone, and picked
up his pace. He was on the way to make a killing at some financial
institution. Many like-minded and anxious professionals impatiently
hustled by, shouldering a person here and cursing a person there.
They too were going to work and knew they were expected to arrive on time. They knew that many prospective employees were
waiting in the wings to take their places. When discussing work on
the weekends, they told their friends that they felt dispensable. The
expression "I am sick and tired of all this," was etched on their faces,
on their bodies, in those tired bodies dragging their feet on bumpy
city rides. Cyclists make matters worse as they cut through the heart
of the Square when the traffic is congested. Drivers give the finger
for no reason and emotions stored up from unhappy marriages spill
out onto strangers on Mondays.
'Do you remember the boy who got caught kissing a girl while

crossing the street?' I ask Neil out of the blue. He still has not asked me any questions.

He scratches at his arms. Thinks back.

'Yes, I remember... That driver almost finished him. If there were no rules, he could have run him over.'

I shake my head. 'Cursing, cussing, so mad. It was brilliance in the end. The boy did not even care enough to check the driver. In fact, he kept on laughing.'

'I think you said something to them, if I remember.' Neil says in a faraway voice.

"Live your lives right,' I told them, 'Never mind the jerk. They called me handsome, said they needed more people like me. I was surprised by their sincerity. Not all of them in Cambridge were stressed and angry all the time. Some could not wait for dawn to arrive so that they could go to their well-paying jobs.'

I look to Neil, waiting for him to join in. He could not stand the Starbuck's double latté early in the morning, lunch from that pricey Thai Restaurant, and a candlelit dinner on Newbury Street-type of people.

'Did you ever even go into a restaurant on Newbury Street?' I ask him. He just makes a small noise, something between a grunt and hmm. While I want to distract us with talk about the jet-setters who commanded huge salaries, lived in the most prestigious addresses in town, who ate out five times a week, Neil was lost in thought.

If they ever ate at home, they brought in orders from outside, I think to myself, talking to Neil's camera that now lays at his feet. They had house cleaners, dry cleaned their clothes, and attended charity fundraiser events on the weekends. They had summer homes and boats in Cape Cod. And perhaps someday they would have liked to have children, if thoughts of a family ever crossed their minds.

I am a one-man, one-act play, I laugh to myself as time drifts on and still, Neil does not speak. That is because Neil is thinking about Heidi again.

**

When Neil had asked Heidi to marry him, she told him that both love and marriage were political matters in her life. As a black person, she was expected to marry within the race. Flings and affairs were frowned upon. Marriage to a white man was absolutely condemned, as evidenced by the titanic anger that erupted when the rare interracial marriage occurred. Neil believed she had simply not been the type who would ever cross the racial line.

Heidi's book says that black women are invisible. That they are not only invisible but that their invisibility is taken for granted. They have been ignored. She also argues that black women in white society are even more invisible, and more misunderstood, than black men. Neil cannot help but think that Heidi is somehow talking directly to him. As his mind rolls over into the past, he remembers what a struggle it was for Heidi to make this point to him, he sees how many of his actions made her invisible. Heidi's lifework was to make equally visible black women's achievements and sorrows. It seemed that Cambridge, the bed of Harvard and 'a multicultural' would have supported her. No woman was let off easy for choosing to make her lifework to be struggle and Heidi was not just any woman. She was a black woman. Neil told Heidi to ignore people who made judgments. 'They are just ignorant,' he said. Neil never scoffed at Heidi even when he did not understand and he made sure to turn his back on anyone who did. This did not stop Heidi from hurting. 'Turn the other cheek, Heidi,' he begged. But she did not have any fresh cheeks to turn like he, a white man, could. Neil did not want to be a white man to her. He wanted to sweep Heidi's claims and hurts up under the mantle of their love. He wanted to learn her dance but she blocked him. In so many many words, she said that a dance would have been nice, if the world were kinder. 'Neil, you do things that you were not aware of that hurt women.' Neil could finish the sentence for her. 'Hurt women…like me,' is what she meant. She explained to him, patiently at first, that privilege is having a fresh cheek to turn and to this, Neil replied she was accusing him unfairly of being unaware.

'It is not my fault the world is cruel,' he said on the fated day.

'I know,' Heidi said sadly, 'but I have to leave anyway.'

At least that is how Neil remembered the end of their relationship. In the hard years that followed those awkward dances of racial tension, Neil had moments of anger when he thought Heidi had allowed her heart to be a coward. But there was something that neither he nor Heidi could know. Loving each other in the world is one hard thing but no couple is an isolated entity. The whole world will attempt to live inside them. Loving the world despite its crude ways of taking up a home is quite another. It was only after Neil realized his heart would never stop burning if he did not just understand what Heidi was trying to tell him. He had also to learn to from it.

Near the time he was due to fly to Dar Es Salaam to meet me, Neil threw the largest fundraising party he was to ever hold for the homeless in Cambridge. From the time Neil arrived in Cambridge until the time he left it, he was an artist of sorts and a fundraiser for homeless people. He never sold a single painting in Cambridge, and never tried, but he spent a lot of time on the phone raising money for the homeless. This fundraiser was intended to be massive, a blow out. It would help Neil to usher out his life in Cambridge and invite in the new one yet to come. It was mid-August, and the event was held outside on a hot summer night. Very wealthy, and mostly very young, Boston professionals attended the party. He spent the entire event trying to concentrate but with his impending relocation to Tanzania so near, Neil's heart was far from the crowd. Heidi had seen Neil straightaway when she walked in. Twenty years had changed his dressing habits little. He wore an untucked shirt and loafers, a sore sight in the middle of trendy young professionals. Her heart warmed as she watched the way he moved, methodical as he had always been, as though each movement had its own ending before it linked into the next one. She noted they were also the only ones in the room with silver streaks in their hair. While the young professionals doted on each other over wine near the end of the evening, Heidi approached Neil. When he saw her, there in the flesh before his eyes, he dropped the speaker he was holding and did not even apologize when the technical support man dashed over. The man was not sure, upon seeing tears running down Neil's cheeks, whether to ask him if he was OK or to scream at him for the damage. Neil would not have cared either way.

They shared a cup of orange tea behind the stage. Heidi did not cry, but she said yes to Neil this time. She told him that she had been in search of fulfilling a dream to join him in her waning years. 'I will come to Tanzania,' she told him. On the first day she arrived in Dar el Salaam, just to visit, she added that she could, in fact, stay there 'for life.'

Neil turns back to me just as a light appears far out on the horizon. The waves reflect the moon chasing the sun. The light we see is an orb that appears for less than the blink of an eye, it bobs as though it is a ship on the waves. And then, before Neil and I can even confirm the existence of any thing at all, it disappears.

'I think it was the constant turnover of people in Cambridge that guaranteed her pristine illusion stayed in tact so well,' Neil says when we have both finally pried our eyes from the mysterious orb on the horizon. 'Every year saw new faces, every hour a new mood,' Neil says.

It has been nearly an hour since we have spoken.

'It was easy to be charmed.' Neil is skeptical. 'Even you have to admit, Neil. Did you ever walk the Charles on a sunny day?'

I say this on purpose. He often met Heidi at the Charles River. She liked to feed the ducks. As much as I would like to continue with our script, my mind wants to wander. Neil seems to want the same. He does not reply to me. So I let my mind wander into the snow white clouds of a sunny day at the Charles. People were in a festive mood. At the restaurants people tipped generously. On the streets they laughed easily and made contact with strangers by talking about the gorgeous day. Young women did not mind some mild flirtation. Some people made actual efforts to smile without much calculation at a dashing black male. Mothers, letting go of the customary fear of strangers, allowed those passing by to admire their toddlers. The toddlers loved the unconditional adulation. Older people accepted help from younger ones without belligerence. Touchiness briefly disappeared. Painters, poised on their ladders under the shade of stern trees, brushed vibrant colors onto nice homes on Irvine Street. Poets described what they felt. Writers emerged with their laptops and seemed as if they had a lot to say.

'It would almost seem disloyal to deny Cambridge was not all it is cracked up to be,' Neil says as the pretty images dance around in my mind. The sky above me is expansive. I do not think of death, disappointment, or Adowa.

'True,' I force myself to say. Neil has brought me down again. 'But did not this parade of illusions make us all'...I search for the words, 'into liars.'

'Liars?' queries Neil. 'Well, yes, I suppose it does. We were all searching for the truth beyond the illusions....'

I realize Neil has hastened us to the end of Scene 1. I am thankful and take up my part.

'The truth....beyond the illusions...Neil repeats, '...that is what we sought. We were...'

'Searching for ourselves...' I add.

'...The truth of ourselves...'

'Freed from the identities imposed on us by others...'

'And imposed on ourselves...'

'by our own selves...'

'It was a painful journey,' I wince, unable still to say this line without feeling, quite literally, the jab of that pain, 'but now...we are at the beginning again.'

'Cut!!!' yells Neil into the night. The night shatters into a thunderous applause. We have timed it perfectly. The tide has just rolled in. What a performance. Neil lobs the rest of his drink into the air and it arcs up in a flash of silver. I look into the crystal-studded sky. Relief. It must be nearly two o'clock in the morning and tomorrow is the first day back to school. We pick up our empty glasses, the unsmoked cigar and say goodnight. I head right, Neil goes left. The stars look merry. My heart is light. I have an urge to skip.

I think back to my decision to come to Tanzania as I walk to my house. When I resigned from my role as professor, I knew I would have to get used to the idea of liking work, respecting it. I would have to rediscover the dignity of labor, any labor. After I decided I was leaving, I had to deal with a question. What are the limitations a professor is willing to accept? Was I willing to do any job, by any means necessary? How far would I push to get back to Tanzania? For years I had been afraid of work, thought that work was wearing a tie, driving a car, covering oneself with newspaper, snubbing cleaners, cashiers, waitresses and parking lot attendants for making a living through what is available, without bothering anybody, but going about the cycle called life. While they were marrying, raising children, sending them to school, aging and dying in a dignity bestowed by their labor, I toiled under the burden of an unsatisfied self. I knew I would have a lot of explaining to do to all those who called me "professor." Maybe they would think me mad or worse, a failure. I anticipated hearing my name again. I had missed that light and informal way of interacting with people. I had always felt uncomfortable with the formality, I asked that people let me return to the old days, when they called me by my name and I called them by theirs.

Once I decided I could work, I decided I was willing to earn money by any means necessary. I worked hard. At legitimate jobs. Some weeks, eighty hours. The money collected rapidly because I worked so hard.

Within a month of having saved enough, I packed and left Cambridge. I came to Tanzania. My childhood home. A place of memories and new beginnings. A place I recognized, and did not. I did not feel as if I had to wear any masks in Tanzania the moment I stepped on the soil. No one tries to take anything away from me here in Tanzania. I built a school, the youth are enthusiastic. I have employed the best teachers around, my best friend is here, and Adowa is coming soon. Life could not be better. Again I have the urge to skip. I am an old man now, I say to myself, though I am not in the least bit serious. I may be over fifty but I do not feel it and I know I do not look it. I stride longer, the muscles in my thighs working.

Adowa. My heart breathes her name in and the sea salts sting my lungs as I breathe her name deeper, and deeper still. Like Neil, I too am in the mood for love. When love dances, she can really dance. I have forgotten completely about the earlier visions of the day, the fact that I have not spoken to her for two weeks. All I can think about now is the day I met her. I was in the Coffee Connection. Actually, I had just entered. As soon as I came through the door I saw an amazing figure. A sculpted frame standing in line, tall, two persons ahead of me, dazzling dark skin covering long fingers. She looked determined and focused to conquer something I could not name, although I wanted to. My body vibrated. She looked at me from the corner of her eyes, and then made contact with the server. She picked her order and walked to the far end of the coffee shop. I followed her too, but did not have the courage to make contact. I made sure that I sat down where she could see me. I checked her out two times, without turning my head, and I felt that she saw me seeing her.

I found myself at her table before I had a chance to decide what to say, and then I heard myself being introduced.

'Hello. This is Nyerere. From Tanzania.'

She did not invite me to sit. She replied coolly but her eyes danced, 'And this,' touching her hand to the slope above her breast, 'is Adowa. I am from Ghana, finishing a dissertation here at Harvard."

We settled in the atmosphere, sharing the moment after our introductions; briefly, our gazes searched each other.

Adowa said nothing but she heard it. A snore, a stirring then, a musky smell. It rose from the crack in her heart widening, she thought, with each breath. Something was hatching. Her pulse quickened so she looked to her watch. Ten minutes until she had to meet her advisor. Her palms began to grow sweaty and she reached toward her head and laid them flat, one beside the other, smoothing her hair. Focus yourself Adowa, the voice whispered from the crack. The smell spread out of the crack, out into the open, so heavy that when she tried to move her mouth it felt like she was moving it in gum. So this is what it feels like, she mused while polished introductions moved themselves out of her mouth and through the gum. I haven't forgotten. Adowa felt surprised she was so overwhelmed. But she had no interest to fight it. She had long since buried desire and did not think at first that it had much power left. Desire was too confusing. She ticked through why that was. Too many disappointments in the past. More important projects to focus on. A life of the mind to cultivate. But as unexpectedly as could be and with creeping persistence, Adowa felt movement deep inside when I, as slowly as I could, opened my mouth to breathe.

I watched Adowa's neck. It was only there that I could see her pulse raced too. Every other part of her body was relaxed into a firm composure. I watched her neck and wondered about desire. I thought that in the farthest centres of desire mind does not always have its way. My mind had fled the moment I saw her. In the place where breath begins, all the hurt and memories cannot live. I was in a mood for love and there was no way I would deny it. The pulse of her neck alone made me ready for anything.

'That is fascinating,' Adowa heard the dashing man in front of her saying. "What an interesting idea, this notion of the African Biological Self. I can understand Biology, but African biology?'

She must have told him about her dissertation. She straightened, aware suddenly of her thin cotton shirt. It clung to her because she was sweating.

'I know what you mean, because, one would think that Biology is just that, Biology, right?' She opened her mouth into a small oval, waiting for an answer.

'Exactly. Biology is Biology,' I said. 'Why Africanize it?'

'A long story.'

I thought I saw her sigh faintly. She pulled in her shoulders and I watched a small pocket appear underneath the delicate bone of her clavicle. When she rolled back, her bones curled up to meet her shoulders.

'It is precisely that question that my Professor wants me to explain carefully, since many hasty listeners can easily misunderstand my project.'

She stood up feeling disoriented.

'I must go.'

I knew she had to meet her advisor and that pushing luck was always a risk. Yet something more than the love of a gamble pressured me to talk on to her, to hear her words, to feel her world. I knew she had to go but I had to leave an impression.

'We should meet again sometime.' I said. Silence.

The room was blazing suddenly. I was hot and something was searing my eyes. They stung and then as I realized what had happened, they widened. Adowa had smiled.

'And I would like that very much,' she nodded to me, her face a prism. I radiated. She reflected. She shone bright. I boiled. My breath caught in mid -air and hung there in front of us. I wanted to move it away. It distracted my view. Adowa saw it too. She paused, her eyes searching mine through the breath. It seemed to gather into a cloud in front of her eyes, blocking me from her. I watched as her hand withdrew from my extended palm. The chair scraped the floor as the backs of her legs jarred against it. Her hand reached for the bag at her feet.

40

'I must go now,' she said again, picking it up and dusting the bottom. I waited for the answer to what I should do. She meant what she said, I knew that. She would like to see me. But what was the impression I had given? My confidence waned as she deliberately shouldered her bag. Perhaps the despair for love, or as I dreaded more, the marks of loneliness had shown through. Repelled her. The restlessness that had become my nature embarrassed me suddenly. I thought she could understand these things. Her presence felt my pain, somehow composing it into a picture that did not look quite so bad. But I had a disease, a metaphysical disease. I was consumed in the search for self, a restlessness for joy, for meaning. My disappointment at having found none so late in my life made me feel like a marked man. Caution played slowly at the edges of both of our minds.

'Maybe then I will be able to develop an explanation of what I mean by "The African Biological Self,"' she said as she walked out. I heard my voice. It said, 'Yes. Yes, that is a wonderful idea.' But then before I could get the words from mouth, to ask for her telephone number, she had turned her head and vanished out the door.

'Nyerere!'

My name in the darkness suddenly pierces me. I stop mid-stride, eyes bulging out into the darkness. Adowa has just vanished, it cannot be her. The moon does not give enough light to illuminate the speaker.

'Nyerere!' It is a man's voice. This the second time today my own name has confused me. Where is it coming from this time? Surely I am not sleepwalking.

'Nyerere!' I hear a pounding at my back. My heart is beating. Maybe I am an old man, I think to myself, finding this thought only half funny. The beating increases speed. It grows louder. Someone is approaching but I cannot run. I am frozen.

'Hey....' The hand reaches my shoulder, 'phew....'

Someone pants.

'I need to exercise more.' It is Neil. Again.

'Why are you just standing there?' he asks, breathing hard, chin down.

I push down the unexpected flash of anger that bolts through my head.

'You scared the hell out of me, Neil,' I tell him flatly. I am not accusing him so he accepts my tone. We amble along. I do not ask why he is not home already and why, at this hour, he has come running back to me.

'Tell me about Adowa,' Neil says as we walk. He is casual. His arms swing. I do not understand.

'You must have been thinking of her,' he insists, 'you were standing stock still forever.'

'Pardon me?' I do not mean to be brisk but it is late and we have school in the morning. I do not easily give over my fantasies. Especially of a woman like Adowa.

'You always play so cool about love, Nyerere. I don't know how you do it. I remember that even when you thought you had lost her in the bottom of Boston Harbor, you still looked cool.'

I could not believe my ears. Neil could be relentless. His honesty, which sometimes seemed tactless, was his best and most devastating quality. Those six days after her supposed death at the Boston Harbor were the most tortuous of my life.

'I suffer silently, Neil.' This does sound accusing.

Neil does not notice. 'Yes, I know. And if you would let on with how you are feeling more often, then maybe small things would not pain you so much.'

Neil is being very bold and I am unsure I like his uncustomary pushiness around my affairs. I do not want him to ask me if I have heard from her. It has been fourteen days since I last spoke to her and he does not need to know this. Luckily, he does not. He pushes on with the first track. He wants to remember the incident at the Boston Harbor.

'I thought we finished our play for the night,' I say. I am now in a mood again. I had been quite happy in my memory before Neil stumbled along into it, unable to keep his curiosity contained. I am sullen but he keeps on at my side. He wants to talk. I need to reserve a fraction of energy to prepare for my teaching tomorrow. I might be an ex-professor, but I am still a teacher, a professional and an intellectual. Creativity takes energy. Also, I still like to prepare the night before.

'You thought you had really lost her,' laughs Neil. He has clearly been thinking on my situation.

'It is not funny. It was not funny at the time either,' I snap, my voice momentarily losing the soft edges I like. The late hour has made both of us careless.

'Those were tortuous days, Neil.'

'I know, I am talking about Adowa the wrong way,' admits Neil, 'I just got to thinking that I have been spending so much time talking about Heidi, remembering Heidi, wondering about Heidi, there has been no room for you to tell me about Adowa.'

Neil obviously misreads my needs sometimes. I do not mind he is in love with her. I am happy for him.

'Do not worry yourself, Neil. Adowa is fine. She will be here soon.'

'OK.' Neil says. He looks disappointed. I realize then that he has only half asked me out of curiosity. The other half of the question is about him. He misses Heidi and cannot escape memory. The book must be pounding some important things home to him. He needs company. Wants to commiserate our bachelor lives. They are almost over, but both of us, for the time being, are without women. We are instead waiting on them.

'Fine.' I say to Neil. He turns his head to me, surprised. He had been walking sideways, turned toward the ocean.

He did not think I would cave. But I cannot fight what he has already set into motion. Memory is like a prancing child. When you resist, it prances closer. I glance at the sky. It will be morning not too long from now. I gauge it is at least 3 am. My house is another fifteen minutes' walk.

'I will do it. I will tell you about the time I thought I lost Adowa.'

I do not pretend to be a character. But I do know how to tell a story. So I begin.

**

I walk into the Coffee Connection. I hear a conversation.

She went over the rails.
At Boston Harbor?
Yes. Right over the rails. They aren't short, you know.
I know. The storm was strong. Are you sure she jumped?
She jumped, I said. The water was so high.
That explains it. What a shame. What a beauty she had been.
Yes. Long body and built strong. A silent grace.
Still, you could never imagine she could jump. Over the rails!
Are you sure about this? The details just don't add up.
She jumped, I said. It's all over the papers.

'Pardon me,' I say as I pick up the loose newspaper lying next to
the two guys arguing about something that happened at the Boston
Harbor. I am curious about what they are talking about but I do not
pay any mind because I am thinking about Adowa. I sit down close
to them and begin leafing through the paper. Maybe I will find the
story about the harbor they refer to. Let me tell you about how it was
that I came into these guys' conversation at the Coffee Connection.

I came to here in search of Adowa where we met for the first
time nearly three weeks ago. I called everyone I knew who might
know her in the last three weeks. I was desperate to see her again,
but I had not gotten her number. She was going to develop an explanation of what she meant by "The African Biological Self" for me. I
could not wait. I was in love. After the first moment she opened her
mouth I cared about her. It did not matter we had one conversation, I
wanted to have one hundred and then a thousand conversations. But
I was also distraught. This had to do with Elias.

Someone told me I should contact Elias and that he would give
me her number. I did not know him but he and Adowa were old
friends. But whenever I tried to call Elias no one would answer.
Finally, someone picked up the phone last night. It was a young
man on the other end. He was very wary of me. He would not let
me speak to Elias and he would not say why. I asked him if he knew
Adowa. I was so desperate to talk to her I did not even think about
how foolish that sounded. The young man did not answer me at first.
Finally, he said he did, and that I must be crazy to be calling for
her on Elias's phone. I had asked why, confused, but the guy just

kept yelling at me. I think he was telling me that something bad had happened but I was not sure if he was talking about Elias or Adowa or something completely different. 'If you don't know what I am talking about then you do not know Adowa!' he yelled before he hung up on me. I was so confused that I did not sleep. So, I came to the Coffee Connection with the feeling I might just see her. But the longer I waited for her, the louder the guys' voices next to me seemed to grow.

'I know so many people in this damn city with unfulfilled lives,' said the tall thin one.

'I know, I don't understand why they keep coming out here even though they know well that very, very few make it in this place. The dreamers never make it,' said the shorter one.

I wanted to lean over and say, 'Forgive me for interrupting you, but I am one of those dreamers that you speak of.'

They seemed like the types who talk bitterly about life in Cambridge and complain endlessly about it. I was in the mood for love and did not want to listen to them. But I held my tongue and kept reading. A headline caught my eye, 'SHARK COMMITS SUICIDE. CAMBRIDGE IN SHOCK.' I flipped to the front page wondering if I had picked up The Onion or another local daily satirical leaflet. The headline was outrageous. I realized when I turned it over that I was holding the *Boston Globe* which is a reputable newspaper. I started to read the story only I could not concentrate well because my curiosity had been now piqued and the men had begun arguing.

'A she, right?' the tall friend said. He was taller but had the same clean-shaven face and tired eyes. 'It was a she right?' he repeated, 'or was it a he?'

'A she I think. But, actually, I don't know. You never know with those kind. She. He. What's the difference?'

'Ok, let's just say it was a she. But she was black right?'

'Black! No way, man! White. Who are you kidding? Aren't they always white this side of the Boston Harbor? This is the harbor we're talking about not the Red Sea or Indian Ocean!'

'But they've got killer whites out there, too.'

I peered over the paper, sick at them. Killer whites! This was an amusing thought but I despised what I was hearing them say. First they had been talking about someone who jumped over the rails, a tragedy no doubt and one that I had not, surprisingly, heard about. Now they were debating that person's color. As sick as it was, I was only mildly surprised. People in Cambridge were obsessed with race, difference, and multiculturalism. They were the buzzwords of the eighties. The radical politics that brought them into language have no place in Cambridge, I thought to myself, especially among students. Everyone wants to talk about identity but they don't want to talk about gentrification. These guys were over the line. It was some of the most racist and sexist dialogue I have ever heard, and in public, at one of the most popular coffee shops in town. I set the paper down and unabashedly folded my hands, cleared my throat and listened to the conversation. To my amazement, they looked at me and kept talking.

'I just know the black ones don't live in this side of the harbor, that's all I'm saying. We might be the multicultural city,' he laughed conspiratorially, 'but that mixing only goes so far past the city center.'

He leaned in to his friend, I leaned in closer to both of them. "Behind the effortless merging lurked an impenetrable world of Multicultural illusion," he said to his friend and then burst out laughing. 'That's what that columnist wrote in the *Globe*.' I thought about saying something to them. To tell them what was what and then, perhaps even kick them out of the shop. They had no business being anywhere public with this kind of talk. What was striking about this conversation was that they did not try to hide what they were saying. I was so used to scripted conversations about race that this one caught me off guard. But I did not want to have to think about this right now, I wanted to think about Adowa. But instead of doing this I turned away from them and got bored with the conversation. I considered moving tables until the tall one said something that made my heart drop.

'I can't stand that columnist you're talking about. He's a Liberal lefty nobody. And he doesn't understand what multiculturalism is all about. I say she was black,' he glared at his friend, sealing the argument over the color of the person who had jumped. 'What I want to know is about the splash,' he continued.

46

'Oh, at the harbor you mean?'

'Yeah.'

'Well I heard that the reason the whole thing was so crazy, was because she hardly made a splash.'

'She was a professional suicide artist then,' one of them said.

They both paused. The tall one surveyed his friend.

'You forgot the most unbelievable thing about the whole story. They found that umbrella, didn't they? It was a light blue umbrella open, hanging from the rails, and busted up. Like the shark had tried to eat it or something.'

'Yeah, so?' the short friend seemed irritated. 'What's your point?'

'Well, it was hot out right?'

'Yeah.'

'So why the umbrella?'

Up to that point in the conversation I had listened with half an ear. As frustrated as it made me, I did not want to concern myself with their jabber. But when they mentioned the umbrella my heart trembled. I could not believe what I was hearing and suddenly, the pieces of the story began to fit together.

Adowa always carried a blue umbrella in the heat. She looked beautiful when she carried it, it fit her profile just perfectly and people would stare at her as she walked with it. She was majestic. But, also the only person I have ever known who carries an umbrella in Boston in 100 degree heat.

I began remembering the earlier parts of their conversation. Long and strong body, they said. Black. 'A she.' African. The room began to blur and my heart picked up pace. My mind raced. Jumped over the rails. Cleared them. Hardly a splash. Their words circled in my mind like an seagull wheeling overhead. Boston Harbor. Blue umbrella. A 'she' ... jumped into the Boston Harbor. I could not speak the words to what was pounding in my heart.

'If it wanted to die, it wanted to die,' the tall friend said to his shorter one. They were getting up, packing their bags. How could they be so inhumane? Since the beginning of the conversation they had been saying 'it, as though whoever jumped was a thing. Not a human being at all. White people can be so cruel, I thought, imagin-

47

ing Adowa's beautiful black body floating in the waters of the Boston Harbor. She looked peaceful. My mind screamed.

'See you later, man,' the tall one said.

'It was a 'she' and she was black,' the tall one said. He wanted to have the last word in their argument over the color of the person who had jumped. Jumped. Over the rails into the Boston Harbor. My mind could not comprehend what I was hearing. But I could not escape it. I wanted to stop them but one had gone to the bathroom and the other was already at the door. The room began closing around me. I could not think. I could not hear. I wanted to rush to somewhere. Anywhere. But to where? My love. My new love, my life's love. Gone?

It could not be true, I decided as I pulled myself up, jerking at the *Boston Globe* that clung to my shoe as I started to walk toward the door. 'SHARK COMMITS SUICIDE' I saw again as I thrust it across the room, and I thought, what a cruel, twisted headline to see today. I ran all the way to the Boston Harbor after that. I thought I would find her there. Of course, I found nothing there but too many tourists. I ran down one end and then up it again. I kept running until I saw a very happy woman with small children who looked like she had all the information anyone could ever need in the world. But when I asked her if she had heard any word about what happened to the woman with the blue umbrella at the other side of Boston Harbor she just looked at me in disgust and pulled her children close to her.

**

'The week that followed was horrendous,' Neil says to me. We are at my gate now. The sky is velvet and deep. It is the time before the morning begins to come in. The darkness will soon fade into light. I look at Neil, his eyes half closed. He is remembering what happened next. He picks at the crumbling part of my painted brick fence, waiting for me to continue.

'Do you want to come inside?' I offer. We could make ourselves something hot to drink.

'No. That's alright. We have to go to work in the morning.' He smiles. It is already morning. 'But I do not want you stop with the story. Please go on Nyerere.'

I am pleased he wants to hear. The air is moist and thick. It feels good on our skin. We sit down, right in the front of my fence on the unruly ferns and grasses curling their way into the street.

**

The telephone rang at the coffee counter. No one picked it up. It kept ringing. We were at the Coffee Connection. Neil, you convinced me to come because I was so depressed and would talk to no one. I thought I had lost Adowa and the worst part of it was that no one could tell me what happened. I scoured every newspaper, called Harvard, called people I knew, searched for her in every part of town. No one could tell me anything. Some hung up on me when I asked them about her death.

The phone just kept ringing at the Coffee Connection.

'Why doesn't anyone pick up the phone?' I asked the silence. Then I chided myself for the image of Adowa rising in my mind. The phone stopped ringing. I thought about leaving. The sky was fresh and Neil was sullen today. I picked up my cup to finish my drink, but then, the phone started again. Maybe it is Adowa I thought suddenly. The idea rose luminous in my mind like her smile. Someone picked up the telephone behind the counter.

It was Adowa's voice on the other end. My own voice disappeared and I could not even say Hello 'This is Adowa, remember me?' she asked. The woman behind the counter must have handed me the phone.

'Remembering you is all that I have done for the past two weeks,' I said to her. The silence was electric over the telephone lines.

She asked me if we could meet at Harvard's Barker Center for a lecture on the 'Foundations of Identity.' I readily said yes, my lips quavering from the desire to simply see her once again. I would tell her, if I could muster the courage, that I had fallen in love with her. Of course I knew that she would be shocked, but then again, why not? Let her be shocked. I would only speak truth.

She hung up the phone first. I was left with the receiver in hand, wondering how soon a week could pass.

'Double skinny caramel soy macchiato with whipped cream!' shouted the server at the counter, shattering my reverie. A man in pressed white oxford and pencil tie hurried up to the counter, just in

49

from the door.

'We don't usually make coffees to be picked up, sir,' the server said curtly. 'Next time you want a drink, please don't call on the phone. We are not Dominoes and everyone else waits in line.' The people at the counter glared at him. I thought I even heard one-man growl.

The man with the pencil tie looked bewildered, as though he thought people called coffee shops every day to have their favorite drink pre-ordered and ready. He reached for his coffee and did not even say thank you, brushed past us out the door, his cell phone ringing in his pocket.

'What a jerk,' the server muttered to herself as she jerked out the phone cord from the wall. 'See if anyone calls again with that kind of prank today. On the day of the lecture I prepared myself carefully. I looked good. Before I left the house, the phone rang several times. Each time, I thought it might be Adowa. Each time it was a different person. First Neil. Then Makau. They felt sorry for me. They believed I had lost my mind and they probably had good reason to. I saw Adowa everywhere. Heard her voice. She lingered with me over breakfast. Sat with me while I graded papers. She even whispered in my ear during lectures. My eyes combed the streets for her when she was not near. I searched lines in other people's faces for some clue about life, looked deep into the cracks on the old sidewalks of Brattle Street. I wanted answers about life. I wanted to know why it could be so cruel. Neil insisted I had imagined the phone conversation with Adowa, when I told him I had to hang up because I was on my way to meet her at the "Foundations of Identity" seminar. Makau pointed out to me that it was the man with the coffee who had called in to order. 'He was calling to order in his drink, Nyerere, he jested. No one was calling to order in *you*.' I thought Makau was being crass. I ignored them and checked my self in the mirror one last time before I got my coat from the closet. The phone rang. I stalled in front of it, unsure if it would be yet another person, harassing me to stay indoors and save myself the trouble of traveling across town to a woman who had jumped over the rails at Boston Harbor. I put my coat on, willed the phone to stop ringing and turned the doorknob. It did not stop ringing. My heart fluttered, faint. I reached out for the

50

phone and before I could stop myself, I said hello.

'Hello. Is this Nyerere?'

It was a man's voice and it sounded unsure. I considered slamming down the phone. I would be late for the seminar if I did not hurry this person on in whatever it was they were calling about.

'Yes. It is. Please, I do not mean disrespect, but please be quick. I have somewhere to be,' I said to the stranger on the other end.

'I understand,' said the voice, 'but I am calling you with some news I thought you would like to hear.' A silence.

'By the way, my name is Elias.' I recognized the name. Adowa had mentioned she was going to meet him after she saw her advisor that day we met in the Coffee Connection. I bit my tongue. I could not alllow any excitement into this moment, whatever he had to tell me would not bring Adowa back to me.

'Go on.'

'I think there has been a big mistake.' A pause. 'About Adowa.' Another pause. 'I heard you were worried about her. That maybe…' his voice was getting quiet, 'you thought that maybe…'

'Go on,' I said to Elias, 'there is nothing to fear.' I meant it. I had no energy left in my body to let anything he said destroy me more than I was already destroyed.

Elias cleared his throat. 'Adowa is not… I mean, Adowa is alive. She is well.'

'I know.' I said firmly down the phone lines. What did this man want with me? I thought.

'Yes, but, what I mean to say to you, because I heard you were upset is… that she did not jump over the rails at Boston Harbor.'

I waited. He began speaking quickly, 'she would never do something like that. She loves it down there…and besides, I saw her, just a few days ago… last week I think it was.' Another pause. 'Like I said. I think maybe you heard something wrong. Adowa is fine.'

'She is fine.' I knew that. What was with this guy? But then it began to register. What had he said?

'Last week?' I asked. All the moisture in my mouth had been sucked out, I could not form even enough saliva to swallow. My voice drifted and then fizzled out. Clearly this man had not heard the news himself. Only six days had passed since they said Adowa had last been at the Boston Harbor rails.

'I know, I know…' Elias cut in, 'I saw her. Recently. A few days ago. Six days ago. On the day you are thinking she… well… on the day you are thinking she was at the Boston Harbor. I mean to say that she was there, she went to the rails after I saw her. We met up first, had a drink, and then she walked down there. I called her, at home, later in the day. She is fine.'

The phone lines seemed to buzz in my hand, come alive.

'I spoke to her, Nyerere.'

'I am sorry my friend. Elias?'

'Yes. Elias. But I don't think…'

'You are right, I cannot understand what you are talking about.'

I held the phone away from my ear. My head was ringing.

'I'm trying to tell you…'

I slammed the phone back up against my ear. 'I know what you are trying to tell me,' I nearly shouted, but I need to go.' My voice sounded even but I was crumbling inside. My reserves depleting, I wondered for the first time in six days if maybe I should listen to my friends. I should not go to the seminar. Maybe I was going crazy, seeing apparitions. Maybe Elias had been put up to the task of doing reverse psychology on me. The more he insisted Adowa was alive and well, the more I insisted she was gone. After six days of seeing nothing but her, I began to wonder if in fact, I was imagining her. No one can be everywhere at once, I chided myself.

'I will not go to the seminar, then,' I announced to Elias, 'but, still I need to go. I am very tired.'

'But, did you…' Elias was talking past me, speaking quickly, loudly, making me more and more tired.

I breathed through my nose loudly into the receiver. 'Hear?' I asked him calmly, 'Yes, I heard you. Thank you for calling.'

I hung up the phone before I could hear what it was. My heart had turned from lava, to jelly, to stone and back to jelly again in a matter of moments. I grabbed my cap and pushed myself through the door. Once on the step I realized I had left my keys inside. Though I have never done it, for some reason it seemed natural I would not be able to get back into my house, would have to crawl through a window or call a locksmith or…. my mind began running from me as I walked down the first step and then backed up again. I continued like this, up, down, up down, until I had made up my mind about what to do. I would trust this man knew what he was talking about. I had no idea what this man Elias was talking about but I was going to see Adowa. The seminar started in twenty minutes.

I arrived early because I jogged the entire way to the lecture hall. I sat near the back so I could see each person in the room and all those coming and going through the door at the side. I did not see Adowa. In fact, I did not see many people at all. I looked at the clock. It was five minutes to the hour. I relaxed into a daydream and let the people filter in around me.

'Nyerere?' A voice interrupted me. It was musical. Like charms on a bracelet. I looked up. There in front of me, stood Adowa. I knew she would join me.

'I wondered if I would see you here,' she said. 'Do you mind if I sit?' She motioned to the empty chair beside me.

'Of course not, please do sit,' I motioned to the chair, but I wasn't sure whether to stand or to sit. With an entrance like that, I wanted to say, you need a man with finesse. She sat. I decided to stay where I was. My pulse ran wild.

During the course of the talk, our eyes locked twice, and both times, I was convinced, we whispered to each other without using our mouths. I am in the mood for love, I said. Are you? I am in the mood for love. She said. Are you? I thought I had lost you, I whispered. I never left, she murmured back.

The speaker bored us. We tried not to yawn. I concentrated on the current between us. Finally, the question and answer period arrived. A lot of people asked the right questions. One particular question interested us immediately. A young female asked,

"What is identity after all?"

The question was deceptively simple. The speaker was dumbfounded, for he had assumed that everybody knew what identity is, but he himself had never asked the question. He was simply convinced that since everybody knew, he could proceed to discuss its foundations.

We talked about this question on our way out into the night air. 'Color, race and gender are really appearances,' I said to her, 'we wear them because we have too, but when we are alone, all of us are nothing more than incomplete projects, unfulfilled selves.'

She agreed and then we let the night be. We walked toward her place, our legs nearly touching each other as we stepped in time. By pure accident, our ankles kissed as we crossed Memorial Drive towards the Science Center at Harvard Yard. Our eyes locked again, and we were both embarrassed by it. It had happened three times in a single day.

Adowa told me that the question on identity went to the heart of her concerns, as she was working out her dissertation on the African Biological Self. 'I must first figure out what identity is, before I can examine its biological organization. 'What do you understand by identity?' she asked, 'if you ever think about it?'

I told her that all that most people know is that they are black, white, and brown, female, male and so on, and that these masks are taken as real. I told her, I myself, simply assume that to be a black person is so natural that it does not deserve any further scrutiny. My philosophy courses helped me much later to at least begin wondering about what being human means, long before knowing what it means to be a black person. I learned how to separate masks from essences.

Adowa's mind had already turned back to her project before she even looked at her watch. She had a new inspiration about how to begin the chapter she was working on. She would start it by examining first the components of identity. She would have to decide where she must read to supply a definition she found fitting. I floated next to her, my mind as clear as the night. She looked at her watch, said she had to abort the conversation, promised to talk again soon. She strode away. I was left hanging in the air, suspended on a love that was so high off the ground I could not even see that she had stopped, just a few feet away from me, and waved goodbye.

Impossible, I mused to myself as I turned the other direction to go home. The dream is the truth. Indeed, I thought, I will remember this, whenever I think of you.

**

I have finished my story for tonight. I look over at Neil in the dawning light. He has fallen asleep. A smile on his face. I lean back against the fence, move a rock that digs into my calf. The early morning is delicious. I think about the big day tomorrow of opening the school back up after the holiday. Seeing the kids. Teaching.

'We must be ourselves, no matter what the consequences,' I have always told my students.' I mean it, though most of them think this is cliché. We should live life honestly, only once. We should live it honestly and courageously. I think Neil and I are living honestly now. Courageously, too. This gives me a sense of peace. We are entirely free though. Our play has no beginning. It has no end. It is also tiring. Sometimes, I wonder if Neil and I are not going in circles too. We plunge memory to free it, but the more we plunge, the more it lives. As our nightly script writing shows, we can tell the same stories a hundred different ways. I am not sure if this is a good thing anymore.

I watch a young woman swinging a large and empty petrol canteen from her hip. She crosses the street to the left of me and then disappears around the corner. She is up very early, running an errand for someone. The struggle to be free of Heidi's struggle is Neil's struggle is my struggle. The struggle to be free does not look the same for her as it does for me. I think about Neil as I watch him, sleeping so contentedly in the grass outside my house. He often insists that he sees what I see, hears what I hear. That he struggles over questions of race, of place, of meaning. He told Heidi that, long ago, and she left him in frustration over it. He made her invisible with those words. I also know that my particular struggle with all of these things is different than Neil's. We do not have the same history. Some might say we are not cut of the same cloth.

'Let us go to sleep,' I say to Neil. He does not stir. I look to the sky and the moon winks one last time at me before it begins its slow retreat from the day, making way for the sun. We have about three and a half hours before we will need to be up and ready to go to school. I cross my arms and close my eyes. The grass is prickly then soft. I do not want to skip right now. But I do want to sleep.

INTERMISSION

ANNOUNCEMENT

We are in the intermission and we are sleeping now. I am dreaming and so is Neil. The dream is good. In it, I want a new script. An entirely new script. Neil has agreed. He said he was up for the challenge.

Wait.

Neil just told me he is no longer ready to begin a new script.

'I think we need to fill in a few more details first,' he is saying, 'set the scene. Explain what got us here, to Tanzania.' I wonder if he still needs to tell more of his story. This is probably true. Maybe I do too.

'Maybe we can divide each person's life into chapters,' Neil is now saying. 'No interviews.'

I agree. 'No long diversions.'

'We knew many people in Cambridge. We should tell their stories. Each chapter a different person.'

'There will need to be at least eight chapters then.' I think about all the people we knew in Cambridge. 'It can be a long book.'

With that conversation out of the way, we can now begin again. We look at each other. We do not smile though the situation is funny. We have a similar problem as last time. We need to decide on whose chapter we will begin.

ACT II
IT BEGAN, AGAIN

ADOWA

'Hey! That hurts!' exclaimed Elias. He looked up and then reached for his head. It was wet.

'What hurts?' Adowa asked, alarmed. She was used to Elias saying unexpected things when he was uncomfortable. Elias shifted in his seat. Strange things often happened when he was nervous. He thought he had felt cold water drop on his head, but maybe he was just imagining things. They were sitting in their familiar surroundings of the Coffee Connection, it was not raining, and Adowa looked perturbed. He did not like when she did not have on her cool smile.

'Maybe you take life too seriously.' Elias repeated.

He had spent the last fifteen minutes advising her on how to relax. He had meant the advice as compassionate. She did not look particularly stressed, but she always had to go after they had spent more than two hours together, 'to get back to her project.' She knew this bothered him but it was the truth. She arranged her face into calm to divert his discomfort. He did not need to know she was bristled.

'You don't have to take so much responsibility,' he said for the fifth time, 'be free. Express yourself. Be a little reckless sometimes. You won't be young forever, Adowa. A little serious here, a little reckless there. It cannot hurt can it?'

She was weary to explain herself, again. She was not at home any more. She thought she had escaped these kinds of expectations. Cambridge was the city of knowledge, was it not? Why did so many people seem to think she needed sympathy for her chosen way? Suffering and thinking was Adowa's way of expressing herself, of being in the world as a vigilant human being, as an African. It is the dignities of resistance that makes us African, Adowa thought resolutely. She picked up her teacup, rippled her cooled tea with her breath and then made her eyes gentle for Elias. Elias felt better after he saw her face like that. They sat in silence for a little while, watching the passersby from the window.

'I will be patient,' Adowa said aloud.

'With what?' Elias asked. He looked concerned.

'Oh. Nothing, Elias. I am just thinking aloud.' She turned and looked out the window again.

I have done well by myself, in spite of the lonely nights, she thought to herself. Her relatives had been right after all. Concentration attracted men, but it did not always keep them. They wanted her concentration in measure and her beauty in full. She wanted both and could not explain that to her, beauty and concentration were hand in hand. One without the other did not exist. She sighed deeply, expanded her lungs and pushed out the air. My work on the human body gives full meaning to my life. I will not trade that for anything else.

While Adowa sat and pondered, Elias watched her. He always watched people and this often made them uncomfortable. He was often anxious but he meant no harm. Adowa knew this. They were friends. He had arrived early because he had been so excited to see her. Indeed, they were friends but Elias felt more. Elias had been the first to arrive at Harvard Coop. He kept pacing up and down. He grabbed a newspaper and attempted to read it. He could not. He put it down, and went to the bathroom for no reason. He stepped out of the bathroom and returned to the table and sat down for a few minutes. He got up again. He walked to the far end corner of the floor where he indulged himself in the Self-Help section and immersed himself in reading on love and relationships, an obsession of his. He returned again to his table and sipped more of his coffee. He covered himself with a stuffy magazine on love, and got bored with it and put it down. By then Adowa's arrival had fast approached. His hands began shaking. Anxiety spread its wings. His entire body changed. But he tried to put up a show, and exuded confidence. Unlike Elias, the ever-anxious one, the controlled Adowa arrived exactly on time. On the dot, as the English say. He got up to greet her, and she extended her thin hands, and his large hands embraced her generously. For a moment he thought that he might have actually hurt her. His sweaty hands rested on her confident hands. For a while his eyes could not shift themselves from the focus on her body. He was embarrassed when he noticed that she had caught his eyes surveying her body. She did not know whether to forgive him or enjoy the attention. She smiled and said,

'So how is life treating you, Elias?"

'Oh. I really didn't know the ups and downs of life could be quite hard on the soul. But I remain alive.'

"Oh, well. So you are not the hardy type then," said Adowa.

"Certainly not. I have never professed to be," replied Elias. "By the way, what can I get you from the restaurant?' he asked.

'Let me think about what I want.' She put her hands around her chin and a few seconds later she told him what she wanted and he came back with an orange tea.

"I love tea in the afternoon. It is an English thing," she said.

"I guess so. We Americans are obsessed with our coffee in large mugs, which offends many real coffee drinkers around the world, who prefer their coffees in small cups," he said.

"Oh, yes. I was startled by the obsession also, when I first observed it in America."

After she finished that last statement she glanced at the far end side of where Elias sat. There was a book on love that Elias had leafed through quickly while he was waiting for her. She asked for permission and leafed through it equally quickly.

"Love. I am shocked that it is being written about," she sarcastically said.

"Why are you shocked? It's a hot topic in this country. You're so cynical Adowa," Elias declared.

"I know it is on everybody's lips. Really though, most people cannot even love. It is as if they are afraid of it. Surely, there is the phenomenon of infatuation. That I am aware of, and everybody is into that, young and old," said Adowa.

"Fear you say. What has fear got to do with love?" said Elias.

"I would not even know where to start, on the topic of love. I have so much so say, but I do not know how to say it in a condensed way. We English-speaking Ghanaians love to speak in rather longish sentences. We indulge in language," she said.

Silence. She looked like she was organizing her thoughts, before starting a lecture. She self-consciously said, "If we get into this topic, you will have long sentences to put up with, Elias."

"What do you mean?" he asked innocently.

She replied, "I cannot converse about this topic without lecturing you in long sentences. I am going to bore you. It is a real warning," she repeated.

"Really. Try me. Really, go at it. I don't get bored easily, least of all with a speaker like you," said Elias, and raised his eyebrows.

"Well then, for me, Elias, love is a memory of experiences. It is a recollection of the meaning of every gesture, every laughter and pain you shared with the beloved. Long after the relationship is over, the one who loved continues to love and remember, and it is that remembrance of things past that hurts, that haunts," said Adowa.

She removed a falling tear.

Silence again. As if she were remembering. She closed her eyes and scratched her ears.

Elias broke the silence, and said,

"It's remembering the past that is the cause of the fear, then."

"Precisely. You really got it. When you really love, and the love is over, you have memory to fight. Forgetting the things past is the struggle of the lover. And love itself becomes a struggle against memory. That kind of love is hurtful, and people are afraid of that hurt, of that memory, of that struggle with the past, a past that will never come back. Although it is a loosing battle, the lover nevertheless tries, and fails over and over again. That is why the smart ones protect themselves against love, by not falling in love. That is my humble thought on a very complex matter," she concluded.

They left the conversation at that. Agreed it had been a good afternoon together. Adowa said she wanted to go for a walk at the Harbor. Elias bid her good-bye, watching her intently as she walked on, a secret desire stirring deep.

**

Adowa kept walking until she had passed through all the crowds of South Station and the shops of the Harbor. She turned heads as she walked. Left to right, right to left, their approving eyes measured her gait with a studied awe. No one could make a walk so beautiful as Adowa. Bold measured strides with an Umbrella. It was Boston Harbor, it was 100 degrees outside and the sun was fierce. Of course she carried an umbrella. The eyes thought the umbrella gave her presence a mystique. Some women stared directly. A few men took secret shots at her. Older women told her out right how beautiful she was. Older men simply smiled in admiration. Everybody, however, looked on this Black beauty. She wore deep smiles to welcome the stares, the unsolicited admirations and the profusion of acknowledgements. She welcomed them all with a demeanor, reserved for princesses. For she was a princess as her mother used to call her, when she was barely five years old. She maintained that stillness of manners, that silent grace, which has earned her a place among her admiring colleagues. But Adowa always walked on, right foot in front of the left; she walked on past the admiring eyes, shifting right and then left, to that place beyond to her destiny.

She arrived at the rails at midday.

She held on firmly to the rails as a single powerful storm swung by and scared the hell out of her. She jumped in fear, but regained her cool in a few seconds. Waves flew by her eyes. Adowa stared at them all. The deafening noise and the force of their movements forced her to acknowledge the overwhelming presence of nature in human life, and for the first time realized that Ghanaian waves were the same as the Bostonian ones. She laughed at the comparisons of her imagination, and was charmed by her silliness. There is time for silliness too, she said to herself.

**

Adowa let go of the harbor rails and felt the breeze lift her. She saw the trees, the high church steeple and ring of its bell, the sloping roof of home. The wind eased her down toward to her aunts and her uncles under the shade of the tree. Laughter seeped out from the big open pores of her elder aunt, and the older ones sucked in their teeth, waiting for a climax. They were telling Sunday stories and it was her middle uncle who had them baited now. Adowa settled in between them just as the laughter exploded through mouths and shook out through limbs relieved to let go the anticipation that uncle had been building up for far too long. Adowa felt her face contort into a lop-sided smile, she had forgotten this struggle with laughter. Adowa only laughed sometimes. Most times she felt embarrassment for the interloper, sympathetic to the lover who found his wife with another man, intrigued by the young seeker looking for God. She knew why her aunts and uncles laughed. Their laughs had a purpose; to ease the interloper and the hopeless lover they giggled and prodded, to encourage the stubborn farmer they hooted and with long deep belly laughs they comforted the hopelessly challenged Christian who knocked on all the wrong doors asking if anyone had seen God. They themselves knew from experience that if you cannot laugh at the confused self you cannot begin to set it straight.

'Adowa, stop frowning!' exclaimed her uncle as the laughter separated and eased itself into the air, preparing way for the next good story. As always, Adowa pulled at her face upwards and raised her eyebrows to the sky trying to mold her cheeks into a smile. 'Good, good,' he said, pleased she was at least trying. She had been making progress with her smiles lately and for that at least, they all had to be grateful. God only knew how much her poor mother worried about Adowa's insistence on frowning all the time, even when she was happy.

Adowa had to hide the way those words scratched. She was thinking, not frowning. Adowa wanted to know why the searcher could not find the open door. From when she was very young, Adowa also wanted to see God in the face. She understood the searcher. Like him, she looked for God everywhere. In the sky, at the ocean, even on the glossy underbelly of the beetle and the skin of a green mango saved over from Sunday school. Adowa was a thinker-dreamer. Many people might have known this about her, but it was not a condition they envied. She concentrated so much that her mother worried. Her father remained indifferent. Her aunts and uncles tried their best to teach her. They understood a mother's worry.

Her mother was afraid of the things that could grow because of such concentration. Of course she did not want her daughter to be silly, to take smiles for granted. More than just the smile it was the absolute absence of smiles that worried her mother. It was the things that grow in the smiles' place. Things like thin lines around the mouth, a long nose, a reputation that would leave her barren and her body hard. Adowa's mother fretted and picked but Adowa still only smiled sometimes.

'That is for the men to do, Adowa,' her mother said when she caught Adowa bent on her knees in front of the of the lemon tree in the front of the house. She thought Adowa was holding a scythe in one hand and a ruler in the other. Her mother thought she was out to cut the grass. But Adowa surprised her when she said she was measuring the circumference of the trunk. Adowa knew that if she were to cut the tree in two, there would be rings inside that they could count together and guess the age of the tree.

'That tree is at least as old as this house is young,' her mother said, 'and I can tell you now that it bore lemons long before you were born and it survived the master too.' She was proud of that tree and was not about to let her daughter saw it in half. Like her, the tree had seen many days, many of them not easy ones, and yet, it stood, still, and bore fruit. It did not matter the lemons were too small and fleshy. Like her, the tree was getting old.

'Your face will harden into that stare,' she said to Adowa, picking a green lemon from the branch and placing it her daughters' lap, 'like this hard old lemon.' Adowa had seen lemon-faced women before. She wanted to know the stories in between the lines on their faces, but she also understood she did not need to defeat her mother. 'I will learn,' Adowa said to her mother, to which her mother replied with one word. 'Good,' she said and then made the motion as if to walk away. Later she would tell Adowa how it is that women are to be soft, she decided, and said instead, 'You are becoming a woman now. It is time now to make your face.'

From that day forward, Adowa began practicing her smile in earnest. She chose to practice on Sundays because it was on Sundays that everyone smiled and laughed and celebrated. It would be easy, she thought, once she put her mind to the task. Adowa found it was hard to stretch her face and expose her teeth. Her cheeks would ache and she pleaded with her relatives to let her rest. But they were insistent she could learn and that she only needed patience. Adowa was a smart child, she knew that she needed patience, and diligence and strength and faith too. The real problem was that Adowa did not really understand why it was so important to smile. They tried to give her reasons. Shamed parents, hostile neighbors. Already some people said she had a locked heart. Her family knew better, there was no child more compassionate than Adowa. Perhaps they would sigh, she was just born this way. Your beauty will not keep you up high for so long, they teased instead. One day you will put your hand to your stomach and feel a wasted womb. You will reach to your breast and there you will find useless old sacks of skin, just hanging there, down to your knees. They laughed at that. Many of them knew about long breasts spent from years of nursing. Boring hours, toiling days and hot lonely nights, they would joke. That is the life of someone who does not smile. You will cry, Adowa. Do by the right way, Adowa. Life is hard but you are a child. The time will come when you need such a serious face.

It was her youngest aunt who unlocked Adowa's smile finally. It happened on a Sunday afternoon after the church bells had come and gone and the breeze had stultified into bright heat. Most people were getting restless to go home. Her youngest aunt had not got to tell her story and though it was getting so hot, she began. She looked at Adowa when she asked them all if they had heard of the girl and The Black Cloth. The Black Cloth was about a young girl named Aiwa.

Little Aiwa lost her mother at the same that she was born. She was fated to live with a vicious stepmother, who made life unbearable for her. She labored her to death, insulted her pointlessly, and yet Aiwa bore all these sufferings with remarkable patience and unusual grace. The elegance and depth of her manners of dealing with her anguish was, in turn, unbearable for her stepmother. Yet, Aiwa kept on smiling, and these smiles of resistance irritated her stepmother to the point of wishing Aiwa's death. Finally, the stepmother gave her an impossible task, which was to get the whitest piece of cloth available. In that part of the country, at that time, white cloth was impossible to find. There was blue cloth and red, black and brown and grey. But Aiwa took the challenge and left home. She traversed miles of rivers and mountains to no avail. She nearly gave up until one day, high up in a mountain it began to snow. In between the great flakes, her dead mother revealed herself to Aiwa, white cloth in hand. Aiwa thanked her mother and took the long journey back to her stepmother. When she arrived back home with the cloth, her stepmother gasped. She was shocked to find out that the white cloth was the one with which her first husband was buried. Aiwa was vindicated and justice was served, fully rectified because it was born of patience.

To everyone's surprise, Adowa's face cracked into the widest smile they had ever seen. It was so unexpected to everyone, including Adowa, that they all fell silent. Adowa basked in the newfound pleasure of this smile. Her cheeks massaged her eye sockets. Her forehead lifted to touch her hair and her ears stood on end. Teeth kissed the breeze. The oldest had to shade their eyes with the backs of their hands from the glow. Adowa understood. After all the threats and the jokes and the worry, Adowa had found a good enough reason to smile. After that, her mother never said anything more about Adowa's future. People who first met her would say she looked as though she were always on the verge of a smile. Adowa had made it her philosophy to smile as Aiwa did, in the face of all struggle.

Adowa relaxed as her hands dipped into the icy water. Boston Harbor was not the place to swim. Her mother did not like them going to the public beaches when they were young because Adowa was always searching for tide pools while the others played in the waves. Her mother worried she would lose herself looking. Adowa raised her heart in silence to her mother. Her mother always wanted the best for her, even when what she thought best stood in the way of what Adowa thought she wanted. Adowa wanted to major in philosophy in college. Her mother disagreed, her father, in his indifferent way, agreed with her mother through his silence. Adowa was glad for their foresight now. She might have just flown up into the clouds and lost her anchor to the world if it had not been for her knowledge and love of biology. She was committed to the biological world. Her passion for thought, for looking at things deeply gave her a deftness that other rigid scientists found difficult. Many of her colleagues believed science was a series of stages and seriousness, a face one wore to the laboratory. And patience? They thought patience was born through proving those stages—writing theorems and heavy textbooks, scrawling diagrams that made sense to just a few.

They do not know the subtleties of patience in this country, she mused to herself. People in my country name their children Patience. Patience breathes, patience lives, thought Adowa. Seriousness does not sleep when the body does. Adowa made her hand into a cup and scooped up water. She let it fall between her fingers like splinters of glass. The light caught on the drops as they fell, twinkling little drops of light plummeting back down to the ocean floor. She smiled to little Aiwa as the ocean mixed the water she had dropped. Like you, I accept my destiny with a smile.

**

The sky was blue like the ocean and the harmony soothed her eyes. Thanks to the Transcendent, she whispered. I could not live without these giants of nature. A rumbling shook out loudly in reply, the sky and the ocean. The waves seemed to be moving faster the closer Adowa flew to them, alarming speed and deafening noise humbled her. The curving lips of the waves danced and leaped and she couldn't help but laugh. Long and hard she laughed, and then she kissed the winds. Destiny for those who wait, triumph for those who are patient she sang. And then something happened. Adowa opened her eyes wider in astonishment. There in front of her was the face of the Transcendent. On this special day, she had finally a childish longing visit with her, and she succumbed to it. She understood now why her aunts and uncles laughed so hard at the searcher who knocked and knocked on so many doors. If he had wanted to see God so badly he should have just stopped knocking.

**

Suddenly, she began thinking about her work on the African body, the subject of her dissertation. The body, she mused, is so fragile, so vulnerable to sickness and death, and the African body suffers even more, because of political princesses of African leaders and health experts. Why is it, she asked, that Africans, as the founders of world civilizations, such as Egypt and the Great Ethiopia, Songai and Mali, Great Zimbabwe and The Sudan, have yet to conquer dis-

72

ease and hunger, amidst plenty of resources? She closed her eyes, as she asked these disturbing questions, the sources of her anguish and pain. To be sure, she said, death and sickness are dimensions of the human condition. We Africans, however, get huge dosages of these venoms, sickness and death.

The African body, she said to herself, is really in jeopardy, and those who are in the position of protecting it are not up to the task. The diseases which are afflicting millions of children, who do not live beyond the first five years of their lives, can easily be cured, but the funds, which should be earmarked for services for the African poor and sick are being pocketed by the wealthy and the powerful. Her eyes were filled with tears, as these words of the heart flew out of her. She took out a notebook and began jotting down notes, as she firmly held to the rails, and focused on the determined waves which invaded the ocean. A couple of times she saw the tails of sharks floating with the waves and resisting their force to swallow it. The shark too was fighting for its life, by protecting its body. You see, Adowa remarked, every being wants to live, to affirm its existence. Those words went into the notebook.

She looked down as she was reminiscing about her first trip to the historic Ethiopia and was hit hard by the memory of this young girl, whose name was Aster. Aster was the mother of a two-year-old. Aster was never home. At times she comes home for two hours, feeds the child, and hands her back to her baby sitter. The child is always looking for her absent mother. One can see the child following the contours of her mother's shapely body, as she comes in and out of her mother's life. The two-year-old says, 'Mother, will you stay and play with me?' The mother can only smile and leave immediately. Aster goes out to wait on her customers at the bars of the city. On her way, she sometimes offers her body to her cab driver, so that he can her drop at work. Aster works at several places. Aster, a young girl in her early twenties, has three jobs. One is a secretary at a news room, which barely pays for a tiny apartment which she shares with a sort of a baby sitter. One of the rooms is the home of her second job, where she sells drinks, after she gets off from her first job. There in that tiny room, she witnesses some of her drunken customers passing out and urinating on the floor. Her customers drink there, sleep there. Those who manage wake up the next day; go to work in that vile form to oxidize the morbid bureaucracies in which they frittered away their unfulfilled lives. A few times, Adowa remembered, Aster confessing to her that she has actually made out with her customers while her child is sleeping right next to her. Aster has a third job. She is an escort in a hotel, where she is forced to make out with any customer with money. On one of those days, the father of her only child catches her making out and hell breaks loose. He savages her, calls her names, and she does the same. She swings her hands to his face and manages to hit him on his nose. He bleeds profusely. Shortly, he avenges and throws his huge arms on her face, smashes her nose, tears her lips, rips her hair, and drives away to the depths of the city, with a singer on the radio saying,

Fate has it right
Everything is relative.
No condition is permanent
Do you get it man?
Kick a woman hard she will love you
Love her hard she will adore you.
Never give a woman your heart
Will destroy you with it.
Do you hear me you fool?
Give a woman just a little love
Make her think that you love her
Keep her running
Then you will get what you want
Sex and all will be in your hands
For the rest of your life.
Keep it cool and firm that thing you got.

She did know whether to laugh or cry, when she remembered Aster's fate, for the abuse of the African woman's body for the sake of living had been a subject of her thoughts for many years. For her, Aster was the living example of anguish and pain in the lives of millions of African women who sold their bodies by way of fighting for the right to live. As she put it, in her notebook, life for these women is literally not a right, although it ought to be, but a happenstance that could be taken away from them by poverty and disease, both of

74

which are preventable by intelligent public policies. She herself, who is physically the ideal beauty for everyman, white, black, brown and yellow, has taken another track of living it, another track of fighting for women's lives. She does not want to sell her body for anything.

A group of ducks and their ducklings had come to the shore. She changed her mind, and reached into her purse, and brought out two bagels, cut them to little pieces and threw them at the ducklings. They must have been so famished that they came in perfect lines and remarkable discipline and gently pushed and shoved each other to feed themselves. So she was reminded of the story and the African experience. She had witnessed African victims of the story in Ethiopia, clamoring for her face, encumbered by pain and by helplessness. While thinking, she fell asleep, as the heat progressively tired her.

Dreams invaded her soul. She saw herself inside another person's body, a person who was about to die, and reflecting on the life she lived. A woman in a man's body, a young woman, who wanted to be a writer, a writer on human pain. The work needed independence of mind and a lot of freedom, but the woman also one day wanted to be married and have children. The two dreams conflicted, and she entered many disappointing relationships, each of which ended because the men in her life loved her in the best way they knew. They all wanted to possess her and control her time. For these men, love was possession and full control. That is what their parents taught, and what their grandparents taught their parents. The men who loved her were upholding a tradition. Even the mothers believed in these myths. The aspiring woman writer wanted to break from all these, and yet, it came at a heavy price. Reconciling freedom and tradition had never been easy. That is why the woman was trapped in a body and soul she did not want. She had no friends to confide in her secrets, her sorrows, and disappointments in life. She neither became the writer she wanted to be or the fulfilled mother, whom she hoped. One day, she entered a nearby river and committed suicide at the tender age of twenty-one. The village in which she grew remembered this story, and it was told to many aspiring women writers as an example of what a woman should never aspire to be.

Adowa woke up in a shock wondering about the dream.

She saw them all, and listened to some of their worries and dreams. She said to herself, "How wonderful it would be if medical science could make it possible for us to know exactly what a person is feeling and saying in his heart and brain, without articulating it through words." She smiled at herself for thinking that way.

It was late in the afternoon when she reached home for a quick bite. While she was about to hang her jacket, the telephone rang, and it was an unexpected call from Elias.

"So finally you are home. I must have called about three times today, to see what you are up to."

"I am sorry. I went to my club and then decided to shop at the last minute. And once I started, I could not stop looking around."

"You are getting Americanized so quickly, Adowa. Shopping ha…"

"Oh, Elias, you Americans, and your exceptionalism. You really think that shopping, like going to war, is an American obsession, too. I have a surprise for you. It is not so. People with money shop. Period."

"Anyway, Adowa, what are your plans for the rest of the afternoon? Anything special?" "Not really. I was thinking of going to the Harvard Coop this afternoon, to do some mindless reading at the Café there. You are welcome to join me, if you like."

"Perfect. That sounds like an excellent plan for a Friday afternoon," said Elias.

On Friday, as agreed on, they met at the Harvard Coop, on a bright summer day "Maybe you take life too seriously."

Elias meant this as compassionate. He did not see the bristling. Adowa's face remained cool.

"You don't have to take so much responsibility," he said. "Be free. Express yourself. Be a little reckless sometimes. You won't be young forever, you know."

He sensed he had said too much. What he meant was that she could do both. A little serious here, a little reckless there.

Adowa just gazed at him calmly. She had heard these words before. Her mother had said them. Her aunts. She was weary of explaining herself. Suffering and thinking was Adowa's way of expressing herself, of being in the world as a vigilant African.

She believed for a reason, and she smiled to suffering. Aiwa dealt with life this way, and in the end, those who arrogantly inflict suffering on others will have a day of judgment.

"Hmm. I get it, although, I never saw it that way before this evening. But it makes a lot of sense. That explains why I am afraid of love," said Elias.

"Like most people. You have just joined the crowd. You are smart, Elias," said Adowa.

Elias laughed and said, "You have just called me a coward, and I confess I am."

Her thoughts struck at the root of Elias' sexuality and silenced him. He blushed a little, and his ears became brick red, and his hands were traveling all over her face, nervously reaching out for something out there, which he, himself, did not know about. He was looking for thoughts.

"Have you ever fallen in love, Elias?" asked Adowa.

He hesitated a bit and then said,

"To answer your question truthfully, I have always wanted to fall in love, and now I know why I did not. It is fear, the fear of loving without being loved."

Adowa interrupted and added,

"Not only that, if I may speak from experience, it is the greater fear of fighting memory, the memory of the existential events of our lives, the fleeting joys, the laughter, the fights and the making ups, the eateries, the summer motel about, love making in cars, all that stuff of existence. It is all these contours of life which haunt us. When you come to think of it, love is a burden and not a light weight of joy. Is it not?"

"Well said, Adowa. I am too weak to deal with memory. So I refused to give my heart to anyone. It is still that way. I come dangerously close, and then something controls me, something stops the feeling from blossoming into love. When a relationship is over, I have nothing to remember, since I was just there for a month or so, and I go through relationships just like that, a sort of changing shirts, without thinking much of the routine," said Elias.

"I understand, Elias. I, too, am in the same situation. I have loved once, only once, very deeply. I gave the man my entire being, soul and body, without getting anything in return. I am now left with a memory which refuses to die. For now I am in love with my work on the African body. The man I went for took pride in being the type who could love and hide it, after the relationship is over. I do not believe in that kind of love. I do not even think of that as love, as I understand it."

Elias nodded his head in agreement and then said,

"How does one hold love in one's heart without suffering? It doesn't make sense, not that love is sensible, but still, I don't understand this hiding thing," said Elias.

"That is the point. I, too, am puzzled. Just like you. I did not believe him then and I still do not believe it now. Frankly, when he told me that, I concluded that he really did not love me, although he thought he did. Oh well. That was the guy I loved, without knowing why. I loved him so much. I don't know why, may be it was his sex, since he was good at it."

She was a bit embarrassed and was thinking how heroic it was of her, an African woman, to refer to sex, so fearlessly.

Elias was impressed even more, and credited her openness to the fact that she is a biologist, after all.

"Even now there are streets that I cannot drive by, restaurants in which I could not eat, theaters to which I could not go, suits and pants in which I imagine him and which I could not bear to see, because of this man, whom I still see in those places, and he dared me when he told me that he still loved me, and has buried that love in his heart, and of course he had many lovers after that, whereas I still have not seen another man, because I am still in love," said Adowa.

She broke into tears, and Elias ran to the counter and came back with a napkin.

"That makes sense. I agree with you," said Elias, as if either he has done it to a lover or a lover has done it against him. There was an experiential dimension to his declaration of love.

Silence.

Adowa's eyes were pregnant with unshed tears.

Elias added, "I agree with you even more. One does not bury love in the heart, one lives it courageously and lovingly."

And then she said, at the end of the summer, I met this handsome man, Nyrere, briefly, and I find myself thinking of him, wishing that I could see him again. She frowned as those final words came out of her, and stopped.

Adowa did not say anything anymore. They both looked outside at the same time. The moon was gently replacing the sun. This scene had always intrigued Elias. He had always wished that was the way humans dealt with one another. He smiled at his own thoughts. Adowa noticed it, too.

It was getting late. Adowa was thinking about her commissioned work on the Responsibility of The African Scientist, and could not wait until she wrote it. Elias felt her anxiety about something, but could not figure it out.

Elias took many secret looks at her, admiring her eyes as they were visualizing concepts and images, and struggling to commit thought to literature, to move the reader towards action. Elias had to be at work very early the next morning. Their eyes said it all. The evening was a success and they both wanted to end it this way. Peacefully.

Ware is a short street around Harvard University, and that was where Adowa lived during her stay in Cambridge. This short street was stretched by Adowa's thoughts on her way home. Remembering every detail of her first encounter with Elias consumed her. She imagined her agony over the question of love, and her hesitation to reveal her true self. The reference to her loneliness exacted her sympathy. Something about his manners projected his vulnerability, his uncertainty about his sexuality. That he did not seem to know whom he was really attracted to, men or women, or both. She sensed his attraction to her, and was touched by the respect he extended to her. His respect of her independence and her mind left a deep impression. This was the first man who treated her like a woman, independent, brilliant and courageous. She regretted her telling him that one can love only once and that all that follows later is infatuation; that love is a curse and a privilege, a suffering, and a joy, while it lasted; when it is over, the memory of it can only kill the lover; very few survive the hurt and the disappointment, the betrayal and the cruelty, the refusal to forgive, the inability of cleansing hurt and moving on. She wished that she could open her heart to this man, whom she feels may be falling in love.

She kept going over these words again and again. As if that is not enough, the encounter with Nyrere began to haunt her. A couple of times, she imagined him in an African context, talking to her, expressing a romantic interest with a polish that charmed her.

After this short walk that stretched itself forever, she arrived home, hung her coat in the corner, went to the kitchen, opened the refrigerator, and made herself a spinach salad, turned the music on, lit two candles and ate her dinner quietly, looking at the rain drops outside, got up, walked to her writing desk, and wrote. She paced up and down, with a pen, that she once put in her mouth, then mounted it on the upper part of her ears, and finally lost it in the thick of her hair. She quickly recovered it. Finally she settled down on her old mahogany chair and her glass desk, and wrote that destiny is calling the African scientist, and morality is chiding him for not rising to the calling, to do something, to act. The African scientist must act urgently. She must be of service to a suffering continent, the birthplace of humanity. She wrote twenty full pages, folded the paper neatly and put it in a drawer.

She forced herself to stop writing, opened the sliding doors in the living room, and sat on the porch, with a glass of red wine on a round red little table, brightened by a flickering candle, which was refusing to die as it struggled against the wind. The wind was blowing the tall trees. The rain had just stopped, and left beautiful drops of pure water on every leaf that she saw from far, far away. Every leaf was happy and spoke to the other. She hoped that she spoke plant language, and could witness their joys and sorrows, as days changed to evening, and the moon displaced the sun. She wondered if plants had moods too, and if the weather affected them the way it does humans. She was amused by her own thoughts.

She briefly remembered Elias' slanted eyes, his large hands, his touch of words, his anxiety, his struggles with his sexuality, but decided to block this memory. She was thinking that this remembrance was not good for her, given her natural disposition towards thinking pain and suffering pain. Again, she thought of Nyerere.

She opened her eyes, as if to say, I do not want to remember, I do not want to struggle with memory. As she sat there, enjoying the scene, the tall trees made music, the leaves sparkled with beauty and youth, the wind blew, the cars roared, and the children played ball, as the squirrels ran by at the speed of time. Adowa squinted her eyes to look at the blue sky, and the golden clouds, clamoring for humanity's attention, the humanity, she said to herself, which is too busy making money, and missing out on the graces of nature.

She saw them all from her balcony on the sixth floor of her apartment on Ware Street. A couple of times, she was tempted by the desire to write, and contained the urge, and remained on her oak chair to think and suffer, and to suffer and think.

She fell into a dream. She saw a priest who held the Bible and preached to the congregation about the duty of the rich to the poor, the healthy to the sick, the patient to the hurried, the forgiving to the resentful. The congregation appeared to be so moved, that a group of women pledged to work for the poor for the rest of their lives. The priest was so impressed with himself that for a moment he thought he was a moving God. Words flew out of him like lava, in powerful volcanoes. He moved the congregation to action. People were pledging, flagellating themselves, mothers carried their children close to their chests; fathers were crying and blaming themselves for mistreating their wives. She saw it all and was alarmed by the similarity between her own work and the priest of the dream. She wondered if she might not have been the priest of the dream.

The dream continued, with rapidity and plethora of images.

Voices replaced sight. Seeing was displaced by hearing. Voices dominated the dream world. Adowa heard, Aster, the Ethiopian, whom she met in Ethiopia, crying; and Konjit, her daughter laughing. They both cried and laughed, sometimes separately, and at other times in concert. The noise was unbearable. Konjit laughed when Aster came home early in the morning; Konjit cried, when Aster left, mid morning. The baby sitter was tired of calming Konjit. Aster came and laughed and Konjit laughed even more. Aster came and left and Konjit cried even more.

Laughter.

Cries and Pain.

Joy and suffering escorted the darkness of dream time.

Pain and joy. Laughter first. Cries followed.

The night was disturbed.

Sleepless dreams.

Adowa was not sure whether she was dreaming or thinking that she was dreaming. For years the closeness of dream and reality had confounded her. She has not resolved the status of dream and reality, to the full satisfaction of her scientific mind. She did not know the difference, and asked herself, whether life itself is one short dream, or a miserably long real. These thoughts reminded her of her philosophy courses at college.

Tired, Adowa frowned. A voice came back. Aster screamed after she was beaten up, by a customer who wanted to take her home after work. Adowa heard Aster say, I am booked for the night. Vexed by her response, the customer descended on her body with his ferocious eyes, his brutal hands, his stocky legs, and sent blows on her face, her eyes, her nose, her hands, her chest, her legs, and left marks of death on that African body. She survived the barbarism of an African man on an African woman. Body on Body.

Adowa saw Aster being beaten to the floor. A stream of blood left its marks on the ground. Tongue silenced by a knife. Ears cut to deafness. Lips deformed. Hands bruised. Eyes swollen. Head squashed like a lemon. Hair cut from her scalp, and smeared with dry blood.

The African body was mutilated by an African man. The body was in pain. The African woman's body spoke through the language of sorrow, of defeat, of endless agony, that felt it would last until eternity. The African woman's body was demolished beyond recognition.

Adowa cried in her extended dream.

Aster's eyes were swollen and stopped seeing the world; her imagination ceased dreaming, and looking into the future. The ears decided not to take the sounds of the world. The tongue silenced itself forever. Those fiery red eyes sunk in a stream of blood. The ears closed themselves to the music of trees, the sound of air, the words of hope, and the cries of pain. Time stopped. Space disappeared. Nothingness triumphed.

Aster's voice remained. Konjit's hands searched Aster's body in darkness. There was nothing there, only a speechless voice, silenced by death. The African body has resigned to its fate, beaten down, and deprived of hope and faith. The African world has stopped singing, playing drums, and circle dancing. The African continent is sad, home to wars, to ethnic strife, to a misunderstanding between the sexes. Hopelessness displaced hope; hate displaced love; the abuse of the African woman replaced the reverential attitude of ancient African cultures. Aster's voice presented itself, and Adowa heard it, loud and clear this time. It was Aster, and her unmistakable voice from the distant past. She imagined her as she first met her, swinging her finely built body for men to see. So proud was she of her breasts, her passionate eyes, her sinewy hands, her long hair, her dark brown skin color. That is Aster, Adowa said to herself. Nothing has changed. She is still poor, and the object of men's abuse.

Adowa cried profusely in her dream.

Aster, the African woman spoke. Adowa listened. Aster said that she wanted to die. She had enough of life. Konjit heard and screamed her lungs out. Adowa saw. Konjit slapped her face. Adowa saw Aster rushing to Konjit and held her close to her body. She wanted to take her back to her womb, where she once was safe, fed, warmed and loved

Konjit complied to return to her mother's womb. She missed the certainty of life there, the predictability of the needs of the body, food, shelter and warmth.

More voices. Aster, Konjit and the baby sitter slept in a single bed. Aster made out with a customer right there after Konjit and the baby sitter went to sleep. The whimpers of sex woke them up. Konjit appeared confused. She asked for her mother in the dark. The mother was not there. She was on the floor, eating her screams. The customer was descending on her with vengeance.

Another night. Her ex-husband caught her with her wealthy friend. He beat them up, both. The police came and took Aster and the man away. Her ex-husband escaped. He came back the next night and took Konjit away. Half asleep, Konjit cried in the dark, when she was kidnapped by her own father.

Aster died in prison. Konjit was never heard of again. Aster spoke from her tomb. That was when she told Adowa that she was in another world, where there is no pain, no time, or space, but a joyous emptiness, a nothingness, where there are no things, but only speechless souls, who fly, who swim, and who live, for ever and ever, in the company of God, who never judges them, but lets them be. She told her how happy she was in this world of tulips, roses, cattle, sheep, stone and fruit; a world of abundances; a world that does know jealousy, and where everybody takes what they need, and no more or less, but just right.

Adowa looked comforted by the voice from the tomb. She took a deep sigh.

After she heard these words Adowa woke up from the dream, and took a fresh read of her hastily written piece on The Responsibility of the African Scientist. On second reading she liked what she said but not the way she said it. She regretted the fact that she wrote it so hastily, only because she was invaded by thoughts, which wanted to be framed by concepts and mediated through images. That she did. It is the writing which did not please her, since she was not a professional writer.

It began raining heavily again, and the gushing wind and the roaring storm hit hard on the sliding door, that for a moment, Adowa was worried that her apartment would be stormed in. It has rained for one whole week, day and night.

Time is already having its revenge, as her work expands, and her young body races against time, and towards death. The movement towards death, she once entered in her diary, is like the natural fact that a stone does not attempt to reach the sky, because its natural tendency is to rest on the ground, and so is the natural tendency of the biological self.

The biological self always moves towards death, said Adowa, and yet people make every effort to deny this fact, unnecessarily. Only a fool, she said, would divert the stone's movement towards the ground, instead, the wise one seeks to understand the laws which govern that movement; similarly, she advised, instead of denying the inevitable, it makes much more sense, to prepare ourselves to live in the place to which death takes us. For that wise gesture, the brilliant Egyptian thinkers have given us the concept of Maat, to make us better human beings, worthy of living a better life in the beyond, in the horizon beyond horizons, at the place were all lives meet, and sit at the palaver with the transcendent.

She credited this luminous moment, which came after one full hour of conversing with the Transcendent to Aster's voice, the voice of comfort, the voice of speechless songs, the voice of the dance, the voice of regret, of poetry and of clear prose.

She knew she said to herself these words were not hers. There was something about them beyond the human. For the first time she understood, how the divine intervenes in our lives, to put us on the right moral path. Nothing that we humans say is complete without the transcendental guidance. We may rave and rant about how great wer are, she said, but we are not great enough in the eyes of the creator. It is this humility which gave the ancient Egyptian imagination, depth, compassion and a great sense of contingency.

While she was dreaming about her second important trip to Ethiopia, she remembered Elias's kindness over the phone, when she was so excited that she gave him a very little space on the phone, and was obsessed with speaking about her very own projects only. The telephone rung several times, as she was ruminating, but she remained focused on thinking and contemplating her trip to Ethiopia.

Twice she heard Aster's voice.

After an exacting exercise, she sat in the corner of the gym and entered a trance and was swept away by daydreaming.

Neil

A tall, thin man with freckles on his face sat alone in a corner of the Coffee Connection just off Mount Auburn Street. A teapot, cup, and spoon were in front of him on the table—signs that his morning routine was underway. He first polished the teaspoon with a napkin. Then, he pulled the teapot forward into a comfortable position close to him. He let it rest after checking its temperature carefully and concluding that it was not ready to drink. Patiently, he spread orange marmalade on his bran muffin, took a small bite and replaced it neatly. He rechecked his tea. This time it was ready. Done the way he liked it, the tea was a perfect light orange color. He took his first sip along with the second bite of his muffin. His face revealed his satisfaction and his day appeared to be off to a good start.

Despite the perfection he demanded of his tea, he did not care much for precision in dressing. An untucked, unbuttoned white shirt, perhaps from Kmart, with a t-shirt underneath, covering his upper body to his knees, and dark blue jeans were his daily adornment.

He had a keen eye and a curious mind that often directed his attention towards those coming in and out of the café. He always fixated subtly. The targets of his gaze were oblivious to it because his body never moved with his eyes. Those of good breeding learn to take in a scene in this indirect way, so as never to offend the observed. Despite having little interest in etiquette, he too had discovered that one should not stare at other people. Neil prided himself in having mastered this skill of indirect observation. He had noticed that people adjust their behavior when they are aware of being watched. But, through his technique of discreet observation, his artist's eye captured people's natural behaviors. In this way, so much more revealed itself to him.

While sitting thus, and entertaining himself, hurried customers came in and out of the café. It was December, and people hustled about laden in winter coats and boots. For them, the café was a toasty, even if only momentary, refuge from the slush and wind outside. The morning rush contradicted the soft blue jazz that pervaded the air in the place. Bob Marley told the servers to stand up and fight for their rights as they struggled to keep pace with the constant stream of new orders. Using noisy stainless steel machines that billow steam and caffeine, they continuously orchestrated the creation of elaborate beverages with names like "double skim cappuccino," "single caramel macchiato" and "grande soy latte." Barking out the names of completed drinks, they summoned customers eager to claim them.

Everyone had to be somewhere in five minutes. A few stormed out in rage because they could not bring themselves to stand in line.

Like a hungry baby they needed instant gratification. The servers had learned not to be bothered by this. They simply ignored it. In fact, some of them even look relieved when the "babies" stormed out, stamping the floor and shaking their heads. It took Neil years to adjust to this madness. He was known to be the patient one at the café. He would never bring himself to the level of the "babies." But perhaps this was because the café was his intended destination, while for others it was simply a brief stop on the way to their workplaces.

After the morning rush of " to go" customers at the café, Neil found himself gazing at an empty paper amidst tea, newspapers, paint brushes, pens and pencils, cigarettes and a filled ashtray, for a long, long time. His large eyeglasses betrayed his age. The glasses sat comfortably on his nicely chiseled nose. Neither big nor small but just right for the rest of his handsome face, they contributed to his intelligent appearance. Although in his early thirties, when Neil sat in that self-possessed posture, onlookers were focused on his stoopy back, his weakened skin, his fading red hair, his proliferating freckles, and his tired eyes. Many mistook those tired red eyes for signs of drug abuse, but they were in fact the result of a sleeplessness that sporadically haunted him for several years prior.

When he was not teaching painting at the Cambridge Extension School or working at his fundraising job for the homelessness charity, A New Hope, Neil could almost certainly be found at the café amidst endless sketches and scribbled notes of which only he knew the destinies. He did not go unnoticed among the regulars at the cafe. They presumed his life was quite pathetic and that his mind was perhaps not "all there." He read the sympathy in their faces and the little offers of help here and there. The waitresses always welcomed him with huge smiles. Although he arrived quietly, not once did they fail to notice his arrival. One particular waitress was always eager for this mysterious fellow to arrive at the scene. Sometimes she would wonder why his eyes were always red. On occasion she had been one of those who thought that he may have been doing drugs, so she would squint her eyes to check him out more closely. He knew that people spoke about those eyes. At least once he overheard her saying, "I hope he is not killing himself with those things." He heard her. She knew he had heard her so she looked away.

Late that morning, but before the transient lunchtime crowd re-populated the café, a woman and her child walked in and caught Neil's eye. The child, perhaps six or seven years old, roamed the room while his mother placed her order. He found himself at Neil's table, and chatted confidently with him. Neil, touched by the attention, ruffled the boy's soft, thin hair. Charmed, the proud mother locked eyes with Neil. She walked to his table and introduced herself as Michelle.

"Todd seems to like you," she began. Neil introduced himself rather awkwardly, but his visible nervousness did not faze her. "This may be too intrusive," she continued, "but what do you do?"

He hesitated a bit, and replied, "I guess I am some kind of painter, creating art when I can, because I also have to make a living. For that I do fundraising for the homeless."

She became even more curious.

"What kind of painting?"

"Abstract art," he replied. "I play with colors. Colors are my themes. I speak through them, along with formlessness. There are no forms in my painting. The formlessness is the theme."

"Hmmm…. Colors are your themes, you say." She paused and looked at Neil. Their eyes locked for the second time as if something was hatching.

Todd pulled his mother's hands to leave. She submitted. Before she left, she wrote down her number and, while handing it to Neil, she expressed an interest in seeing his work whenever he was ready. She had managed to take his number when they first met and kept it. Outside, it was getting dark although it was late in the morning. The weather woman had predicted heavy snow that day. Everybody was ready for it. Numerous shivering pedestrians hid themselves in their coats and furry caps, with scarves wrapped round their necks. Boots trudged through the half-frozen slush. No surprise awaited them. The depth of the cold, the sharpness of the thick air, the heavy clouds, and the penetrating cold assaulted the residents, signifying the coming storm. And all these signs proved the weather woman right.

By noon, thick snow showered down. Gushing wind jostled

strollers like tall ships in the deep blue ocean; umbrellas flew in the air; cars and buses were drenched by the ferocious storm. The billowing wind blew a thin man across the sidewalk, forcing him to cling to a railing to prevent himself from falling completely to the ground. The scene terrified all those who saw it. They had seen umbrellas flying, garbage cans rolling down the street, and even trees falling, but never before had they seen a man feathered away like that. For about an hour, long shafts of snow flooded the streets, rewriting the scene completely. Trees that had been graced delicately by gorgeous ice became laden with heavy wet snow.

Neil put his pen on the table, refilled his teapot, and crossed his legs. He wore a half-smile on his face as he peered outside at the aftermath of the storm and thought of Michele and Todd. Remembering them both filled part of his stay, while he waited for the storm to subside so that he could go to his job at A New Hope. He was in the midst of planning a major walk for the homeless that was scheduled to take place in the spring.

The storm eventually settled down into a steady, quiet snowfall that lasted the rest of the day. The storm turned every part of Cambridge snow-white. With Christmas only four days away, everyone happily anticipated a white Christmas. As Neil walked home from his office at A New Hope, he thought about the holidays. His mother had called him to encourage him to return home to Utah. He had not been invited to any holiday events in Cambridge yet. He was getting restless, for the holidays in Cambridge could be oppressive for those without families or places to go to. The city became deserted for three days. The streets were emptied of students, most of whom returned home. The yuppies traveled to Europe and other places after they joined their families on Christmas day. Harvard College closed its doors completely. All the public libraries closed. Neil had gone through this exodus before. Every time the holidays arrived, he thought of aging. His roommates had already dispersed and he was heading home to an empty house. But the scene in Cambridge was too picturesque for him to leave so he decided to stay in Cambridge for the holidays.

Christmas trees were everywhere—some real trees of magnificent size, others artificial but beautiful nonetheless. Ornamental paraphernalia dramatically adorned a few houses. Most houses, however, had more modest touches. They looked just right. The city of Cambridge was celebrating. The city smelled of pine trees and eggnog. Even the non-Christians responded to the spiritual radiance of the city. Neil too was affected by the mood of celebration. He had been hoping that someone would invite him to a party or dinner so that he did not have to spend the day painting solitude, capturing my loneliness.

As if someone had been secretly listening to his wishes, the telephone rang at his home. He answered on the very first ring. The voice said, "Hello, Neil. This is Michelle, remember me?"

He felt like saying he had thought of her more than he should have but instead he tried hard to be smooth. "Of course I do. What a pleasant surprise. Nice to hear from you.

How is Todd?"

"Todd has been talking about you…and…your ways at the café."

"My ways," he repeated, jocularly. "Meaning what?"

"That you have to ask Todd about when you come for Christmas dinner, if you can." She paused, and then followed up, "I know how popular artists are so I do not expect you to be available. I just wanted to extend an invitation to you, you know, if you have time. No obligations. But we would love to have you. Just the three of us. It would be so nice."

"Umm, sure…I would love to come," he replied.

He almost jumped after she hung up. He had been worrying that he would waste away with loneliness that day. Although only a dinner, this invitation made him so happy that he began thinking about buying gifts—expensive things, personal things, clothes and all. He was afraid that he may be misunderstood, but he decided to be inappropriate and generous.

Feeling strangely exuberant, Neil made a fresh cup of coffee, standing by the coffee maker so as to enjoy the sound of percolation inside the quiet of the room. Leaning against the wall with an intense frown on his face, he thought about what to do for the rest of the day. He put on his robe, combed his ruffled hair, watered all his dry plants, and dusted the shelves, the bed rails, the dresser, and the cupboards before going to the insulated porch to water the plants there.

By the time he had finished chores he was ready to sit on the leather recliner in the hallway and plan the day. Upon tossing and turning his thoughts, he resolved to walk to Fresh Pond to get some air. It was above freezing that day but snow remained on the ground. Along his walk he found a dry bench to sit on. Nearby, an Asian couple sat on a dormant wooden jungle gym that would be teeming once again with boisterous children in the spring. The man sat with his legs open to accommodate his friend who placed herself in the triangular frame formed by his legs. Her hair rested on his hands, which supported her head. At first he stroked her hair and then graduated into brushing it. A young woman with rangy legs passed by the couple with her head turned toward them in admiration.

Neil could not contain himself from sketching the three figures as their lives intersected fleetingly. Later that night, he transformed the sketch into a painting he titled "Fleeting Beauty at a Pond."

The day before Christmas, he decided to stay home and draw. He continued a series of a female body that he had recently been working on. The vagina had always fascinated him. He traced the deepest and most private part of the vagina in deep red, surrounded by meandering orange on the edges. The inner layer was deep with barely visible layers inside. The inside was simultaneously dark and deep red. On first blush, it looked like a pupil. The vagina was rarely distinguishable from the human eye as Neal lived it in his world of forms. His paintings treated the viewer to this ambiguity, complexity and intersection of differences. He spent one whole day on the painting. He left it to dry and went shopping for Todd and Michelle. He fought off his urge to be excessive and bought modest Christmas presents for each of them: a bouquet of daisies and tulips for Michelle; a teddy bear and a painting book for Todd.

That night he tried to sleep but was restless with anticipation. As a rule, he never drew at night. Night was exclusively for thinking. Sometimes he went to bed early to interact with images, forms that revealed themselves only in the dark. He took mental sketches. Occasionally he cheated and got up to draw a line or two, but generally he was satisfied to work from what he could remember in the morning. He had done this hundreds of times. But, just as dreams sometimes escaped his memory, so did the forms. Whenever

91

he could remember them, he was inspired to draw. When he could not, he busied himself with work for A New Hope.

On Christmas day Neil arrived at their place on time. Todd welcomed him at the door and Michelle greeted him inside. He hung his coat on the rack and Micelle led him to a tastefully decorated living room. He sat on a beautiful blue couch with a matching love seat and a multi-colored coffee table made out of glass. The glass itself was painted in light blue on the surface, with purple trim; the top was unpainted glass except on the edges. Directly facing the love seat sat simple black chairs decorated with splashes and dots of colors that transformed the ordinary chairs into unique living room chairs. They looked deceptively expensive. Michele herself had decorated all of them, but was too modest to take credit.

Shortly after Neil sat down, Todd beckoned him to go outside with him. In the backyard, the two of them created a huge snowman, an art that Neil had mastered in the snow piles of Utah. Todd had never seen anything like it. As they rolled the snow boulders around the ground to increase their circumference, Todd's mantra encouraged Neil: "Make it bigger. Bigger."

As they put the finishing touches on the snowman, Michelle tapped on the window and summoned them in. They both brushed the snow off their pants, Todd following Neil's lead, and took off their boots. Todd excitedly relayed the tale of the snowman-building project to his mother while Neil washed up in the bathroom. Neil then stepped into the kitchen to ask if he could help. Through the door he spied candles flickering on the dining room table and Christmas lights in the windows. Michelle offered him a Cotes du Rhone wine and asked him to open it while Todd took the food to the table.

Dinner, like the house, was simple but elegant. The main dish was lemon chicken, accompanied by potatoes in roasted garlic, boiled spinach, and a huge bowl of salad. For desert, there was carrot cake with vanilla ice cream. They took their time and had a long candlelit dinner. Neil and Michelle sat facing each other. Todd sat to the right of his mother and to the left of Neil, and yakked away throughout the dinner. A couple of times he mentioned his dad and the good times. He dropped his plate and was embarrassed by the mess he caused. Without a word, his mother knelt down and in no time cleaned the floor and served him on a fresh plate, assuring him that such things happen but that he should be more careful in the future. Todd grabbed his mother's hands, reached to her cheeks, gave her a kiss, and told her how much he loved her. The scene touched Neil, and it reminded him of the days at that sweet age, when his mother was his entire universe.

Todd ate a lot and looked tired. He went to bed shortly after dinner, giving Neil and Michelle time to get to know each other. Michelle sighed as she told Neil that he should think very hard before having children. One is enough to change your life around completely, she emphasized before excusing herself to go the kitchen. She returned with a bowl of fruit, an assortment of cheese and another bottle of wine on a round Japanese tray which she gently laid on the coffee table. She sat down close to him, pushed her hair behind her ears, made herself comfortable, and asked, "So Neil, are you originally from Cambridge?"

"No, actually, I'm originally from hillbilly country Utah. But I've been here in Cambridge for a good ten years, and I am quickly forgetting my Utah life. And you, Michelle, were you born here?"

"Yeah. I'm a Somerville girl. I am a Somervillian in every sense. Italian. Opinionated. I wear all the stripes with the exception of bigotry, thank God. I don't have that disease."

"Oh, is bigotry a Somerville thing?"

"You better believe it. Many immigrants who should know better do sickening things here. I get so upset by them. I guess they don't know any better…. What brought you to Cambridge?"

"Fate, I think…if you believe in that. When I was very young, I loved to write, and later I picked painting. While in college I took a creative writing class. Boy was it hard, but I managed to do well. My teacher thought that I should pursue it. I didn't do that, though. Instead I began painting and have never stopped since then. I have no idea where it is going, though. I know one thing: I am no Van Gogh. Anyway, one thing led to another and one day I ended coming to Harvard for my brother's graduation. I fell in love with the place, packed my things after a year, and now I am here, talking to you, ten years later."

Michelle got up to get the bottle of cognac he had brought. As she re-entered the room, she subtly reached for the switch on the wall and dimmed the lights. This did not go unnoticed. Neil could feel himself shaking a little with nervous anticipation. He concentrated on relaxing, but became more nervous when Michelle appeared to be waiting for his response to something she said but he did not hear because he was too focused on my shaking. He decided that he would not be able to achieve relaxation through concentration so instead put his faith in the cognac. He took several sips and felt the cognac traveling down through his body. He felt good when it joined his blood stream. It made him feel bold, confident, chatty and exuberant.

Michelle engaged him again. "Wow. So that's how it happened. Interesting. I'm curious. What do you like about Cambridge? Somervillians hate Cambridge, and vice versa. I know people who have lived here all their lives and never set their foot in Harvard Square. It's another country for them. And here you are having come all the way from Utah."

"Size is a factor. It's a small place that I can manage without a car. It has that academic culture that oozes from Harvard and rubs off on the residents. I guess I like all that. I guess you're not really a fan of the Square?"

"Well," she said, not really answering the question, perhaps due to the cognac, "I am a Somervillian all the way and Italian on the top of that, which makes me passionate and emotional…in some peoples' eyes, that is. That's good and bad, of course. The emotional part got me in trouble very early on. I met this guy at nineteen, a dark, tall, skinny, charming boy that I blindly went for—you know the type that little girls call cute—and ended up marrying him against my parents' objections. So I fell in love with this guy, and married a couple of months later, at city hall, just him and me. The first two years were lovely. He hid his true nature very well, I must say."

She lit a cigarette, puffed smoke to the air, frowned a bit and continued,

"Then he began changing on me. Jealous like hell. I had to account for every minute I was late. Every phone call I received was a subject for argument. 'Who is that?' I hated that question. I'd be like, 'What the fuck is it to you?' When we went to parties I was not even

94

allowed to look at another guy. He would watch my eyes. If my eyes
locked with another guy's, he would drag me home to listen to his
insecure ass telling me I was a slut. I couldn't leave because I was
pregnant with Todd. After I delivered, I could not take the shit so I
ran away with my child. My parents hired a lawyer so I could get full
custody of Todd. I have not seen his father for the past five years. I
don't know where he is, dead or alive, and it is better that way. I have
my kid, my health, and my job...."

She suddenly realized that she had compressed her life into a
paragraph filled with very personal matters and that she had surely
scared Neil. Why did she always do this? she berated herself silently
while trying to recover the festive mood with a coy smile. Neil had
listened with great interest and compressed her hand a bit while she
spoke. Her forwardness made him feel connected and helped him
forget his nervousness. They sat with a comfortable space between
them but occasionally, when making a point, she would harmlessly
inch closer to him and lightly touch his body. After a while, they
caught each other looking into the darkness outside through a sliding
door that opens to a large backyard crowded with leafless trees.

Directly across from where they sat, the snowman that Neil and
Todd had made faced them. For a moment it looked real, as if it was
struggling to tell them something. With its mouth half-open and big
red eyes, it seemed to be taking in the world's pain through its large
ears and struggling to release it through the slightly opened mouth.

The trees outside looked cold. Neil commented "Their leafless-
ness has always intrigued me. I have always wanted to paint their
loneliness, how they feel, their suffering in the winter cold."

"Oh, trees suffering. You're a trip...." Michelle shot back at him.
But, her "are you for real?" response soon gave way to consideration
of the idea. "Well, maybe they do after all. It reminds me of my college professor who once told us that all beings suffer, but we do not
understand their language, and do not have an access to their world.
That stuck in my mind. I tremble when I see a slaughtered animal
and wonder how it feels, what it thinks of its situation, you know."
Silence followed. It was getting dark outside. One could almost hear
the quiet. The flickering candles and the slow moving cognac began
affecting them both.

Neil removed his thick eyeglasses, cleaned them a bit, massaged his tired eyes, ran his long, powerful hands through his thinning wavy red hair, and rested his head on the couch. Michelle, once again, drew her body closer to him, but he did not respond. He appeared to be somewhere else, imagining forms for a drawing, perhaps trees in the dark. After a while she realized that he was not present with her in spirit, only in body. She withdrew a bit. Maybe she had not been artsy enough to stimulate him. Maybe she had killed the mood with talk of her ex. Although unsure of the stimulus for his distance, she came to the sad conclusion that he was not going to have her that night. Yet, she was in a mood for sex, and he, it seemed, in a mood for sadness, for thought.

Neil had been thinking about leaving for quite a while but could not find the courage to tell her. When he finally stood up and told Michelle that he had to leave, his abruptness did not sit well with her. She looked a bit startled and almost asked him to stay a bit longer but did not. Before he left he thanked her for a special Christmas, reminded her not to forget to kiss Todd for him, and emphasized how happy he was to have spent this special day with her. She called a taxi for him and he left her home before eleven o'clock. His taxi driver was a chatty one. The driver talked about the weather before moving on to discuss how he had spent the day.

"My friends slaughtered a chicken right inside the apartment, shared it among ten people, and we drank most of the day. A few passed out on the dinner table. I could take this, but not the very drunken ones who became abusive toward their wives. Abusive men are not true according to my standards. After all the abuse, some of the men even had the nerve to ask their wives to serve them with food and drink. A few of us napped after dinner while others, like myself, came directly to work after emptying the last glass of whiskey. Fortunately, I am so sober that I feel like I am on the top of the world."

Amidst all this talk about drinking, he assured Neil that he was in control and never had a problem driving even while dead drunk. Neil replied sarcastically, "I'm sure I have heard that before."

...

A few days in March had hinted at spring, but this day was cold. Sit-

96

ting at home, Neil looked around: table, sofa, chair, lamp, painting brushes of various sizes, piles of paints, canvass, pens and writing pads. He has been looking at these objects for years. They were always the same. Some got half-empty and were refilled; others got old and were replaced. Neil, however, reflected on his own aging, realizing that he could not be replaced. Unlike the objects around him, he moved steadily towards death.

While deep in contemplation, he glanced out his window and witnessed a very sick bird choking to death while still struggling to live. It was lying on the cold ground, shivering in the midst of one of the coldest winter days. One of its legs was half rested on the ground, the other quivered, suspended in the air. And, what remained of it was determined to fight to the bitter end. The bird's breathing was weak, and its end appeared imminent, but its body would not relent. The will to live! Neil came to a stop. He looked at the desperate bird in terror. He walked away, but could not resist the urge to watch longer. His legs brought him back to the same space, where the helpless being rested. He looked at it again and imagined the number of people who must have passed by without looking... and those who looked but did not see.

Neil wept from deep inside. His sense of helplessness saddened him even more. There was nothing he could do. He so much wanted to help, to make a difference, but could not make such a thing happen. All that he could do was remove the dying body from the street, cover it gracefully, and place it by the garbage can. That angered him beyond measure. Many pedestrians had passed by. Only a few noticed the suffering being, a dying soul, struggling. Some of them thought that their lives were not any better, but their pain couldn't be witnessed like that of a being without rights.

Neil returned to his apartment and turned his stereo on. The Bee Gees were singing "Staying' Alive." He was immediately reminded of the bird that he nursed to death, a few days ago. It too, he said to himself, was struggling to stay alive. (After some time he went down to the café, and, shortly after he put his writing pad on the table, neatly hung his coat on the chair, and ordered a cup of coffee and a bran muffin with orange marmalade on the side, a couple of unfamiliar faces walked in, talking away and continuing a conversation that they must have begun earlier. A middle aged man said, "So you think that there are unfulfilled lives?"

The female companion replied, "Of course there are. And I think it has something to do with imitation."

"Explain."

She hesitated a bit to organize her thoughts and replied, "Well, I think it is because people like to imitate the past, imitate the so-called greats who become standards after which we must all model ourselves. In this way we burden ourselves as we try to climb unnecessary heights. When we fail we are crippled by the intensity of defeat."

He continued her thoughts. "So if I understood correctly, unreachable standards from the past harass us. The heights that we erect are neither necessary nor attainable, and yet we continue to do this to ourselves."

"Right. You hit it on the head. That is what I had in mind," she excitedly replied. "Exactly right. That is how we oppress ourselves. By imposing unnecessary standards."

He continued, "Mmm, we feel that our lives are unfulfilled because our failure to meet these standards and be like the 'greats' belittles our ordinary efforts to be ourselves. We belittle ourselves. We ridicule our otherwise meaningless (meaningful?) lives."

"Indeed. Were it not for the imitation of standards, the use of the past as a measure, we would be well. At least we would not be so sick. We could somehow lighten our being, which is already heavy. The sickness is self-inflicted. I truly believe so."

While saying this, her eyes locked with Neil's. Neil was taking in every word and got caught in the act. After they left Neil took my notebook and wrote, "Suffering is self-imposed. We create heights that very few people can reach, and when we cannot reach them, we stop creating. We belittle ourselves and profoundly affect our self-worth." In the margins he wrote. "True. That is why my painting is not going anywhere. I am not proud of my own creations when I measure them against the Greats. I have to work on this stumbling block."

As he was scribbling, another conversation attracted his ears. Three young people were engaged in a heated debate about gender roles. A young man with an African accent who professed to be a Muslim declared:

"My great-great-grandfather, my grandfather, and my father all thought that it was in bad taste for a man to cook for his wife, that such a situation is simply not meant to be."

His friend, who described himself as an Armenian, responded, "It is crude to think that way." He admitted proudly that he cooked for his girlfriend and happily, and remained unbothered by the knowledge that she had three other boyfriends as well.

The third person in the group reported that her husband cooked for her. The African protested and called her husband's behavior unnatural.

She rebutted him, stating, "You are behind times, my friend. Wake up. We all like to be waited on. That is what you seem to want. It has nothing to do with nature. Whether we admit it or not, we all want to be waited on. And women are beginning to say no. Good for them. They are just beginning to wake up."

Neil was amused by all the conversations, and jotted down his observations in his diary.

...

Spring had finally begun to erase the starkness of winter. Greenness was returning to the city. Neil sat by the Charles River and bent his head as if he were looking for something, which is what he does when he is either planning the day or is worrying about something. Lately, he had been thinking a lot about a young girl, Heidi, from Barbados, whom he had fallen in love with at first sight. He had made the contact and she had responded. He had not begun dating her yet, but she occupied his mind quite often.

Meanwhile, Michelle had called half a dozen times over the last few weeks. He had spoken to her a few times after Christmas and they had run into each other once in the Square. Both had vigorously asserted that they should get together soon, but he had not followed up. Recently, he had not returned her calls. He worried that any response might be construed as interest. On the other hand, not responding was rude. He agonized over what to do. When the telephone rang repeatedly, he would know it was Michelle and grab the phone, almost making contact before changing his mind at the last minute. How dare he forget the fabulous Christmas dinner at her place, and especially Todd's unconditional love for him, he thought. Perhaps he could find a way to preserve that encounter as pure friendship and approach Heidi as a lover. He toyed with the idea but, realizing that it was merely an idea, did not pursue it further. Besides, his heart was taking him somewhere else, and he knew it too.

As he sat on the bench, his mind wandering, he watched the geese and birds that have come back to town singing and mingling peacefully. Visible. Present. Unworried. Certain about their lives. He sat there watching them for a long time before rising.

He began his walk by the Charles. From far away, he spotted a familiar figure sitting on a bench and looking at the ducklings on the banks of the river. Tall, dark brown, with soft silky hair and slanted black eyes, she had large hips anchored on thin legs that looked like they might break away from her hips, a short skirt, big feet, and a small mouth. From a distance she appeared to be contemplating the early hazy afternoon, which threatened rain. She was examining the sky, which sky had brought down some heavy blocks of darkness to the earth. In Barbados, from where she came, she could predict with remarkable precision the arrival of the rain. She was trying and failing to do the same. She opened her purse and took out a bag of stale bread, which she always brought with her when she came to the Charles. The moment she spread the bread on the ground, ten ducks and ducklings came to the party. She smiled as she bent down and sat very close to them; they circled her, eating and quacking as if they were thanking her. Neil observed the entire interaction and was smiling away as he approached her, still circled by the ducks. Instantly upon Neil's arrival, the group broke apart. To his painterly eyes the beautiful form of her sitting with the ducks disappeared. Beauty dissolved. Some walked back to the river. Some flew away. All were gone. Now it was Neil and the good-looking woman.

That was Heidi. A book, which she had forgotten about when the ducks landed in her corner, rested on the bench. A few had camped very far away at the other end of the shore. A daring one came very close to Heidi. Her happiness encouraged Neil to make contact so he quickened his walk.

"Hi!" she said, unmistakably excited to see him. He was taken aback a little, but happy at the same time. He blushed, and the redness in his face temporarily masked his freckles. Initially, he pondered what he should do, how he should behave. He wanted to be himself. Overwhelmed with happiness upon seeing her, he wondered even more if he should display it earnestly or hide it. Would she recoil? Would she be afraid? He asked himself. Something, a kind of rendezvous, propelled him towards her. He followed its course.

Neil held her tight in his arms. He was beside himself. She remained attached to his grip for a few seconds without protestation. The warmth of his hands comforted her. He rubbed his body against her, almost unconsciously. Heidi remained in his hands. She must have suddenly felt the closeness and withdrew subtly. Her short skirt was ruffled a bit. She pulled it down.

"How have you been Neil?" she asked in a convincing tone.

"Considering everything, I guess I'm fine. One thing is certain. I am happy to run into you. This is the last thing I expected today, so it's a nice surprise."

They were both quiet for a while. The day was cool and Heidi wore a light scarf and an Irish cap turned backwards. She tucked her arm under his. The ducklings continued to come and go. One bird strutted over to check out the new figure. Neil broke the ice with crumbs of bread. In less than a minute about twenty birds joined their pioneering compatriots. Heidi became sprightly when she saw her little friends. Neil got into it, too. He, too, enjoyed birds, but had never fed them. The pair remained near the bench consumed by pleasure until it got dark.

After the crumbs were finished the party was over. Neil and Heidi thought the ducks looked disappointed either because the food was finished or perhaps because their friends were going away. The ducklings left the scene as well to float in the river.

"So, what have you been doing lately?" asked Heidi. Before answering Neil put his hands around his chin, kept them there for a while, and struggled to contain a short yawn that hit and overwhelmed him. He then slowly removed his hands and answered, "Many things, really. Perhaps too many. I am trying to focus. And you know, it's so hard. I want to do so many things. But…they are just not getting done."

"Yes. I know what you mean," she said.

He laughed a bit and continued, "The difference is that I am still there. Trying to figure things out. Even now I still do not know where my life is going. Nothing is moving."

He closed his eyes, fixed his glasses, which were hanging loose on his sweaty face, rubbed his eyes, and kept quiet.

"The same here," added Heidi.

He adamantly tried to distinguish his situation from hers. "But we are at two different points in our lives. You see. You are not supposed to be focused now. Your age allows you to explore, to change. Really. It is wise not to make up your mind at your age. I am at that age at which I must know in absolute terms what I should want and be."

She yawned and was embarrassed by it. She stood up twice and stared at the horizon, gave him her back, and began to slowly dance. Then she turned toward him to say something.

Her little dance made him a bit nervous, for he was not much of a dancer. He worried that she might have been sending him a sign about what she liked or what her values might be as a young black woman who might be into the dance scene.

They interrupted each other to utter the same words. They were both having trouble focusing; perhaps they were both also stressed. They laughed at their fates and made fun of their ages by declaring that age is just a number. It occurred to Neil after a while that he was being too intense with the young woman and that he should lighten up a bit. So he changed his pace, took a deep breath, and shook his anxious body to get rid of those cobwebs of anguish that had been tormenting him of late, since he turned thirty.

They both noticed that they needed to chill out in a place where they would not have to use words, but could just sit and look and enjoy one another. They decided to go to the Harvest, a famous bar-restaurant in Harvard Square. The street lamps were lit. They could see students in their Harvard dormitories. A group was studying outside in the well-lit gardens. Others were inside with their books. Such scenes took them both back to their college days.

On their way to the bar, they stopped outside an antique shop. Lured by a few items—a Victorian plant holder, a mahogany coffee table, and a chest of drawers from the eighteenth century—they decided to step in. A youngster in her teens followed them around before calling another teenager to take her place so that she could call the boss. Then, a heavily accented middle-aged blonde man came over to explain to them what they were looking at. As they looked at each other, the man left. The previous teenager followed them around again.

Neil gave the teenager his briefcase to comfort her, but Heidi still had her purse and Neil had his pockets. Neil almost suggested to her that perhaps he should take off his clothes to reassure her, but refrained from doing so. As the teenager continued circling their paths with Neil's briefcase in hand, they decided they had had enough and left.

"You see what I mean," said Heidi.

Neil replied, "Just a silly kid."

"Really?" Heidi muttered with controlled anger.

...

Harvest was full of people. Layers of conversation combined to fill the dimly lit bar with a noisy energy. Neil wondered how people listened to each other in such circumstances. But they must be able to, he reckoned, because the talking continued. Heidi must have been thinking the same way because she too noticed how difficult it was to hear amidst the talking. As they walked through the crowd to their table, they felt a wave of hush following them. A young man with a pipe hanging out from his tired mouth stared without shame. He accidentally inhaled smoke while busily staring, almost choking himself to death. A mother reprimanded her two teenagers not to look their way and smiled reluctantly at Heidi. The husband looked without looking. An old couple at the back pointed in their direction. The buzz of overlapping conversations returned as everyone talked and stared. They sat there for quite a while before a black waitress attended to them. When Heidi was deciding what to order, the waitress's eyes roamed all over Heidi's body. She began with her shoes and went up to her golden earrings. When Heidi looked up to order, the waitress averted her eyes and took the order feigning complete disinterest. Heidi had to repeat every word at least two times before the waitress understood her. The waitress was much nicer to Neil. She reappeared after ten minutes and roughly deposited their drinks on the table. As the glasses clinked, a few faces turned towards their table.

Flickering candles cast a glow on their faces and gave their drinks an orange look, which blended with the evening colors. Neil's face looked radiant. Heidi's color changed into light brown under the dim light. They toasted to their health. Silence frequently punctuated their conversation—sometimes awkward, sometimes not. Neil took a deep look at Heidi when she was looking elsewhere. Heidi did the same when he was distracted. She focused on his sharp face when examining him from the side. Only once did their eyes meet while traveling on each other's body. They both nervously looked down.

They ordered more drinks. They were both in the mood for gin and tonic. Like their first order, this one too arrived after a long while. While waiting, Heidi drew herself closer to Neil. Accidentally, so it seemed, her hands rested on his shoulders. He complied by holding her hands tightly, but she gracefully withdrew them.

The waitress arrived with the drinks and slammed the glasses against the table even more loudly than the first time. The noise provided justification for additional stares. Heidi and Neil looked at each other in recognition of a familiar scene.

Around 2 a.m. Heidi and Neil walked out of the bar hand in hand, starry-eyed in each other's presence. The waitress and a bus boy stood in the kitchen door watching them leave. The waitress muttered to the bus boy some commentary that ended in an audible snicker.

The cab dropped Heidi at her apartment in Central Square and continued on to Neil's destination.

Neil was so drunk when he arrived home that he fell asleep immediately. Throughout the night he fought a man. The intruder, a tall dark-skinned man, came in the nakedness of the night and shared his bedroom. A large web occupying the full entrance to the bedroom door hid the man's body as he stood smiling and looking larger than life. When the intruder first appeared at the entrance, the door made a squealing sound and his wings showed themselves. The one on the right hand side was vital, in tact. The one on the left was bruised, dying slowly. The man was inclining toward the right. His form had been disfigured by the condition of the wings. For a moment he appeared to be in pain, but he was also smiling.

After surveying the situation, the intruder walked toward Neil's sleeping body wielding a kitchen knife. At that moment, the sleeping body awoke briefly, terrified by the howling of a dog announcing death. The body screamed, terrifying the intruder, who suddenly dropped the knife.

Walking backwards, he said, "Leave Heidi alone. She is mine. I am her kind."

In his dream, Neil awoke again and stood on his feet, pulling a sword from under the bed. He ran after the winged man. Upon catching up to him, he lunged onto the man's back and strangled his neck. As Neil's victim fell limply to the ground, Neil slit its throat. Its head separated from the rest of its body, but the man did not die. He jumped out through the window while his lower body remained motionless.

Heidi did not have much better luck sleeping that night. She tossed and turned for over an hour, busily thinking about the stares at the bar, the waitress and the bus boy, haunted by what she always called the "invisibility problem." That night her thoughts focused on the process of not being seen, even when one is as visible as billowing cumulus cloud on an exceptionally clear day.

* She asked herself, What are the processes through which one is rendered invisible? How do people make others invisible? How does one see, without seeing? The experience reminded Heidi of a college course she had taken. She had read Ralph Ellison's *Invisible Man*, a book that examined the subtle processes by which the black in America is made invisible, transformed into a being with a body and soul that others do not see. White people go out of their way not to see the black man's looks, his accomplishments, and his virtues. In full daylight people do not see the black man as a human being. They erase his humanity. The eyes, the eyes that are trained not to see, do the task. The black man is made absent. He is relegated to the zone of non-being. Of course sometimes the black is perceived as the white man's servant or as a rapist or a murderer. If he is seen at all, he is seen as the example of the negative. She remembered one of her professors referring to this process of invisibility as the "architectonics of the racial gaze."

Heidi could not take these questions and the thoughts off her mind as she tossed desperately tried to sleep.

That Ellison's observations still applied to contemporary life amazed Heidi. People surely saw her at the bar, but she did not have any control over the way they saw her, the images white people saw in her. She wondered if black women were rendered invisible in the same manner as black men. If not, she wondered about how white people saw black women. The course that she had taken in college unfortunately had not addressed the specificity of the black woman's experience. Given this void, she had considered writing a book one day that she would have liked to call *The Invisible Black Woman*. Thinking about these matters kept her awake for the whole night.

Heidi's hobby was dressing well. Every day she went to work sporting different styles. Her spring colors consisted of black silk pants with a lilac scarf and high heels. On cold winter days, she wore a blue suit with matching shoes. Tight pants with high heels, her usual Friday outfit, were also among her favorites. During the rest of the seasons, she changed every day. She rarely made mistakes, but noticed that on the days she did, people actually saw her. Some people would tell her how nice she looked. Her appearance, of course, determined their visualizations of her. Although she could not control the images others rendered of her in their minds, she enjoyed dressing well.

"What am I if I am not capable of controlling images of myself?" Heidi questioned.

But no one went out of their way to say a word to her. Some it seems even forced their eyes not to see. Her boss, for example, made a point to discuss black crimes and her, goading comments out of her. She did her best to ignore him. A Communications major in college, she had learned not to allow racism to easily provoke her. She had trained herself to either walk away when provoked or to not hear racist comments if possible. For years, she had been applying that formula when she found herself in uncomfortable circumstances. As a communications consultant, Heidi did her job meticulously. She always kept her table clean. Her work was piled vertically and numbered in accordance with the importance of each task. Before she left work, everything that had to be done the next day was always neatly piled. When she arrived at work, she made coffee, carefully read the papers, and took notes. Then, she moved to her desk, listened to the voice mail, made all the important calls, and took a short break before changing gears, opening the computer, and checking all new emails. She always answered all of them immediately and carefully. After going through her morning routine, Heidi took a half hour for lunch and returned to work to attend to the piles, on which she worked systematically each day for two hours. She scheduled all of her appointments in the afternoon. If she had no appointments she would return to working on the piles, sometimes well into early evening. This was her daily habit of work, but it remained invisible to her boss and coworkers.

Heidi's boss approached her only when she made mistakes. Her virtues were invisible. Any mistake Heidi made always sparked a reaction, sometimes a scolding. Her boss, however, would excuse the same mistake if made by a Caucasian, male or female. He consistently erased any job well done by Heidi. Most did not even travel to the boss's brain, but were selectively blocked from entering his memory bank. When it accidentally made it there on a few rare occasions, he quickly erased it.

One day two employees were fighting bitterly over an assignment, when open violence broke out. The situation captured Heidi's attention. One employee had bitterly complained that another secretly interviewed a rich fund-raiser that he had located. Heidi, with remarkable ease, appeased the disgruntled employee by immediately hooking him up with an equally rich and even more generous donor. The employee, as well as the boss, said nothing, not even thank you.

Heidi smiled in response. That is all. Not a word was betrayed, as if she had not anticipated any other outcome. Events of this nature had happened to her numerous times—events of invisibility, as she called them.

Heidi found it ironic that America is so obsessed with the black female body. While not seen at all, the body is simultaneously seen too much. Television quarters the black woman's body. Her powerful legs, her supple black skin, her buttocks, her hips become the source of the powerful white males' pleasure. Images lock the black woman into the roles of lover, nurturer, and achiever. They stole her from the black male. Tossed between males, blacks and whites, Heidi felt dehumanized. As she had told Neil, "I am now surely visible, but only as an object. I am admired like a car, a stereo, and a body. You see Neil, I am now visible as a commodity, but not as a person."

Heidi worked with a black lawyer. He was tall and highly intelligent with powerful shoulders and a huge chest. He was able to recall the secretary outside asking if he were seeking janitorial employment when he first came to the firm for an interview. When he told the attendant that he was a fresh Yale law school graduate, she flippantly commented, "Oh, I like your sense of humor. That will get you the job. With that humor, you'll make a fine janitor." Then, she laughed. He made a point to ignore it even though his reddened eyes surely told the world that he was boiling with anger. He decided to remain quiet. She examined his body from top to bottom. Then she proceeded to display her legs, move her hips as she walked away from him, and wink at him several times. Once he sensed that there might be a setup with which to heckle him he ignored her all of her flirtatious gestures. He had read somewhere that these were techniques people used to black males before they were even hired at a job.

While waiting in silence, he was rescued by Heidi, who took him in to be interviewed by the Director.

The Director was snide. "You have time on your hands, I see. You have done well with your body. The Gym is nice to you. I am too busy for that. Well, I'm glad somebody has the time…. So what can I do for you?"

"I would like to work here as insurance lawyer."

"Is this your first job?"

"Yes, indeed. Fresh graduate and ready to have my first experience as a lawyer."

"Well. We are looking for experience."

"You got it. This will be my first experience. Everybody begins somewhere, right, and I am ready to begin here."

At the end of the interview, he extended his hands to the Director and thanked him for his time. He flashed a smile as he left the office and stopped by the secretary's desk to thank her for arranging the interview. The prospective employee's confidence and perseverance, as well as his capacity to shake off demeaning jabs directed his way perturbed the Director. Nevertheless, the moment the young man left, he went to the secretary's desk and told her to call the "boy" after a week for a second interview.

The secretary followed through on the boss's request and the boss ended up offering the young black man the job. Members of the company insinuated that the business was under pressure from Affirmative Action, suggesting that he was hired simply because he had come along at the right time.

That was how the second black face had arrived on Heidi's work scene. Heidi recalled how exuberant she was to work with someone with a similar complexion, but, contrary to what others may have thought, their two souls shared nothing in common, except their skin color and subjection to invisibility.

He liked cars, iron bars, drinks, and parties. She loved poetry, painting, books, writing and skiing. She felt tied to the poor left behind on the island of Barbados where she was born. He cared primarily for himself and believed in personal responsibility. He loved to sleep with white women because they, as he claimed, made him "feel like a man." She felt obligated to marry within her race, although she secretly loved Neil. Despite their vastly different personalities and ambitions, their blackness led people to assume that they were essentially the same: sex maniacs, incompetent, prone to lying and stealing. Others treated them not as individuals, but as members of the black community. Sometimes, out of the blue, her boss would say, "So. Heidi, how is the black community?" Then he would add, "How are your people these days?"She would ignore him, as if he were not there. Although he resented being ignored, that was Heidi's way. When people got out of line, she simply ignored them, erased their very existence. Heidi remained awake all night long pondering such things. She felt like calling Neil to tell him why she could not love him, even if she wanted to, why love for her was not a personal decision. Everyone in her family, she felt, should be involved in her decision to love someone. They should decide with her, even though they may have no inkling of how she felt. She opened the window. The cool spring night softly breathed in her ears, comforting her, blowing her hair, kissing her face, massaging her eyes, gently tiring them to fall asleep. She projected her neck into the silence of the night, looking at the deep beauty of darkness, with the blue sky as her roof. She felt for a moment that she owned the world, that, in the silence of the night, the world belonged to her, just like the soft feeling of joy she experienced each time she walked alone upon rustling leaves on a quiet country road, taking in all there was to see. She recalled the sky, the struggling sun, the silent moon, the cold trees, the dog chasing a frightened squirrel, dogs barking at dogs as frantic owners chased after their pets to prevent them from eating each other up -- all the elements of nature surrendering themselves to her eyes, her ears, her feet, to every part of her body.

The night captivated her. She felt free, unburdened by life. Light, hopeful, and radiant with thought she went back to her bed and fell asleep. She even forgot to close the window and left the door half-open. She had always taken great pride in living in a safe black neighborhood that the news reporters and cameras never visited.

Heidi did not wake up to the world again until four o'clock in the afternoon. Waking up to clouds suffused with heavy weight, she thought of Neil. The first thing she did was take a hot shower mixed with a cold shower—like life itself, she liked to say. She went to her blue kitchen with bright teakwood. Although a heavy look at first, the colors grow on the viewer as she looks deeper into it. The blue delights the heart through weight. Only the heart can handle weight. The blue absorbs sadness, sadness that delights only the human heart. The teakwood invites the eyes and lightens the heart by mixing itself with the blue. Heidi felt that blue, light brown, and black, were colors of compassion, a compassion that pleases the compassionate through the power of blue thought inscribed on solid wood.

Black coffee with sugar and two slices of toasted wheat bread with a light spread of apricot jam rested on a table waiting for her taste buds. That was her breakfast. As she did every Sunday morning, she sat with the morning paper, put on her glasses and read every part of the *Boston Globe*.

As Heidi struggled to finish her second cup of coffee and dry her hair, the telephone rang continuously. The hour after she woke up passed rapidly. Rising from a difficult night, taking a long shower, preparing a pot of coffee, drying her long silky black hair with natural curls in between, walking from one end of the room to another doing this, looking at that, and touching this and that had filled almost her entire day. Although she had been part of the world for only two hours, she already began thinking of evening, dreaming of night. Of course, she was divided between going to sleep and meeting Neil, whose company she enjoyed. But she might decide to tell him that they might not have a future. But she liked him, too. She did not know what to do and fought herself. This was not a pleasant day for her.

While sipping her coffee, she fell into the usual spell of thought, of anguish, as she wondered what to do next. She mulled over calling Neil, since it was he that she had first thought of that afternoon. She liked that idea. She thought, It is a rare gift to fall in love, even though it may not be reciprocated. Love is the gift. Sometimes it comes with enormous suffering. That too is a gift. She put her cup down, lit a cigarette and puffed smoke into the clean afternoon air. Circles of smoke danced in the air and gradually settled on the dark green kitchen wall. The smoke darkened the area where her collector's plates were displayed; a long line of plates from all over the world hung on the kitchen wall. Walls stared at her from the living room as well. She became fixated on the plates, studying them, and thinking about their creators in Iran, India, China and North Africa. Every time she gazed at that area of her house, she surveyed those plates. They took her back to the geography of the world: through them she imagined the richness and creativity of human hands, underpaid artists who produced beautiful objects under a blazing sun in Africa, the barbaric winds of India, the shivering cold in Guatemala.

Beauty distracted her from hypnosis as she grabbed the phone and inhaled her last smoke. She called Neil.

The telephone rang a few times before Neil answered.

"Hello, Neil speaking."

. "Oh, hi, this is Heidi. Good morning, Neil," she added and laughed. "It's me, your nightmare." She laughed again. Neil did not.

"Hi, Heidi. What's up? How was your night?" He inquired hesitantly.

She excitedly answered, "If you really want to know, we can discuss it over drinks tonight. We can have a bite to eat here, with drinks, if you would like." She waited for an answer, but not for too long.

"It sounds great. What time?"

"Say, at eight."

"I'll be there," he replied.

Neil arrived that night exactly at 8 p.m. Heidi welcomed him at the door. He hung his coat on the rack, moved right into her lovely kitchen and began chatting there. He checked out the decorum. The plates attracted his attention. Her collection of dolls from all over the world also tickled his fancy. He had never cared for dolls before, but this time he took an interest. She told him where they came from and what they symbolized. He was intrigued by the uniqueness of her interests. After a while, and after asking for her permission, he opened a bottle red wine, which he had brought. They were both quiet for a while, as if they were both thinking about how to say what they wished to say without offending one another. Neil broke the ice for the first time. In the past Heidi had always started conversations. She had less difficulty with words. This time, however, Neil took the first plunge, and seemed quite happy with the move.

"Well. What happened last night that kept you awake?" he inquired.

"Things. All kinds of things, if you care to know. How could you be so insensitive to all that mistreatment at the bar, Neil? I guess it does not get to you. You are mister cool."

"Not that. But, having lived in Cambridge for a good fifteen years, I have learned how to brush it off from my body, like drops of rain. Really, as they say in Utah, one shakes off bad talk. That's all. I don't let people get to me. Not anymore."

"Oh, Neil. It is so easy for you white guys. You have it all. You can get what you want. Good jobs, black women, Asian women. Just about anything. You stare. Hire and fire. Recognize and not see. You hate black men. You see to it that the bold ones die early of defeat. The ones who challenge you die from envy. You put them out of business, and, if that is not enough, you finish them. You kill them. Look at Malcolm, Walter Rodney, and the countless others."

"I really don't understand you. Two things. First, all these insinuations have nothing to do with me. I am an individual. A farm boy. A painter. And still unrecognized. Without a career. You have the audacity to link me with those rich white guys."

He grabbed her on the arms, and said,

"Hear me. I have nothing to do with them. For all I know, they may secretly refer to me as white trash."

He stopped, rubbed his eyes, which looked hot red and said, "Or, even worse, they may call me a nigger lover. Second, all of these things have nothing to do with you. You are gorgeous and smart with a dream job. Cut it out. This political correctness kills me."

He stopped again, and rubbed his eyes even more and said, "Don't give me that shit. It doesn't work with me. I am in hell myself. Too bad for a white guy. Right, Right. You cannot make me feel guilty about anything. If anything, I love black people."

Heidi lost it. She raised her voice at him for the first time. "It kills you. Right. Your ears cannot hear it. I hear it all day long at work. My ass, my breasts are scrutinized by my boss. I am the black bitch who fucks all night long. I carry that damn company. And what do I get? Nothing. I am treated like a whore. You get it. I get it from black men and everybody else. I am called bitch when making love. You don't get it. Do you? Do you, Neil?"

She sat down and drank more wine.

Neil got up from his chair and walked around, with a cigarette in one hand, a glass in the other, searching words of anger. The redness of his face communicated anguish.

He started, "Perhaps, you're a little too sensitive. You consume things. Your heart sucks sorrow. You let words seep deep into your soul. Dear Heidi, that is a weakness in this world. I do not know about the next."

He paused and then said, "I cleanse myself of human words. Still, you're out of line to bombard me this way. I too have my sorrows. But you are too self-involved to pay attention. I guess we are not meant to be. I suffer like you."

He briefly stopped and added, "Years of male literature have bombarded me with the ideology that I should never appear to be hurt in public, but rather suffer privately when no one is around. But even then I have been taught to not ever cry, to not ever despair."

She calmed down and said very sadly, "You're right. We are not meant to be. Not in this city, and not at this time. Sad as it sounds, it is the truth. I cannot live as an object of stares wherever I go with you. The price is too high and life is too damn short."

She walked around and added,

"I am not free to love whomever I want to. Love for me is an obligation; it comes with a commitment to my family, my race, and my people. It is an act of collective affirmation. Most importantly, it comes with the silent expectation that I cannot love the whites who enslaved, whipped and killed my people." Then she got up and walked away.

As he always did when he was sad, Neil looked down to the kitchen floor, in search of an answer, in need of guidance, from somewhere, from the depth of the dust to which he will one day return. He remained fixed in that position, as if words froze in time. He looked at her several times. She looked at him also as she stood on the verge of tears. Then, she could not control her tears. She rushed to him, grabbed him by the shoulders, shook her head and said, "Remember that I will always think of you, and will always regret that I have lost a man who really cared for me. The joke is on me and not on you, Neil."

Neil's eyes were also weighed down with tears, but with much effort he pulled them in. He said to himself, She thinks I have chosen the so-called white race that I wear. Shit, it's nothing more than an imposition. Shit, I am still looking for a self, for a person to be... As he thought of these words, he shed those impregnated tears, and felt release.

The moment he recovered from the depth of anguish, he almost immediately got up to leave. He did not turn his face. He walked one-dimensionally, head strong and fast-paced, as if he were trying not to remember anything, sucking out the past, his heart. Heidi tried to stop him, pleaded with him to wait a little longer. He said, however, that he had to leave.

Before he left, he told her that she was afraid, that she was the type who lived for others. From afar, his reddened eyes examined her entire body, as if they were taking a mental image for a future portrait.

Then, he left.

...

"Yes," Neil muttered to himself. "We all live for others. We have all become performers. No one has the gumption to live for oneself. This is particularly true of Americans. Everything is about race." He recalled a story that Heidi told him about her time at Smith. She was at a café meeting with an American student to whom she was teaching her native tongue when a tall, blonde, graduate student of French at Harvard entered. She smiled at Heidi and the student and asked them what language they were studying.

When they told her, she replied enthusiastically, "Oh, so exotic!"

The American students answered, "It depends on where you're standing." And Heidi added, "To me, French is exotic." The woman answered, "Oh no, French is beautiful."

Heidi and the student decided not to engage in the conversation anymore. They looked at each other, nodded their heads and carried on with their task.

Neil remembered this story to make a point about close-mindedness, to illustrate that people were becoming increasingly provincial, if not directly racist. People, he felt, approached the unknown as not only different, but also weird and inferior. He watched as hostility, replaced curiosity, the virtue of childhood. People, he believed, no longer loved freely, but rather distributed love calculatingly. He shook his body from hate and sat back on his old mahogany chair with his face looking at the ground.

Neil rearranged his hair a little, rubbed his eyes, and rose to look at the night outside his home. The wind was boisterous as if it were the end of the world. Only the flickering stars in the sky were alive. Everything else was inundated by thick darkness. Neil took a deep breath and accidentally bumped his head against the window as he desperately positioned himself to look at the depth of the rampant night. The emptiness of the street devoid of life moved his heart. He could feel life without seeing it.

It was past midnight. The power had gone out an hour ago and the lights were still off. No TV or radio. Neil's roommate and neighbors had nothing to do. It was terrifying, Neil thought, to see people without their gadgets. People got lost. He saw it all in their eyes— the bewilderment, the boredom with the world, the utter loss when the familiar preoccupation with watching TV vanished from their sight.

Silence.

All that he could hear were occasional whimpers when, suddenly, the lights came on, just like when a letter appears in a mailbox with a job offer, when its intended recipient has already taken it off her mind to protect herself. Everyone looked up in utter wonder and relief. TVs soon illuminated living rooms throughout the neighborhood once again.

...

Neil sat in his usual spot at the Coffee Connection. Sometimes he looked to see who was coming and going. Most of the time he held a pen in his hand. He peered at the floor a lot that day, often breaking the trance by rubbing his eyes, cleaning the lens of his glasses, or slowly refilling his teacup. The waitress had come to visit but she already knew him. He could stay there the whole day if he wanted to. They were used to him. He always took his time when ordering.

At the far end of the shop he saw a dark-skinned couple make a very happy entrance. They were walking hand to hand, with a spring in their step. A couple of times they kissed each other lightly. They were giggling, talking black, and singing a little, until a collective gaze silenced them. Upon entering the café, they quieted down, reluctantly, and stood in line. The girl looked more anxious to be served than the young man did. She appeared to be on the verge of exploding on account of being ignored, while the young man pleaded with her not to make a scene. They looked at each other as if they understood the unwritten laws in the city. The conversation at the café became considerably quieter in their presence. A few chose to stare. The couple, however, decided not to make a fuss. They waited for their turn and changed their order to take-out.

Neil watched the scene intensely, sketching outlines of disappointed faces in his painterly mind. For years he had been attempting to capture sadness without sad faces. This time, however, he settled for faces. He overheard them whisper? "These are the 1990's, mind you," whimpered the guy to the girl. "Oh, yes. But it never changes for blacks in this country, and most particularly in this part of the country. I cannot wait until I get that degree to assure white people that I have a mind. Not that a degree will stop discrimination." The guy comforted her with a gentle touch on the cheek.

They left the restaurant outraged. Both aspiring lawyers, they

116

took mental notes of the situation, silently planning to address the issues at a later time. But middle-class blacks like this pair had learned how not to show anger. They left with forced smiles on their faces, although it was inevitable that they would explode the moment they were alone. For a brief moment they had fooled the cashier who made them wait by not betraying emotion, but rather doing exactly what whites have mastered—the apparent control of emotion even when one is bleeding inside.

...

One day I decided to take a break from the drudgery of work, and entered a coffe shop at the Square. I accidentally sat directly across from Neil. I sat with my medium height, stocky, strikingly brown young skin in my late thirties, writing away. Like Neil, I sat alone. I intuitively knew that he was my type, the kind struggling to find a place in the world. For a while I alternated between reading the papers and writing things. The waitresses at the bar, who appeared to be students, talked about me.

"Look at that pretension. I bet you he is writing shit, probably hoping to be picked up," one commented.

The other one replied, "Leave the guy alone. He is trying to be cool. At least he is not selling drugs."

"I hate it when they pretend. They should be themselves. You know what I mean. He looks funny. Really out of place. Trying to write. Give me a break." Nyrere heard this.

The conversation was interrupted. They went to serve their customers.

I could feel in the depth of my bones that Neil was dying to make contact with me. Something about me intrigued him. He looked as if he were straining himself to locate me, for he sensed that I am a foreigner. Neil had always felt more comfortable with foreign blacks than African-Americans. He wondered about his interest in me. Perhaps it was my intense concentration, or maybe my looks. Shortly, we subtly checked each other out. Both of us were interested in starting a conversation, but the question of who would take the first plunge into the sea of the unknown remained unanswered . "I'm Neil," Neil finally blurted out rather directly.

I said,

"Nyrere is my name, from Tanzania originally. I am sure you know where Tanzania is, right?"

"Oh yes. I have lots of African friends who have schooled me in that."

"I take it that you may be affiliated with Harvard, here."

"Yes, I am remotely associated with the University, although I went to school in Columbia and studied Creative Writing there."

Silence followed.

Neil was composing more questions in his head.

We talked about work. I told him that I had a Ph.D. in Sociology and had no real job yet. I had been looking for one for the past eight years while working part-time at six different Boston-area universities to end up with a salary of twenty thousand a year, published my writings in prestigious journals, hoping that would make a difference. But time was catching up with me. In America, I told him "people believe that age determines prospects. Unless one secures a career in his thirties, one is doomed."

Neil commiserated with me that he, too, had no career. He explained that he thought he was a painter, but perhaps he was only a lonely fund raiser who is treated like a telemarketer, a pariah.

"The way people judge you around here is beyond belief," he said, "They take one quick look at you, notice your dress, your shoes, and your tie, then they ask you what you do and create a category for you." He then advised me not to be too trusting. "If you can," he further advised, "give very little information. Keep the intruders in the dark."

We did not talk any further, as I suddenly began thinking about Adowa, and comforted myself by re-reading her long letter.

Conrad

On a gorgeous day, Conrad and Kim met amid the breathtaking view of Harvard Business School. They sat on a bench overlooking the Charles River surrounded by tulips. He came very close to wrapping Kim in his big and lanky hands, known for their firmness. Rightly, he decided against it. They sat very close to each other instead. It was so quiet that he could hear her heart murmur. His passionate eyes,

118

the thick black hair, his biscuit skin color, his long hairy arms; but what she liked the most was his eloquence, his way with language, his elegant tone on the phone. For her these were windows to his soul. She hoped that the inside would live up to the enticing outside.

She averted her eyes from his body, and was distracted by the beauty of the yellow tulips. She had always preferred the yellow ones to the bloody red ones.

Conrad discovered that Kim actually wrote poetry for herself and, on occasion, for her friends. About them she said,

"They give me company. They are my concrete anchors to the world." He begged her to read just one, only one for his soul. He held her hands softly, looked her in the eye, and asked her to read him one, only one. She insisted that she simply is not good. She was hesitant. She kept on telling him that she is not good, that she wrote them for herself, that they are a sort of therapeutic, but nothing to share with the world. "They are too mediocre for that," she said.

He insisted, nevertheless. Finally she gave in. "I will read only one."

> There under the beautiful moon
> The evening winds kissing me
> Late at night
> Those visiting hours of despair
> Come angels on wings of desire
> They blow wind of comfort deep into my ears
> I laugh.
> I cry.
> I laugh and cry
> Sometimes I don't know which
> Hands of love stroke my face
> Then I wake up to the same world
> So much better was the world last night.

She was so bashful that she covered her face after the reading was over. Her head fell on his shoulder, with her face still covered.

He said, "Extraordinary. To my ears."

She told him that was it. No adjectives. No analysis.

"Promise Conrad, never to discuss my poetry."

She threw a smile at him. The cool wind blew her short hair and jostled her like an old ship caught in a storm. After staying for a while he took her home. She did not invite him in, for she had to leave for Japan very early the next morning. She bade him farewell and said, "I will drop you a card from Japan. Be well in the meantime."

Walking and Thinking

Neil's new acquaintance, namely, I, was a short man, with protruding eyes, wide shoulders, and sturdy legs. My legs were built for playing soccer; my wide shoulders were fit for carrying the weight of life. A careful observer might notice that my head was physically large relative to my body. Neil's artist eye noticed this and speculated that perhaps a life of serious thinking could swell a man's head the way weightlifting creates bulging body muscles.

Like Neil, I was observant of my environment, but I felt it to be a sort of curse. "I am born to see all without being able to change anything," he liked to say when describing himself. My friends described him as hyperaware and hypersensitive, a charge he did not deny.

After Neil left the café, I turned my attention to apartment ads in the newspaper. I hoped I would have better luck that day. After finishing my coffee and circling half a dozen new prospects, I departed from the café and hopped on my bicycle. I headed to Newton where one of the colleges at which I taught rests on an expanse of land in the rolling hills of Chestnut Hill. The ride usually took about an hour when peddling at a reasonable speed, but I slowed down often that day to admire beautiful women. When they glanced at me, I generously returned their gazes. Eros was present everywhere and I made sure to respond to its summons.

I also slowed down on the stretch in Brighton that was filled with shops, bookstores, and cafes. Here I seemed to completely forget that I had a destination. But along the deserted areas I zoomed fast, without seeing or hearing. Occasionally, I turned to look at an assemblage of nice furniture thrown out for garbage pick-up day. I could not help but wonder how grateful Tanzanians would be to move the chairs, tables, lamps, utensils, television sets and radios into their barren homes. Even the middle-class in Tanzania would not hesitate to take in this furniture in the middle of the day to furnish their tasteless homes. Garbage here is wealth there, I noted to myself.

After peddling rapidly, I slowed down again, this time to defer to an old couple, pain-racked, as they crossed the street. I had learned quickly how not to be myself freely in this country. When interacting with women or elders, I offered my seats to others and greeted people on the street. Habits are habits. I did it again. I deferred to the couple. So many elders had refused to take my seat on buses and trains. Memories of being humiliated on a few occasions made me extremely hesitant to let the elders cross first. I was pleasantly surprised when they thanked me for it. This was the first time ever someone had thanked me.

The big and elegant trees on Beacon Street moved gently with the cool morning breeze. For a fleeting moment the surroundings transported me to Tanzania where trees shuffled in the same way and to the same kind of breeze. They happily reminded me of the universality of nature, which I hoped would carry over into the human world. How nice it would be, I thought, if everyone responded to abuse and honor in the same way, with equal sensitivity.

Everyone I passed on the street amiably noticed me. My invisibility momentarily disappeared. I found himself thinking that good weather could change everything. It has such a hold on our moods I muttered to myself, and then laughed as I took a bite of the ripe banana while waiting for the old people to cross. People were beside themselves as they emerged from a bitter cold winter and prepared themselves to embrace the New England Spring. A few people were already wearing shorts, anxious to show their bodies to the world. Many were wearing light pants with white shirts, prematurely imitating summer attire. It was obvious that people were looking forward to the summer. For most people the past winter had been particularly long and cold.

Dogs ran with joggers. Squirrels hopped from tree to tree. People affectionately held their cats on the porches of gorgeous colonial homes. Others sat relaxed by windows checking out the street scene.

Some cyclists were huddled against cars at red lights. At one location, however, the peace was broken as the cyclists, the strollers, the runners, and the casual walkers met at a red line. The cyclists tried to be the first to pass, but the runners blocked them. The walkers tried to catch up with the slow runners, but the runners would not allow them to. To make matters worse, the cars blocked everyone. Impatient cyclists fingered drivers, and the drivers screamed back. A stroller brought the matter to the attention of a police woman who was on a break at a coffee shop. The police woman appeared and broke the impasse. The scene charmed me. I spoke about that day so many times when the subject of the aggressive Bostonian was the topic of conversation.

I pushed my way past ferocious and notoriously impatient Boston drivers. I had my ways of putting them in their place, without ever loosing my cool. I was nearly hit a couple of times, but I adroitly cranked hard on my pedals and brilliantly overtook a rapacious driver without getting hit. The surpassed driver fingered me. I laughed it off. I even thought that the driver may have called me "Nigger," but I brushed this off from my soul and body as well, without letting it pollute my ideals for humanity. When I finally arrived on campus, I went to my office and changed into my professorial garb before entering my classroom just in the nick of time.

As I always did, I put my textbook on the podium, cleaned my reading glasses, placed my lecture material on the podium, quickly gathered my thoughts, looked outside at the meadow, paced a few times, took a deep breadth, and said," Good morning students."

Not a pip. Not a word, until, a mulatto student, an admirer of mine, shouted from the top of her lungs, "Good Morning, professor." I smiled, and started right into my lecture on "race and identity." I prefaced the lecture by making the statement, "I hope you are not upset about the reading. Remember that your responsibility is not to agree or disagree, but to read and master the material and then critically and judiciously evaluate it. That is the purpose behind reading. Of course, you can express your disagreements and agreements, if you are so inclined, but that should not be your main purpose. The main goal should always be to understand, to put yourself in the writer's shoes, which is no easy undertaking. Is that clear?"

122

Again, the students gave no answer.

"Race affects our identity in so many ways," I told my indifferent students. They continued to listen in silence until a female student who had been seething in anger throughout the semester, in spite of my efforts to accommodate her conservatism, spoke up. For the past month she had, at my invitation, sat in the very first row. I had hoped that it would facilitate eye contact between the two of us and offer her additional comfort and ease with my accent, my foreignness, my African ways. I had become hopeful that I was getting somewhere with her, lessening the otherness, reducing the tension. I was, however, mistaken. From her old space in the middle of the room, she raised her voice and said,

"I do not know what you mean. As a Greek American, I am proud to announce that my Greek parents have worked so hard to overcome obstacles that others put all around them. We all came in the same boat, but we live so differently now. I don't think race has anything to do with success. It is an excuse."

A group of American students sitting to the right and left of me were struck with disbelief. They stared at me in utter awe, as if they wanted me to denounce her, and defend "the race." My eyes locked with theirs as a special kind of moment emerged onto the classroom floor. I felt called upon to respond, to articulate a position, but I also knew that this was a dangerous moment. Compelled to speak truth to career, I carefully organized my thoughts and struggled to choose the right words to engage her in the adventures of thinking as an exercise in examining the grounds of one's beliefs regardless of what they may be. I challenged the historical accuracy of her statement, noting that some people came to this land of liberty in chains and others free. Her ancestors, I pointed out, did not come in chains but as free people. Africans, on the other hand, were kidnapped, bought, and forcibly brought to this country in chains. Their experiences of bondage and captivity traumatized and embittered them. Their race, I emphasized, marked them as slaves, as fit to be tortured and treated as property, less than human."

"I'm a good person, by the way," she interrupted.

"I am sure you are," I replied. "But don't you think that a good person should necessarily be compassionate, and, at the minimum, empathetic?"

She could not handle it. Her eyes bulged out. Her face became red. Her hands trembled. She threw her notebook on the floor and let the student sitting next to her bend down and pick it up.

"Are you implying that I am not a good person?" she said in an amplified voice.

She screamed her lungs out. Everyone in the classroom heard her wailing. She burst out into hot tears, stormed out of the classroom, stood in the hallway, and disturbed looks on their faces. I, on the other hand, ignored her and continued my lecture until class ended. In the meantime, the girl's friend comforted her in the hallway. I saw the two of them together as I left the classroom and walked toward my office.

Two hours later, the dean summoned me, and told me that a student had stormed into his office and claimed that she had been embarrassed in class and scolded as a racist. I calmly reported verbatim to the dean my understanding of the encounter. The dean assured me that he would not take any position and suggested that I speak to the student in his and one other administrator's company. I readily agreed, but the meeting never took place because the student came to see me on her own. She came into my office, blushing. She invited herself to a chair, stared at me, smiled softly, and took off her sweater, seemingly to display her large breasts through a thin tank top. She smiled at me coyly, got closer to my desk, and asked me questions about the final exam. I handled her behavior and inquiries professionally. I was convinced that she was clearing the air and removing the dust of hate. I was wrong. With my coaching she received an A in the course, but after the semester had ended, I passed her in the cafeteria and, although she saw me, she walked by without even making eye contact.

The school did not renew my annual contract at the end of the semester under the pretext that my services were not any longer required. I knew, however, that the encounter with the student had also surely contaminated class evaluations. I was advised to consult a lawyer, but that was not my style. I left that institution and joined another one although the particular experience continued to stand out in my mind, scarring me forever. I recalled this story when I met

Neil at the café for the second time. Neil was not shocked by it at all. To my disappointment, Neil dismissed the event as insignificant. For Neil, it was a case of a misunderstanding on both sides: I had overstated my case, and the female student had overreacted. Both, Neil felt, had been victims of "political correctness," and my naiveté had blinded me to the manipulative behavior of young students.

"You're not playing your cards right," Neil said. "Do you know that white women are crazy for jet black and muscled black men? I bet she was more interested in you than she ever was in your ideas. She probably thought that you didn't need to possess any ideas of your own."

He stopped. I read through him and killed him with an ironic smile. Remembering that this was only the second time I had met the "the farm boy," I decided we should not bother to "fight" so early on in our relationship. After all, Neil was not the only one who thought that way. My words expressed the ideology of an entire society. I appreciated that Neil was sufficiently courageous and able to speak his mind.

Neil started again. "So you're offended by what I said?"

"Not really. It is just that you hardly know me well enough to speak to me this way. I guess it is cavalier American way of speaking your mind, at other people's expense."

"What do you mean by that?"

"I could have meant only what I said. That you Americans some-times abuse freedom in the name of freedom."

"This goes to prove my point," Neil retorted. "It is your attitude that got you in trouble with those students, not your race, as you conveniently allege."

"Convenient, you say. What is convenient about speaking truth? It is a painful experience. But truth must be told, no matter what the consequences are."

"You are right about that. Truth must be told. But whose truth is the question. The lefty-liberal establishment should not have a monopoly on truth, but it does in reality. That's what gets me," Neil said as he slammed his notebook on the table.

A few customers, alarmed by the noise, turned their faces.

I do not get mad easily, so I took Neil's actions wordlessly. We

125

both took a break from the conversation and hid our faces behind the morning papers. Again, Neil was the first to leave. Since we had shared a table, he made a nice exit with a broad smile, and hoped that they would meet the next day for breakfast around the same time. I remained behind to do more work.

The café became crowded rather rapidly. People lined up to wait for their morning coffee. "Ethiopian Harare" coffee was the day's special. I had noticed that that coffee was so popular that it attracted a huge crowd of addicts. They liked it in different forms: espresso, caramel macchiato, cappuccino, and café latte. Coffee blended well with all permutations. Yuppies in particular, the manager had once informed me, were prepared to spend up to $20 a day on coffee and snacks. As busy as everyone was, almost all of them stared at the studious black face in their midst, dressed better than most of them, disciplined and confident about my being.

I minded my business and continued to work on my lecture notes on culture and relativism. I planned to tell my students that afternoon about the connection between ways of seeing and evaluating what we see. I wrote: "Values and norms are nothing more than various ways of seeing and believing." To prove my point, I wanted to tell stories about how different cultures deal with love, sex and religion. I sat there for a long time thinking of examples from my hometown and comparing them with what I had seen during my fifteen-year residence in the U.S.

I laughed a bit recalling an encounter at a colleague's recent party. An older academic had opened a conversation with me by saying: "I detect a slight accent. Where are you from?"

I responded with, "I too detected a slight accent in you, and where are you from?"

The man blushed. "I am an American, of course," he said.

"So am I. I am a citizen, like all Americans. This is a nation of immigrants. We are all in the same boat."

The academic, Steve, became uncomfortable for a moment. Out of the blue he said, "I am a Norwegian." He pointed to his nose and said, "and this is a Norwegian nose and it comes with reservedness and subtlety."

I laughed and said, "Oh, there is such a thing as a Norwegian nose, and reservedness and subtlety." The comment reminded me of a long and beautifully written ironic sentence in Thomas Mann's *Tonio Kroger*, a novella, in which one of Mann's characters speaks about the difference between northern and southern temperaments, characterizing northerners as reflective, puritanically correct, melancholic; southerners as expressive, emotional and gay. I laughed again, and thought to myself that the world had not changed. I knew that misunderstandings and misclassifications would continue to exist alongside the unexamined beliefs that produced them.

What struck me most was the concept regarding the death of the individual and my inability to choose my identity. I wrote down my encounter with Steve so that I could share it with my students.

***

During my next class, I chose to illustrate this concept by telling my students a tale about an individual who was tormented simply for remaining true to himself.

"During the seventh century," I began "there lived a nameless monk in a remote village in Ethiopia. People simply called him 'Dodo' and that became his name. He was remembered as tall, extremely thin, and resistant to cold and heat, as if he were made out of steel. He covered his body with sheepskin through out the year. His daily food consisted of dates, figs, and water. On special days he would nourish his body a little more generously, adding chicken and fish to his diet, but only three times a year at most. Dodo, without deviation, began his days 6 a.m. and ended them at 9 p.m. He began a typical day by reading the Bible and praying for three hours with hot tears streaming down his wrinkled face. During the final hour, he would enter a trance that led him to take a short nap. Upon waking, he would consume some dates with cold spring water. That was his lunch. Shortly before noon, as the powerful tropical sun overwhelmed him, he would walk for half an hour to a nearby river to feed ducks and ducklings with fresh food he baked for them every single day. There in the silver meadow grass with the tall Ethiopian mountains protecting the river, the ducks and ducklings would always flock to the party, peacefully feed themselves, and then return to their nests in the riverbed with satisfied quacks. Dodo also returned home each day after feeding the ducks and took a long afternoon nap. After the nap, he routinely walked down to a small pond where he did a combination of backstroke and free style for two full hours before embarking own a little self-made boat, and heading towards the market to do any necessary shopping.

At the market, kids and grownups would congregate and call him names. He would chase some of them. He would ignore others. Many would run after him. He always wondered what his crime was. It was his looks— thin, exceptionally tall and frail. If only they had known how strong he was, they may not have behaved this way. For Dodo, coming to the market was a necessity. Getting harassed for it was a curse. After enduring a trying few hours of harassment Dodo would return home the same way he came. At the entrance to his cave, his three students, whom he tutored in Math and Gee'z, Ethiopia's classical language would greet him. Dodo lived this way for 120 years. But one day someone discovered him dead in his dimly lit cave, peacefully stretched across the middle of a straw mattress, with two burning candles to his right and left, the Bible under his pillow. Thus ended the life of one of the most righteous and disciplined individuals who has ever lived."

"He was a real individual," I emphasized before concluding the parable.

"Dodo did not write anything. Dodo lived by example. He showed the healthful and right way of living, unburdened by commodities. One of Dodo's students, whom he had taught Ge'ez, grew up to be the most learned Ethiopian philosopher and an accomplished and prolific writer. From Dodo, the Emperor learned how to live well and how to think well. Yet, during my lifetime, Dodo was an object of ridicule when he went to the market. It was only his students who knew what their teacher was worth." I paced up and down as I related this story. As soon as class ended; I went home, exhausted by the day's events.

Home was a little apartment I had finally found on the third floor of a three-story building not too far from Porter Square. On my way in and out, a pile of garbage that had not been picked up for days greeted me. In the summer the smell was unbearable. Inside, the apartment was sparsely decorated but contained all items essential to my life: a big desk for spreading out student papers; a smaller desk that housed a Macintosh computer and a small TV set. The living room, slightly bigger than my bathroom, had a love seat and a mahogany coffee table, with two side lamps that lit the room.

The burdensome conversation with Neil in the morning, followed almost prophetically by the heavy story of Dodo, had wiped me out. So the moment I arrived home, I took off my day clothes and put on my multi-colored African gown with a matching hat and soft leather slippers. Then I delicately prepared a martini, which I quickly gulped down. I sipped a second martini as I stretched my legs on my sofa. I sighed deeply, as if for the last time, closed my eyes, and in less than ten minutes fell asleep. After thirty minutes in deep sleep, the telephone startled me. At first I ignored it, but it rang again. I continued to ignore it until it rang a third time. This time, I was forced to respond. As I did so, I made sure that I would not burden the person with the slightest hint that the phone call had just woken me from deep sleep or that I was annoyed to have been badgered by three loud rings. For me, civility was an imperative. As I had told Neil during one of our heated conversations in American culture, "Civility commands manners without coercion."

"Hello. This is Makau."

"Hello to you. How are you Makau?"

"To be honest, not too well. It is a long story about the Foreign Service appointment. It did not materialize and as you can see... I am quiet upset. It is better if I tell you in person."

He paused to guage my reaction. I replied, "How about if we meet for a drink on Saturday? We will talk then. In the meantime, be well. Do not be hard on yourself." After that we talked about a few light things—girls, marriages back home, and who was going out with whom—I hung up the phone, and went back to sleep.

***

On Saturday, Makau and I met at the Middle East bar in Central Square. Makau arrived first, dressed like a millionaire. In a dark gray three-piece suit, with a plain blue tie, and glittering black shoes, he sat in a corner navigating the interior of the bar with swift eyes. He stood out in this cool bohemian crowd. His blackness combined with his fancy attire invited attention.

A young shabbily dressed, but attractive, woman remarked,

"Look at that guy. Does he know where he is? He should be going to the Ritz." She stole a quick look at him, and then went back to her business of shaking her hips and much else. A Reggae song blasted in the background while another band raged in the basement. When I arrived I spotted Makau in the back corner. I, in contrast to Makau, was dressed just right for the crowd. Khaki trousers with a white shirt, modest light brown shoes looked very nice on me. After ordering drinks we went right to business.

"Well, what seems to be the problem?" asked I.

With his characteristically formal English style, Makau said, "To put it mildly, I am over attended by problems and problems. Wherever I go I seem to attract unwanted attention. I do not know how to walk problems away. They buzz around me, like a nervous bee."

"Oh, I am sorry to hear that. What kind of problems? Not that I am a shrink, of course."

Makau rearranged his tie, pulled his chair closer to the table, minimized the possibilities of others hearing the conversation, and replied, "I received a letter that rejected my application to Foreign Service for the tenth time. I have been waiting to get an offer from my own country for ten years. I am just beginning to get tired of it all. Sometimes, I feel like ending it all. Abuse here, rejection there. Where is the hope? Why live this way? Can anyone live without hope?"

I, known to be a patient listener, briefly covered my face with my hands, wiped my wet face with the back of my hands, and told Makau that he wasn't alone in feeling this way, that many Africans were in the same boat, that he should not despair, that many Africans were neither here nor there.

"The Africans-Americans have learned the game well. We Africans have not, particularly in professional jobs," I assured him. "Unless of course one wants to work in the service sector, at three different places, and succeed at least in buying homes and sending one's children to live the life that you wanted to live. That option is open in this country. You see, these are the choices. You and I chose the difficult path."

Makau looked convinced by the distinctions, but his eyes were

130

wondering about why it had to be that way. I continued, "Sadly, we Africans are hopeless. Look everywhere around you. Ethiopia and its poverty, in spite of a sustained history of glory and independence, unblemished by colonialism; Kenya and its pretentious modernization; Tanzania and its mismanaged economy; Rwanda and ethnic cleansing, to mention only a very few examples since the list is as long as the continent."

I took a deep breath, for it must have hurt.

Makau burst into excitement and said, "My friend, much of what you say is true, but you are forgetting the role of imperialism played in creating all of these situations. Do you know for example that, according to The *Guardian,* your own country makes 2.2 billion American dollars a year, which it must share with 2.5 million people, while Goldman Sachs, an American investment bank, makes 2.6 billion dollars, which it has to share only amongst 162 people. What do you call that? Who is to be blamed for this state of affairs? Africans again?"

I became quiet and pensive. I rolled up my sleeves before speaking again.

"I know what you are implying—that the continent is mercilessly exploited. But you are forgetting that our own leaders and investors are part of the game. They are hardly victims, but rather willing participants in the exploitation of their brothers and sisters. I am sure it does not take much to get paid handsomely by their capitalist masters. It is like that new debate about the African slaveholders. Were they forced to enslave their own people? I do not think so. We have to call a spade, a spade. I know your dreams of joining them while still screaming racism. What is the point, however, of becoming an ambassador for oppressive African regimes? The problem is that our Ambassadors are mindless baboons. They live for a three-piece suit, shiny European cars, private bars at the Sheratons and Hiltons of the world, fat salaries, villas in gated communities, parties with Cuban cigars and white women, speaking with heavy English and French accents, and endlessly take suffocating orders from their western masters. That is what privileged Africans are good for, and their masters know them well. They choose them carefully."

Makau was used to my style of conversation, which always

sounded a little bit like I was still in front of a classroom. He appreciated my thoughtfulness though, especially in times of frustration. After having a few more drinks, we moved on to lighter conversation, as was our pattern. I felt the pinch of the booze first. He waved at the waitress to bring the bill and we left around 11 p.m.

Makau did not go home directly. Instead he went to see one of several of his girlfriends, whom he is accustomed to seeing just about any time he wants. He arrived at her door well past midnight. No phone calls. Nothing. The so-called African way and her so-called Spanish ways were in unison.

She came to the door in her pajamas, "You woke me up. You…"

Before she finished her statement, Makau pinched her, slammed her against the door, and kissed her mouth and neck. He kept on going after her, carrying her inside. After a while she went along with it, and soon found herself asking him to go harder and harder, calling him names: "you bastard, you fucker." He pushed even harder, tossing her from the back, the front, and the side, everywhere. He penetrated every part of her body. She continued to scream more loudly and the louder she got, the harder he thrusted. For the next thirty minutes banging, squealing, and screaming were the languages of the room. Finally, Makau released her and pushed her back onto the noisy bed. She told him not to get close to her, to stay away from her. Like a pleased lion after a hunt he lay on his back and fell asleep right away. When morning came, she woke first and served him breakfast in bed.

After breakfast, he covered his face with The *New York Time*s and read the whole afternoon. She went back to bed. When she woke up late in the afternoon, she had trouble walking.

"You see what you have done," she said.

"Yes. I see. I hope you are not complaining. I made love to you. Most of your friends are looking for what you are scorning. Some of them go to bars, waiting on suitors. They come back empty-handed, and find themselves in the company of booze and videos. Don't complain, Isabelle. Be grateful."

"Grateful. You son of a bitch. Not when you treat me like a whore. Be a man, have a decent job, and treat your women right, or else just get the fuck out."

"You fucking slut. I will do it again, unless, you stop screaming."

"Get out you bastard. I do not want to see your fucking face again."

He was used to this. He told her he was about to leave anyway because he had things to do.

Dressed beyond his means, Makau walked like a flanneur and a dandy to the T station. All those who knew him could not determine where the money for such glamorous attire originated. As he stepped onto the train, he located a strategic corner and surrounded himself with *The Boston Globe* to his right, T*he New York Times* and *The Atlantic* to the left. With one leg on the top of the other, wearing round Calvin Klein sunglasses, he sat, surveying the scene for the ideal woman.

He located one, and shamelessly changed seats so he was next to her. He flagged *The Atlantic*, did a quick study of her disposition, and shot the first fatal lines,

"Bonjour. Parle-vous Francais?"

He startled the woman who nervously replied, "Oh! I wish I did. I love that language. I assume that you must speak several others."

I speak fluent French, Spanish, and my native language, Kikuyu." My English is not so good, he lied."

"I feel so ignorant," the woman replied.

Makau gently touched her neck, and reassured her, "We can change that. How about I teach you French and you teach me American English? You can help with my accent."

She innocently concurred. Before she got off at the next station, he managed to get her name and phone number.

****

After Makau and I left the Middle East bar, I went home to grade papers and prepare some lectures for the rest of the semester. I also remembered that I was supposed to attend a conference at a famous university.

At home I continued thinking about Makau's doom. During all the time that I had known him, over twenty years since our graduate days, Makau had been dreaming about ambassadorship. Five regimes had come and gone in our home country. And he had applied for positions in all five of them, every other year for almost twenty years; nothing had come out of it. Makau was twenty-eight when he first applied. At the age of forty-eight, my hair was graying and a prominent stomach competed for attention against my engaging black visage. Makau was still a telemarketer, but told people that he was an executive at a bank. Only I knew the truth. Up until this point, I had kept the secret to myself. In this way, I helped preserve Makau's dignity. The abyss that separates the ideal from the real brought me to tears, for I knew that Makau was doomed. One day, I thought sadly, Makau would take his life.

I was right. Makau's real life ended in exactly that way. It is said that he returned to his native country and was infected with HIV, although he may have become infected while still in the U.S. The moment Makau discovered his disease, he took his own life.

...

I woke up to a flood of light on Sunday morning. There was plenty of open space in the living room and the kitchen. I spread my body on a blue and white carpet in the living room. To my left sat *The New Yorker*, which I read every Sunday.

I woke up at six in the morning when most people are either still asleep or recovering from the pleasures of the night before. For me, however, Sunday began with rigorous exercise. My tiny apartment, decorated sparsely, offered bountiful space for exercise.

Each Sunday I would do five hundred crunches and two hundred push-ups. I believed in exercising by carrying my own weight. I preferred my own body weight to dumbbells and bench presses. I divided the push up segments into ten sets, with fifty repetitions in each. I took five minute breaks, during which I read the magazine. This particular morning, I exercised for a little over an hour and also finished a couple of key pieces in *The New Yorker*.

Then, I set some coffee to brew and jumped into the shower. I enjoyed my coffee slowly and read the rest of *The New Yorker*. By then it was close to ten in the morning. I put on my khaki shorts and walking shoes, and set off on a full day walk.

I began by heading to Porter Square. My apartment was two blocks behind the Shaw's supermarket located there. On both sides of the street stood plain row houses resting on very small plots of land meticulously tended by their owners who hoped they could pass for suburban lawns. On the side of each set of row houses sat another portion of yard, but most of the yard was covered with dark and shiny tar so as to serve as a parking area. Some residents even dared to enclose these spaces as garages.

I made my way toward Union Square and then continued on to Irvine Street in Cambridge. At this point, everything changed. My eyes quickly adjusted to the houses, large and painted with great care. I could discern that someone had paid great attention to the design, the size and the appropriate color of the homes. No house even remotely resembled another. The gardens sat on generous land, blending the wildness of the forest with choice plants.

Unlike the Porter Square area, Irvine Street and the other side streets were alive with human presence. I could hear, even if I could not see, children playing in their yards; mothers asking them to come in for lunch; old people hanging out on porches rocking, reading, or simply watching the street scene; students jogging, running, strolling and walking, all day and into early evening.

That evening, as I had planned to, attended a special event with Neil entitled "African-American Response to the Race Concept." The event drew modest attendance. The young, African-American history professor presenting spent the whole hour summarizing a literature review in a monotone. People looked at the clock constantly. An older man sitting in front blatantly fell asleep. Neil and I kept ourselves busy by writing notes, not necessarily on her talk. The sight must have pleased her because we both appeared to be wrapped up in her words. Certain provocative phrases she used, such as, "the community of conditions produced the need for the race concept," or, "blacks were viewed as distinct, wretched and different," or, "for the abolitionists, we are all the same; we descend from the same human family, the same blood," kept me awake.

Neil perked up when she suggested the sameness of humanity with phrases such as "race is a limiting discourse." I, on the other hand, flashed a big smile at her whenever she used the word "difference." After the hour-long presentation, a powerful professor in the audience rose to speak during the question and answer period. "I enjoyed your talk, but I am just puzzled by why the term 'race' is consistently used to refer to inconsistent things." The presenter almost froze. She could find no coherent response, so she simply declared that she agreed with the statement. Many faces seemed to say, "but he asked a question."

Another seemingly frustrated listener accused her of saying that race is a fiction. She answered by saying that she did not say so. I intervened to note that what she meant was that "race is a self-conscious construct by which black people respond to the dominant paradigm of whiteness." She affirmed to the audience that that was indeed what she meant. After a few other barely sensible questions, the talk ended. Neil and I discreetly left first and went to Starbucks for a coffee break.

Since it was a hot spring day, we sat outside sipping Frappuccinos. Neil asked, "Well, what did you think? A good academic talk?"

"Yes, but some things never change."

"What do you mean?" asked Neal.

"What I mean is that I did not get anything that I have not heard before in a better language, particularly by able novelists who write from their heart."

"Such as whom?" Neil probed.

"I do not have any particular person in mind, but someone like Toni Morrison may come close to it."

I informed Neil that this tired talk about race was not going anywhere and that if the world was to finally be cleansed of discrimination based on the idea of race, people would still continue to use the term to distinguish themselves from others, by their looks, skin color, languages, ways of eating, ways of making love, ways of seeing. They would somehow manage to equate race with difference. Even if the term "difference" was abolished, he argued, other words, such as distinctness, would quickly replace it. There would simply be no way of going around that.

'To begin with saying that we are different does not make one a racist," I emphasized.

Neil could not contain himself anymore. He was annoyed. "Bullshit, I. And you know it too. Look at all those who think that Blacks as a racial group are born dancers, born basketball players, sex machines and so on. Your academic friends will not dare to touch these topics. You saw what that feminist did today at the talk. Difference this and different that will not cut it. There is only the human race. We are all from the same cut. Difference, identity, and class are categories that academics created to make jobs for themselves. Imagine all these disciplines we have. What would they teach without these convenient categories?"

No wonder, he mused, that academics keep out all those who question them, and, even worse, those who do not believe in them.

My defense of difference was based on my own life experience. I had been hammering Neil with this point for some time, but Neil resisted it because of its implications if it were actually true. Neil's attachment to the notion of the human race was also an extension of my own ideals. He had used this argument to go after Heidi, when she, like me and Makau, tried to tell him that she could not stand people staring at them anymore. He remembered that Heidi believed that all Americans perceived of race and difference as synonymous. She had told him, "To say I am different in the U.S. is to say you are outside of my circle. We do not belong to the same human race. Our skin color, our hair texture, our language, what we eat, and how we eat are so different that it is much safer to assume that we do not descend from the same human race, that our blood does not flow from the same stream."

Neil had hated this argument then and he still loathed it.

He remembered these words, which at they time infuriated him beyond measure, beyond reason, so vividly that he imagined Heidi's body outlined in the words she chose. He wished then, as he continued to wish, that the creator would erase the word "race" from every human language and replace it with the word "human;" and human only. Neil had gotten lost in his own world, and tuned out of the conversation, when I assumed my turn.

I told him that I too was frustrated with the way the word race is used in this country. I recalled that when I first came to the U.S. at the tender age of twenty, I landed in New York City. It led me to believe that I was the most handsome man who had ever lived. I remembered returning people's smiles with triple generosity, flashing free smiles, deferring to everyone I encountered in elevators, street corners, doors, hallways, parties and bars.

One day when I had entered a bus, I found many open seats, but one right in front of me was waiting for me to sit down. I, however, could not help but see an older man, who could barely stand, uneasily moving around the bus. On closer look, I surmised that the man might be blind. I got closer to the man and offered him my seat. God knows how he knew that I was black, but he said bluntly, "I don't need your pity, boy."

I took the seat for myself and lost myself in thought. I did not, however, easily forget that. The hurt remained etched on my heart for years to come.

I explained to Neil that it took college and meeting African-American students to transform my consciousness. I recalled once going to a bar with my friends. A white boy was heavily drunk and began cursing me, telling me that although I had traveled widely and been to Asia, and had servants growing up, I was still inferior to him. I did not make much of this. I helped the white boy to his car, washed his face in cold water outside, tidied him, and drove him home. Even the young man ended up addressing me as a boy, however, I did not share the overreaction of my African-American friends. They were furious and channeled their rage into organizing a protest on campus. They demanded that the student be reprimanded. They littered the university newspaper with columns on race, on white supremacy, on the notion of color blindness. For them what had happened was a blatant form of racism. Until that day, I had been immune to racial discourse. As I saw it, the boy was simply drunk. Ill raised, I would say. Nothing more. At that time, my vocabulary was not equipped to address issues of race.

I shared another story with Neil. I was walking toward campus to attend a lecture when I noticed that a large white car was following me. It was dark; I could not make out either the gender or the skin color of the driver. The car continued to follow me, inching closer to the curb each time I glanced to evaluate the situation. When the car came to a stand still at the traffic light, I was able to turn my face and make out the identity of the person.

She was white, middle-aged, and brunette with freckles. She threw her arm out, opened the door and invited me in. I had not gotten laid for months, so I jumped in and drove off with her to my

138

apartment. My roommates were not in. She smelled of alcohol and could barely move. Although her behavior disgusted me, I felt as if it were too late to escape because she, too, was desperate for sex and had managed to undress herself almost immediately. In addition, I had already gotten hard by the time she had removed her clothing. Desire had destroyed my dignity; I had allowed myself to be seduced in a disgraceful manner.

What started fast was over fast. I asked her if she liked it.

She confessed, "This is the first time I did one of your kind, a nigger boy. How disappointing."

Neil also had stories of race and sex that he wanted to tell me so he could gauge my reaction.

Neil began, "Shortly after I moved to Cambridge, I went to a party and met this young woman from Barbados. Without physical contact, I fell intensely in love with her. We hung out together a few times, but the only time I made love to her was in my dreams. Heidi would not give me her soul or her body. She was there floating. Long before I developed an actual feeling for her, she had already concluded that she was not going to fall in love with a white man. To do so would be to betray her people, particularly the black island women who had been raped by white men during slavery. She had promised her parents when she left home to study at Smith College that, as a matter of principle, and in spite of the habits of the heart, her mission would be not to fall in love with a white man."

I was saddened by the story. Might Heidi have fallen in love with you were it not for "the politics of identity?" I inquired.

Neil agreed. "You hit the problem on the head. Indeed, it was all about politics. Even love is a subject of political negotiation these days. Heidi was a master of that. But all this comes at the expense of our right to be happy by falling in love with those whom we want, whom we care for. Well, I, it was not meant to be. You see we all have our stories, if we dare to tell them."

Both of us had places to be. As always was the case in our new friendship, our conversation ended in the middle, like an unfinished story. But, we both intuitively knew that we were becoming friends. With every new meeting, something new happened. Before I left, I extended my arm and looked directly into Neil's eyes. Neil returned the gesture, pressed my hands tightly, and tapped me on the shoulders.

"Let's get in touch. Call or visit, will you?" Neil asked.

Neil remained behind to prepare a speech for another fund raising event. He sat outside the café so that he could enjoy a cigar that I had given him. He inhaled deeply and sat for a long time organizing his thoughts. He didn't make it past "ladies and gentlemen" before his mind wandered off.

It began raining slowly, but Neil did not notice it, until a thunderclap took him out of his trance. He went back inside the café and returned to his speechwriting.

"Homelessness is the product of humanity's moral failure. With a changed attitude and a self-willed change, we can conquer and eradicate homelessness along with poverty. But we have not even decided that we need to change ourselves, to transform our consciousness to arouse our sleepy consciences. There are homeless people in our blessed America, the land of plenty. Since 1960, when people in rich countries had a net worth thirty times more than twenty percent of the worlds' poorest people, the income gap has multiplied by more than seventy-four times. The income of the 200 richest people increased from 440 billion USD in 1994 to more than 1 trillion USD in 1998. If rich people asked themselves "What do I need all this money for?" the world would be a different place. Suppose that rich people began to stop pushing legislation that benefited themselves and decided that a million dollars is more than enough wealth to sustain a luxurious lifestyle consisting of a huge house, a maximum of three cars, and no more than three children, the rest of their disposable income could be used to uplift the conditions of the poorest twenty percent of the world. All we need to guarantee to them are decent and beautiful modest homes that cost around $40,000 a year.

Imagine how beautiful life would be if people were free of abject misery, and terrorists waiting to blow up the world on the behalf of the downtrodden.

Ladies and Gentlemen, homelessness and poverty are the result of our folly, our greed."

Neil stopped writing and noted, "to be continued."

Remembering that he had to attend a painting class at the Museum of Fine Arts, he stood up abruptly, gulped down his forgotten ice-cold coffee, and hustled to the T station. On his way, although he was already going to be late for class, his attention fixed on a tulip that that was just joining the world. He practically witnessed the birth of a tulip in the corner yard of a little brown house. The scene reminded him of an old obsession of his — that one day he would be able to determine the exact second of the time he fell asleep. For him, birth, sleep and death were inextricably intertwined. For years, partly because of insomnia that left him tossing on the bed endlessly at night, he would linger half asleep, struggling to know, to really know, the exact time at which he fell asleep. When looking at the tulip, he was overwhelmed by the fact of birth, by the very second in which it happened. He was amazed at the sharpness of his eyes when he actually convinced himself that he saw a tulip flowering into a deep yellow baby that steadily but surely extruded first its thin stem and then exploded into a new flower.

"Ah," he said, "welcome to my miserable world."

Before leaving, he sketched the scene in a rough drawing that he called "Birth." He saw this as a blessing, for he would be able to share the event with his teacher and hopefully convince her to have him work on "Birth" as the semester's project.

This was the first time that he had ever arrived late. Her smile expressed an awareness of that. After he settled into his chair, he wrote her a note about "Birth" and handed it to her. She read the note immediately and came back intense with excitement for him.

"Absolutely. Consider it a gift. Now get to work. It's not going to be easy; you know what I mean, but anyway." She squeezed her fist to emphasize her excitement.

He got busy immediately and drew an outline of "Birth." In his first sketch Neil aspired to appreciate more deeply the struggle of Monet, the impressionist, and his life long commitment to paint air. For he, in his own way, faced the challenge of painting the event of birth, the birth of a flower to which he had been chosen to bear witness. This was the beginning of the birth of Neil's masterpiece, which he began working on in the early 1990s and continued to work on for the next several years. He never spoke about it with anybody for the duration of that time. The project expanded and captured the births of many other beings. He finished them all and they were magnificent, but nobody recognized them because they all hung on the walls of his bedroom, a place that few besides he ever entered.

As soon as he entered home, he sat down and wrote a long letter, with tears dropping on the writing desk. It took two full hours of intense concentration to finish the letter. The letter was addressed to Heidi.

He had been contemplating suicide lately, and his eyes seem to have readied themselves to move towards death. He closed his eyes that night, perhaps for the last time. There was a glass of water, which had turned pink, and he drank from it, turned the light off and went to bed. It was seven o'clock in the morning when he fell asleep.

Conrad

Modest lips liberally spread themselves around his mouth. His long neck made his moves more visible, making it difficult for him to hide his motives. As he walked down the streets his eyes moved in the direction of any woman who passed him. He walked in dark shades that made it difficult to imagine the shape of his eyes because everything else looked so perfect. He lifted the shades for a fleeting second and his sunken eyes made a great effort to look at a woman walking by. He swayed his neck to check her out. For a moment the ease with which he swung his neck reminded one of an owl.

When examining him closely, one could not determine whether swimming or weight lifting produced his fitness. His body connoted both. Its size presented him as a weight lifter. The lankiness and his ease of movement inclined one to speculate that he might be an active swimmer. He walked nervously, never at ease, as if pursued by someone dangerous. The bulkiness of his upper body stood in contrast to his slender lower body, long and thin legs, small buttocks, and thin thighs, which took away something from his otherwise elegant full frame.

His face had begun to look better over the course of the past five months because he had gained full control over his alcoholism. His doctor had warned him that if he ever touched a drink, it would kill him in a few months. He had followed the order assiduously and had not had a drink in 5 months. Conrad wore his black shades all the way to the angle of the cafe's entrance. Betraying good upbringing, he took the shades off the moment he fully entered the café. Those big Irish eyes made themselves present to the world once he removed his shades. From the entrance his eyes surveyed the scene, busily looking for something that no onlooker could discern. Like a squirrel's eyes when it is running through a dangerous street, his eyes moved from left to right, from right to left, and then stared directly ahead.

All those enthralled by the man's presence found themselves trying to guess what consumed the young man. Many thought that he might have had a date of some sort, man or woman. They could not tell. Some thought that he had been stood up; others surmised that his date was there but that his eyes were not sharp enough to locate the person. Suddenly, his eyes shifted toward the far end corner at the opposite side of the café. There sat a young Asian woman with her laptop. She turned in his direction. He stared and opened his large mouth with a precise smile that disguised the shape of his mouth. She smiled back.

He looked around very subtly, for the place was filled with people, and, making sure that others were not judging him, he walked over to her table. Although it was a forgone conclusion, he asked if he could join her, and with a gentle smile she invited him to join her.

"You look busy, with all those notes," he said as he approached the woman.

Like all foreigners for whom English is not the first language, she chose the formal and grammatically correct way of conversing, and replied,

"It takes me almost three times longer than an American student to write one paper. It is an ordeal to write papers, and, at the moment, I have three long papers to finish. You, on the other hand, seem to be free, spending your time meeting new people."

"I, too, am a student. I get busier toward the end of the semester. Writing papers. I'm a Teaching Assistant and an editor of a graduate student magazine."

The woman in a rasping voice replied, "I could have never guessed that you were a student. You look like you are finished.

Coming in like that with those shades, you give that aura of a relieved man who has time in the middle of the day. Chinese men are so studious, so serious looking. That is what I am used to. In Asian culture there are different kinds of looks. Student looks. Professor looks. Married men's looks. It is so funny. We Asians are very hierarchical."

"Yes, you are, if I can be so direct. So what are you studying in this country?"

"I go to the B school and I am studying toward my MBA,"

"Oh. You're one of those moneymakers then. You know"

She was a bit surprised to be called a moneymaker. She told him that she had never been called a moneymaker and that she did not see herself as one. As far as she was concerned, she chose the field so she would be able to run her father's business when he passed away. A family tradition expected much from the children who must keep the family honor going by seeing to it that the business was successfully passed from generation to generation. Since she was the only child in the family, the fate of the generation rested in her hands.

He listened attentively. As a student of Asian culture and language systems, he was highly interested in discussions of values and norms. His way of learning could be quite rough on people. His looks and charms, however, often saved him from many otherwise aggressive people who would not mind punching him in the nose. Women in particular put up with him, they said, because he was ultimately harmless and kind, despite his severe exterior.

She told him that Asians believed in hard work, and that no work was beneath them. That dignity was in work itself, and not the kind of work you do. She went on and on about capital accumulation, investment, and self-help. He took it all in. While she was speaking, he remembered an article that he had read in a magazine about women above the age of thirty in Asia: pretty, wealthy, Asian women with secure jobs could not land good husbands. The wealthy males were always interested in the twenty-five-year- old women, whom they could get without much effort. The modestly comfortable types were already married to women that they did not have to love, because the women were just grateful that they had secured husbands. Their

144

wives tolerated their husbands' protruding abdomens, misshapen bodies, and their unfullfilling jobs. Those women thirty and above, pretty if not gorgeous, intelligent, independent, did not give a damn about these ugly and fat men. They preferred to remain single and miserable rather than always unhappy and married.

For some reason she reminded him of the passage. He was trying to figure out which category she fit into. Her physique placed her with the twenty-five-year-olds. Her intellectual weight exuded maturity. When he first saw her, after his longish darting, she was sitting alone, surrounded by gadgets of success: a laptop, golden cigarette lighter, and a Chesterfield without a filter. She was nursing a caramel Frappucino and savoring a chocolate brownie; the remains of a Greek Salad with smoked salmon were pushed aside.

He looked at her again and again. He determined that she was in her early thirties, but barely looked it.

While he was surveying her as if she were a landscape, in walked a woman, tall, swift, with tight pants that had the insignia "Chick," high cheekbones, wearing a mean and sharp look. She glanced at Conrad and Kwang, for that was her name, and walked to the dimly lit portion of the café, and covered herself with the menu. The young woman checked Conrad out, not caring about the other woman who accompanied him.

Kwang's face turned discreetly when she noticed that Conrad was looking in the direction where the new arrival sat. A couple of times her eyes moved at the same time as Conrad's. Both of them were embarrassed. But this did not stop Conrad from taking many other secret stares or Kwang from taking unseen looks at Conrad looking. The view would have looked unusual if it had been photographed directly. Kwang was of course disturbed that a man whom she had just met was already interested in another woman. She knew that she certainly had no claim over him, less than two hours after having met him. Conrad turned toward Kwang and resumed their aborted conversation.

"So Kwang, what are you planning to do this weekend? Anything interesting?"

She covered her forehead with a hand, as if she were thinking hard.

"Oh. Work, work, and more work. That is what I plan to do. You are forgetting that I am graduate student, and a foreign one at that. And you?" She asked him affectionately, as if she were already developing feelings for him.

"I try to go hiking every weekend in the fall and spring. It keeps me sane. I am doing that this weekend. You're welcome to join me, if you like."

After hesitating a bit, she said,

"Thanks for the offer. It is so tempting. I may. Call me, if you like. Who knows, I may get sick and tired of studying. Would not that be a pleasant distraction?"

"I surely will call you before I leave. Remember though, it's really going to be short notice. I'm just warning you."

On his way to the door, he daringly turned his face to see if the "Chick" girl was still there. She was. Their eyes locked. Both could not help but be embarrassed, but this did not stop them from doing it twice more before he finally walked out the door.

...

For years Conrad had quietly put up with manic-depression. For the past few months he had been on the upside—feisty, ebullient, and confident for days. He had very little need for sleep as he fluttered through his days like a fidgety bee in search of flowers. For days on end Conrad had been hopping from task to task, activity to activity. There was nothing that he thought he could not do. Confidence overwhelmed him; illusions exploded inside his heart.

It was this kind of attitude that propelled him to return to the café, in search of the girl he had spied while talking to Kwang, only fifteen minutes after he had departed. She was indeed still there, and Kwang seemed to have departed, which gave him room to operate. She spotted him approaching her. The moment he sat down, he focused on her firm and large breasts. Without any social graces he asked her if she would come to his place. She protested mildly but gave in so quickly that he himself was taken a back. He laughed as if saying, "God. This is so easy."

The cool breeze outside ruffled their hair. Her ribbed jacket kissed the air. Her truculent hair touched his shoulders. He put his arms around her and pressed her ass hard a couple of times.

When they arrived home, Conrad took her to the living room. She

146

was half his size, which made her easy to maneuver and made him feel especially potent. He had been with women enough to know not to rush. He explored her and let the tension build. He checked to see which items she liked. He discovered that she was a real firecracker. She left scratches down his back and bit his chest as she came.

Overcome with happiness, he asked her if she would like to drive to Manhattan for the weekend. She responded affirmatively and proceeded to shower and toss a couple of items in a bag.

***

Conrad sat behind the wheel, driving with one hand and wetting her with the other. They stopped a car at rest places to make love with the rays of the ebbing sun shining on their red-hot faces. Conrad drove ninety-five miles per hour when he did not anticipate police on the horizon. He drove past hundreds of cars, changing lanes like mad and infuriating others in the process. A few angrily honked at him as he rudely passed by their Jaguars and Saabs. Some fingered and cursed him at the same time. He settled down for a while when his companion put her head in his lap. She whispered suggestions of things he might try with her when they got to their hotel. He pulled over as he was about to come because he couldn't focus. Finally satiated, his companion fell asleep in the passenger seat. He still did not know her name.

She woke up as he parked the car at the hotel. He kissed her deeply and got hard again. At the front desk, she kept her hand in his front pocket as he checked in and got his room key. The moment they entered the elevator, he began undressing her. By the time they entered the room, she was ready for penetration, and he went after her like a hungry lion. He ordered her to sit on his knees and suck him. She did. He commanded her to sit on his top and do him. She did that too. He picked her up with a single arm, put her on the bathroom sink, and did her until she cried. At one point, he screamed the symphony of sexual ecstasy.

"Oh. Asian women. Nothing like them."

"Yes. Yes honey talk to me that way. I love it."

They went out to eat in a Chinese restaurant. He ordered hot mandarin shrimp with vegetables, and an order of fried dumplings, and she had mixed vegetables with orange chicken. Conrad was famished. Not only did he gulp his food down in less than five minutes, but also, with her encouragement, finished hers after she had taken less than two or three bites. At dinner, he learned her name was Ana. She told him that he ate as well as he made love, greedily, but since he filled her so well, she did not mind.

She made sure to present herself as his slave who would live for him. She did not want to work as long as he brought home the money, which she would manage intelligently.

"I am a pure Asian woman who loves to serve my man. I do not care about what so-called liberated women think of me. I am my own woman. I know what I want. I want to love and be loved. But no man will ever cheat on me. He does not have to. I will submit to all his whims."

Their relationship had been non-verbal for the last two days, which he liked. Suddenly she began to speak, but no one was listening. She was not supposed to speak. She was not supposed to have a voice, but rather to help sharpen his voice, and to speak for the two of them. The new development began to disturb Conrad. Hints of loyalty were in chic's voice. Her feminine power exuded confidence and pride. Conrad saw signs that if a lover ever crossed her, she could castrate and, if necessary, kill the lover. For her, submission was not meant to be reciprocated. She saw herself as the equivalent of many women and their multiple appeals to a single man. No man who had her would need to have other women. She expected that she could fill a man's desires so that he would never even desire another woman, that such desire would not ever visit the site of his fantasy.

Conrad listened but still did not hear. He grabbed her and kissed her deeply, as if he wanted to shut her mouth. She complied. She wanted to have him, to contain him. She kissed him back and rested her head on his shoulder. He took out a cigar, puffed a few rings of smoke, paid the bill, and they went back to the room at the hotel.

Both of them were exhausted. They slept through the night until 11 a.m. They checked out an hour later and went to Central Park. Right there and then, Conrad proposed to her. She accepted. Later that week, back in Boston, they exchanged vows at City Hall.

...

Two months into his impulsive marriage, Conrad called Kwang, the woman that he met an hour before Ana that fateful day. He told her that he had been thinking about her a lot, but that he had been away on a trip and could not call. He assured her that the moment he had arrived in Cambridge, he had thought of her. They agreed to go to a movie that weekend.

...

"You see Conrad. That is love," Kwang said as they left the movie, "They loved without loving. The thought of touching put them both in the mood for love. That is what the movie meant for me. It is so different. Sad, yes. But happy too. It is sadness that makes one happy. A sort of perverse many people will say. People do not know that there is joy in sadness. Or, at least there is for me."

She stopped, hoping to get a reaction. There was no verbal reaction. But the expression on his face contained an answer that he did not speak.

In the car, he grabbed Kwang the way he did Ana.

"No," she said, firmly but gently. "No Conrad. That is not the way I want it. That is not love. You would be attacking me, that way, and I will not let you. No. No. Be calm. Relax to love. Move with love and not against it. Follow its ways. Please do not attack it." Conrad did not press her.

His mania intensified during the next several weeks, deploying itself on desire. He continued his affair with Kwang. In the meantime, he nearly finished his dissertation, and lined up a job. To celebrate, Kwang took him to Newbury Street. They ate at the fanciest places and shopped for jewelry, clothing, porcelains, and perfumes; items for Kwang rapidly filled his credit card. His condition amplified his exuberance. He simply could not control the contours of euphoria. Kwang had no idea of what was going on inside his head. Nor did Ana. Both mistook mania for generosity, sickness for health.

Conrad had to be very careful not to descend into sadness, for it attacked him as a contagion. His doctor, in fact, advised him to avoid any contact with sadness. He cautioned Conrad, telling him, "The line between joy and sadness is so thin that those who are prone to both must learn how to nurture their conditions by balancing the two needs. That rule, however, applies only to the so-called normal ones. Manic-depressives on the other hand lack all sense of balance. Extremes mar their lives. They must be prepared to experience both joy and sadness, but never simultaneously. The disease feeds on extremities. When manic, such patients are able to carry only the excessive burden of joy. When the burden climaxes, however, it descends to the gorge of sadness, extreme sadness. At this point, depression ensues."

***

After their day on Newbury Street, Conrad found himself strongly desiring Kwang's body and began to lose his patience.

"May I show you the Chinese way? Please let me," she urged him.

Conrad paused. To his credit, he did no insist on doing it his way. They drove to her place. This was his first time going to Kwang's home. He noticed how her personality grew stronger there, but not in a way that made him recoil. Instead, it intrigued him. The firmness and lightness of her manners sold him on the idea of another way.

Kwang left the room to go to the kitchen and came back with a basket of fresh fruit, bearing the beauty of a Cézanne still life—ripe bananas, oranges, apples, and pears on one side; beautifully sliced cheese on the other. On her second trip, she came back with a bowl of dry shrimp accompanied by homemade prune wine. She offered him some, gently closed his eyes, and lightly kissed him on the cheek.

They sat in her living room adorned with a love seat under pure white curtains, pots of healthy plants on the left and right side of the love seat, a square coffee table with transparent glass displaying a rubber plant, candles on every window corner, two black leather chairs in the corner. Directly across from the living room a triangular dining room was adorned with a round glass table and four leather covered cherry chairs, with velvet curtains dancing to the wind above the entrance leading to a beautiful garden on the porch. All the candles were lit and yet it was almost dark, beautifully dark inside. As they sat in the candlelight, Kwang drew herself very close to Conrad. He consumed her winter grass smell, fresh and light, just like her own nature. She walked as calmly as water. She talked as quietly as a sleepy baby's whimper.

He looked around the place. The Chinese porcelains, chests of drawers, straw mats, vases of all forms, and her traditional dress elegantly sitting on the dining room table captured his photographic eyes. He had been drawing and taking pictures lately. Long trees in the winter; children at the beach; a young mother nursing her child under the shade of a tree on a hot day; an old couple crossing the street aided by elegant canes— these images had recently appeared in his collection of photographs, which he had developed himself at a friend's place.

Conrad found himself gazing at her body from so many angles. Each time he took a secret glance at her, she looked different. His longing eyes discerned her body in numerous forms. She looked one way from the side—pensive, with lines of sorrow. From the corner chairs, where he sat briefly, he noticed her protruding behind, round on the side, tapered at the end, exuding firmness of skin and suppleness of texture. He felt like penetrating her violently, thrusting himself into her as she screamed and resisted him. He wanted to pin her down to the ground, thrust from the top, from the side, from behind, deep inside her mouth as he dripped the seed of life inside her. When he looked at her closely from the love seat while the upper half of her body rested on his, rubbing against his hardened penis, he felt like talking to her forever about the world, about himself, about his pain. They embraced each other with the blanket of desire.

Suddenly, conscience visited Conrad as he huddled in her gentle hands. He remembered his wife. He remembered that he chose her, not Kwang, first. Perhaps, he had known that Ana would be an easier catch, while Kwang would require work. Conrad had chosen the easy way out. Ana had been there waiting for him when he went back looking for sex. Overwhelmed by desire, confidence, delusion, he had felt a grandiose need to prove to himself that he wanted her. He remembered his wife confidently telling her that he would always and hers and that he could never and would never desire any other woman. She had assured him with such a level of certainty that she was the equivalent of many women, that she had scared him. He found frightening the very notion of a single woman fully meeting all of his whims and desires so that he would not even be tempted to glance at another woman. He remembered too that after she had said all these things, she expected an answer from him, which he did not give. He had known then what he now knew so lucidly—that he was doomed to remain in the claws of deceit and dishonesty. His condition needed these infidelities, these changes of body, and these swings of love, the madness of Eros. He would always be yearning for more.

Kwang stood up, walked to the living room, and put on a Chinese song. She sat very close to him with her silky black hair and her big dangling earrings resting on his chest. They kissed again and again for half an hour.

"No penetration tonight. We have to move slowly. Remember that this is the Chinese way. One thing at a time. There is time for everything. I am only in the mood for love. Sex is another matter... if that is all right."

Outside, the sky became progressively darker with each passing second. Conrad sipped the Chinese wine, admiring its sweet and subtle power. His head was light and gay. Kwang recited the lyrics of the love song, translating them into English for him.

The lines read:

> I am walking in the rain
> Remembering my past
> High schools days
> So many loves there
> Spoken and sung about
> I knew a girl that I loved through out high school
> She did not know about my love
> If she knew
> If she knew
> She would feel my shyness
> That was the source of my pain
> Sleepless nights,
> Tired eyes the next day
> But nobody knew

Conrad asked her to stop. The words were too close to his heart, too close to memory. He had been there, in his younger days, when all was innocence, life was beautiful, love dreamable and livable, so his imagination told him.

He sipped more wine. As midnight came around, his eyes began to droop with sleep.

"Time to go Kwang," he told her.

"You are welcome to spend the night here. I have a perfect bed for you. Then, I could bring you breakfast in bed, copies of papers right in bed. Ha! Ha! Conrad, what do you say?"

"It sounds tempting, but I cannot. I will tell you the reason some other day."

She followed him to the door and he left quickly. The wind roared outside, although the weather was mild. He started his car and drove home. At one o'clock, he arrived home, checked the mail, set the automatic coffee maker and the alarm clock, and went to bed, anxious as he embraced his half-asleep wife. It appeared that she had waited for him all night long before finally going to bed.

Conrad fell asleep immediately. Ana spoke to him several times after he continued to blurt out the same name several times. She knew what she did not want to know: Conrad had broken a promise. So, she made up her mind to leave him, without notice, without arguments.

Conrad went to a conference the next day, without coming into direct contact with Ana. Again, she took it quietly, in the "Asian way."

Almost immediately upon his arrival at the conference, he noticed a striking Asian beauty, sitting with crossed legs, short hair resting on the tip of her shoulders, and huge dangling earrings. She displayed an arrogant and academic appearance as she smoked in the lobby of the hotel. She checked Conrad out twice. He was smartly dressed in black pants and a beige button-down shirt with cufflinks. He smiled at her when their eyes met. Then he left to check his room. When he came back down, she was still reading a book entitled *Anthropology and The Mysteries of the East*.

He smiled when she was not looking his way so as to remind himself that he would have no problem approaching her. He already knew that she was an academic, and also that she was reading about "otherness" and identity.

He was right. It was very simple to walk straight down to her. As he approached her, he said, "You're reading an interesting book. You must be an anthropologist."

He was not surprised at all when she candidly admitted that indeed she was an anthropologist from Korea who had come to the conference to present a paper on identity. When she told him that her name was Lee Chueng, Conrad realized that he was vaguely familiar with some of her work.

Conrad was also scheduled to present on the topic of identity the next afternoon. He encouraged Lee Cheung to attend his presentation before he made his way to the hotel gym for an evening workout.

The next day the auditorium was packed with people anxious to hear Conrad's speech. He surveyed the room with his round reading glasses and spotted a familiar person sitting on the first row. She threw a quick glance at him. Her face betrayed a seriousness that cannot be accused of pretension. Conrad thought she looked so much like the women in the magazines—a gorgeous sex fiend who would do everything for you, the type who would, with the snap of finger, would massage a man's feet, cook for him, entice him with high heels and red-hot lingerie. And, on the top of all this, Conrad imagined, this woman could also present a brilliant paper, hold her ground in an argument, and use her feminine ways to lure you in, keeping you only if you behave. She was different from Ana, the type that Conrad was used to.

Following his presentation, Conrad's eyes moved around the room, waiting for questions.

Lee raised her hand and said that she had a long comment to make. "Please do," answered Conrad.

"We Asians are always misrepresented. Others speak for us. Jokes are made about our native languages, our English, if we dare to speak it. All other ethnicities are allowed to write their texts in their own languages. Take African-American language in Toni Morison's hands. There is African-American culture, only because it is expressed in the people's medium. The author represents them through the way they speak. Asians are denied this power, this freedom. Our writers re-translate us into polished English. They make us say what we did not mean. They civilize us. They take away the authenticity of our experience; however, outrageous we may sound to western ears. We are cleaned, polished, and, in the process, unauthenticated. The world is not interested in what we have to say. Our language is transplanted to the shores of the West. Our identity is obliterated. We become neither Western nor Asian. In poetry, our poets' ideas are sacrificed to the context of repression in communist regimes. We are published not because of what we say, but because we denounce communism and embrace democracy. My paper, which will be presented tomorrow, seeks to give a corrective of this. I try to point out that translation is not only impossible but also dangerous. However difficult it is, let the author express directly what is being said in the crudest language available. Let the reader decide for himself what he really thinks and feels about these outlandish others. No need for cleaning and polishing. Let the reader be shocked by what she is reading. No need for shame."

She apologized for the long commentary.

Perspiration covered Conrad's skin, for his paper took the direct opposite line. For him there existed a universal democratic language with a global identity to which languages can be translated. In Conrad's mind, Korean, a language which he could speak, for example, could be translated into English. Sometimes, a Korean poem, he felt, was better when restated in English to an English reader, rather than literally translated from the Korean into English. Equivalent experiences, he maintained, could be mediated through any language, from Korean to English and vice versa. No one in the audience, however, understood his thesis. People squirmed and glanced around during his talk. Lee left as soon as she heard his response to her comment.

Conrad had seen her twice: once in the lobby; again at his talk. That was it. She had appeared in his life through a brief glance and he did not know what to make of their fleeting encounters. He did not attend her presentation, although her paper had aroused considerable interest, because he was scheduled to return to Cambridge.

...

When Conrad returned home Ana had left a note asking for a divorce. She told him that he had not stopped living like a single. He had not changed his ways. His eyes were as shifty as ever. She did not trust him, even with her own sister, and she did not trust herself not to physically harm him if she continued in the marriage.

The letter came as a shock, although he should have known better. After sitting alone and contemplating the smoke in the air, he heard someone open the door. It was Ana. She walked in, threw her shoes in the middle of the living room, laid her scarf down in the kitchen, threw her jacket in the master bedroom, allowed her earrings to fall off into the bathroom sink, threw herself in bed, locked the bedroom, and went to sleep.

After a few hours, Conrad gently tapped at the door. She screamed from inside that she did not want to see him that she wanted a divorce. Conrad discovered that one of his women had called and hung up on her; another had had the audacity to tell her that he was actually seeing her and that she had been wondering where he had been lately; her cousin had revealed to her that he had actually touched her once. During his brief absence, Ana had received many phone calls from his collection of women. She was most aggravated and enormously disturbed by the fact that all of them were Asians. She did not know why he was so intent on collecting Asian women like an over supply of shirts.

"You are a sick man, and I want a way out," she told him.

He left her alone and went to his study, turned the stereo on, and drank heavily.

After this night, Conrad got drunk with increasing frequency, which induced a very slow process of depression. Initially, he had trouble sleeping and then intense feelings of despair began to suddenly pervade one early afternoon. Seemingly for no reason to all, he found himself feeling low sometimes early in the morning, other times in early afternoon.

As the depression progressed and Ana was long gone, melodies of sadness pervaded his evenings. Tears would run down his blotchy face. His voice would fade out on the phone. Whomever he spoke to would ask him to repeat himself, which became annoying. He became a recluse. When he saw acquaintances, he would go out of his way to avoid talking to them. He adopted a new habit of averting his eyes. Parties and social occasions frightened him, so he avoided them like a disease.

Solitude accompanied his heavy sadness and became his new way of coping with his condition. Gradually, acute pain overtook his body, he lost weight and hair, and his libido disappeared. Eventually severe fatigue became so unbearable that he made up his mind to go to the hospital. He could discern no way out so he suffered for a while, alone and quietly.

...

Kwang continued to see Conrad, even though she was upset to learn that he was married. She was more upset and distressed, however, by his transformation. His exuberance, his relish for life seemed completely absent. Conrad's new condition turned him into a totally different man. Conrad repeatedly pleaded for Kwang's company. A couple of times she panicked when he told her that he could not go to work and that she needed to look for a job. In her culture men were not permitted to say that they were sick. They remained healthy until death. She told him that he needed some time alone, no matter how hard it was. She told him she needed to leave and stay with her friends until he cleaned up his life. He could not believe what he heard, but nodded with a bitter expression on his face. His bitterness was not lost on her. She knew she was seeking revenge.

After she left, his situation worsened. He threw up constantly. Dark thoughts pervaded his mind. He could not open a page to read. Thinking caused him pain. The damn TV tired him even more. When he would lie flat on the floor and try to do some push-ups his body was too tired to move. He tried his hand at chess, a game he loved, but nothing came out of that. He denied himself even the possibility of happiness as a minor entertainment. Although, he had done so only once in his life, one evening he thought of reading the Bible. To his great surprise, the idea itself relaxed him, so he opened the Bible and read:

"Because the Lord is my shepherd, I have everything I need. He lets me rest in the meadow grass and leads me beside the quiet streams. He gives me new strength. He helps me do what honors Him the most. Even when walking through the dark valley of death I will not be afraid, for You are close beside me, guarding, guiding all the way."

The words comforted him. Sweat broke through the pores of his skin. Water soaked his forehead, his arms, and his scalp. Afraid that death was visiting him, he clung to the Bible and kissed the verse. For the first time in his life religious experience wrapped his soul. The pain in his body subsided. He actually forced a smile at himself. He stretched his hand toward the floor in search of his cigarettes that had rolled down under the stinky couch where he had been lying for the entire week, without a shower or a tooth brush, and with very little food. His weight loss frightened him. He got up thinking about how God seemed to be showing him how to extricate himself from anguish and dread.

Conrad paced up and down, and gulped some brandy. Drinking fucked his brain up, creating chemical imbalances in his weakening body that sent surges of terror to his brain. He knew that the surges indicated despair, so he picked up the Bible, and read from the book of Psalms:

"To you oh Lord I pray. Don't fail me, Lord, for I am trusting you…show me the path where I should go, O Lord; point out the right road for me to walk. Lead me; teach me; for you are the God who gives me salvation. I have no hope except in you."

He closed his eyes. He had never prayed before. Nor did he know how. So he begged God to teach him how to pray. While he was struggling to do so, Kwang walked through the door. He had heard her coming in, but his eyes were still closed when she stepped into the living room with her hands on her hips, fully tanned, and dressed beautifully, looking radiant and freshly loved.

Conrad looked up to see her. There he sat, his black hair completely ruffled; his thickly yellowed teeth destroyed by tar and black coffee; subtly spread freckles all over his long face; a bush of sudden gray had overrun the black silky hair that had once seduced so many women; his previously leather-flat abdomen rising in a mountain of fat; his lop-sided body snared in-between a monstrous upper body and reedy feet. The sight of him offended Kwang's aesthetic.

Her eyes did not hide the fact that she simply could not stand seeing him in his mood of helplessness, utter helplessness. Evident in the way she stood were disappointment and the inability to love a man in pain. Her inability to respect him overwhelmed her. Perhaps, however, another man on the horizon also contributed to her final decision to leave Conrad.

Kwang missed his old self. She had fallen in love with a different man. She remembered their first meeting at a café when he had flashed his card from a world-class university, charmed her with his looks, his easy manners, and his manipulative intelligence, taken her to bed in the middle of the afternoon. Here she saw him in a different form. She felt cheated. Terrified by the sight, she packed her belongings into three bags and in the mid-morning of that dreary March day, Kwang exited Conrad's life. Leaving was not easy. She broke down in the bedroom. She threw herself onto the bed and cried bitterly. When she got up and gazed into mirror, she saw her swollen red eyes; blotches of red spread down her arms, her legs, and parts of her inner thighs. She knew that she had to break away from the incurable disease of loving Conrad. Without turning her face, she walked straight to the door and left. Shortly before she left, Conrad had tried to speak, but he could not utter a word. Although he attempted to express himself he simply could not speak.

Soon after Kwang left, he found himself in the hospital. He had tried to hang himself, but a neighbor had seen him through the window and called the police. Time and solitude, however, helped him to recover slowly. After his release, it did not take him too long to swing to the other side of his mood life. Confidence and giddiness returned full swing.

***

Conrad was happy again. A month after full recovery, his soul was saturated by a yearning for a woman's body, a body to wake up to, to talk to. The loneliness hit him with panic and trepidation.

One sunny day in mid-May he was waiting for a bus in front of his home when he noticed a woman dressed in black with perfume emanating from her well-kept body who was absorbed in reading just a few steps away. From a short distance she appeared stunningly beautiful to Conrad's eyes. Her skin color and height betrayed a Japanese or Korean origin; her shyness and reticence made him think she might be Chinese; her modernity and flare for fashion suggested Taiwanese. Conrad could not figure out where to place her, but he continued to check her out while she sat quietly and patiently, waiting for the bus to arrive.

A swift glance. A second intense and blazing stare. She remained unaware and returned neither. She remained focused on her book. Nothing could divert her attention. Not once did she move. Conrad could see only her long black hair, with two glittering golden earrings hidden struggling to be seen.

Before the bus came, she accidentally moved and noticed a someone, a stranger keenly observing her. Finally, she turned her head without looking directly, as if she were simply staring at the air. Unbothered by curiosity, however, she returned to her reading. She had just ended a long and unhappy marriage, and was enjoying her solitude at that moment. Her eyes seem to be swimming in the ocean of a newly found freedom uncluttered by another human being. Just to make sure that the intrusive eyes were still there, she turned again. Just as she turned her head, the bus came. She took the very first seat. It was a full bus so Conrad ended up at the far end in the back. When she got off at the second stop, Conrad remained inside and headed toward Porter Square.

The next day, their paths crossed again, at the same time and the same place. She noticed him right away. This time, he did not beat around the bush. He simply told her, "We are synchronized."

She smiled generously. He gathered that she must have been kind and added, "We must be neighbors after all," to which she reluctantly nodded.

In that short period of time, Conrad noticed that she had a very small stature, sharp features, a large forehead built for thinking, and a very quite demeanor. In addition, he gathered that she was a rigorous observer, the loyal type who would give her very self to others in both health and sickness. She was his complete opposite.

He asked her if he could interest her in having a cup of coffee on the weekend. She agreed to meet him so they set up a date for the following Saturday.

Saturday came quickly and they at met at the Coffee Connection in Harvard Square. The coffee shop was full of people who did not fail to notice the appearance of two beautiful people in their midst. Although the place was full, Conrad and Kim, for that was her name, managed to sit in the coziest corner of the café shielded by dim lights. Kim liked the atmosphere.

160

In the far corner of the small coffee shop, two people engaged in an animated debate. These people were Neil, me, and a third friend of ours, Elias. Elias had been roving in Europe for the previous two years and had just returned to the States a few weeks prior. He was the first to notice Conrad and his lady in the dark corner. He pointed them out to Neil and me.

At the same time, Neil and I, responded,

"Oh, him."

Neil said, "Oh God. Another one. This is one of the finest in his collection."

He paused. Everybody laughed. I smirked and said,

"It is one after the other. What does the guy do? He must be eating steel to keep up."

We all laughed again.

Neil said,

"We must be jealous or something. Look at us. Three guys. Saturday morning. Obviously none of us got laid last night. The lucky ones are having breakfast in bed, getting pampered, for a job well done."

We laughed again, this time louder than the first. People turned.

In the mean time, Conrad and Kim sat quietly. Both were calculating their moves. The atmosphere enhanced their natural beauty. Her hair became luminously blue under the yellow light. She was the first to tell him her life history condensed into precise language. She must be a poet, he thought, a fact, which he discovered much later. Before she began telling her tale, Conrad who was back to his chatty self made sure to impress on her the weight of his brilliance and his deadly charm. She could not help but be seduced by it. He kept on telling himself, perhaps genuinely, that she was unlike any other, that she was physically staggering, but additionally, beautiful inside and outside. He had repeated these words all his life when describing her, especially when he remembered her late in his life.

She told him that she was Korean-Japanese, born in Singapore and adopted in the U.S. by adoring American parents who loved her more than they loved themselves. She lost her parents at the age of two, she was told; she was briefly orphaned until her adopted parents saved her. She was a little over two years old when she was taken to the U.S. She still does not know her real parents. She lost them. She was the only child in her American home. "You can imagine the way they doted on me. No one has ever matched that love. Perhaps, no one ever will," she stated.

She resumed her story.

"I studied architecture in a leading college in California. That is where I grew up. After graduation, I applied everywhere and fate brought me to this place at the age of twenty-three. I have not stopped working since then. Many boyfriends came and went. I did not love any of them deep enough to marry them. Meanwhile, the biological clock kept ticking and my parents became worried to death about my destiny. So, in a way, they pressured me to catch a man. I did all the right things—joined clubs, dressed to kill, attended balls and wine tasting, traveled to Asia and Europe twice a year. I finally landed a man. I did not jump up and down when I met him, but I decided to settle for something tolerable. To make a long story short, a year into the marriage the man's colors begin to show up. He was sexually abusive, an alcoholic, and on the top of that a notorious gay. I simply could not trust him with anyone, man or woman. He desiccated any sacred ground and slept with anything that moved. I abandoned our beautiful condo and divorced him."

"I told you so much in our first meeting. I felt like clearing the air. How about you Conrad? What is your story?"

Conrad looked visibly disturbed. He realized that his story was so similar to the story he had just heard. He did not know where to begin or what to say. After collecting his thoughts he decided not to say much. He told her history of his past love life. He told her that while he was a graduate student, he madly fell in love with a white girl. Not long after he courted her she became pregnant without his knowledge. She gave him his first and only child, and forced marriage on him. The marriage lasted only a few months. He divorced her when he found out about her affairs. From that point onwards he decided to "go oriental." Never again did he date women of his complexion. He concluded by saying,

"That is the shortest version of my story."

She replied,

"Exactly like mine. We will deal with the details of our lives

162

some other time."

After that they parted company, and Neil, Elias and I were still chatting away in the back. After a short stay, Neil and I split off while Elias remained behind.

Elias

Elias was a fascinating figure. Those who knew him variously described him as "enigmatic," "queer," "strange," "restless" "shameless" and "confused." Indeed, he was all of these at once. From the back corner of the room he canvassed the place. With his stupefied almond eyes in a small face, ivory-biscuit skin, adorably curly brown hair with emerging shades of gray, a goatee, and receding hairline, people could not help but look, especially when they see him practically everywhere in the Square, at any time of the day or the early evening. Of course he worked there and lived close by. That explains part of the story. "You cannot figure that guy out," was a common way of capturing his personality, and was what Adowa, my Ghanaian friend, used to say about him. Today he is this, tomorrow that was also another way by which many described the essence of this ageless man, who loved to wander the streets of Harvard Square. On any given day, Elias is there, roaming the streets and crowding the little shops, and going in and out of places. He walked into a tobacco shop, and stepped out with a brand new pipe, readying it for a weekend use; he entered a café, surveyed the scene, always looking for anything that moves and quickly left, and then immediately entered a bar, nervously looked around and left abruptly. People used to say that nobody knows who this man is. The waitresses at the Café speak behind his back, every time he meanders in and then leaves without buying anything; the cashiers at the clothing stores are tired of answering his questions, because they know that they are just being checked out under the pretension of interest in what ever they are selling; the young barber laughs his heart out when the balding Elias enters the barber shop for no particular purpose. A little boy once described him as a squirrel, God knows what he saw. For years, the cashier, the barber and the saleswoman have been laughing behind Elias' back. Elias however does not care. He continues to roam the streets of Cambridge, day in and day out, oblivious to people's reactions. Adowan used to call him, "the shameless," who is interested in sleeping with anything that moves. For Adowa's Ghanaian instincts Elias was truly indescribable. Over the years he had exhausted peoples' curiosities. They had stopped talking about him. For most people, he was just there in some human form, who spoke, walked, and roamed the streets of Cambridge.

Adowa had known Elias for five years. Through these five years, Elias refused to make up his mind about her, and she was utterly confused about him. Adowa is a thin, shapely, and extremely intelligent Ghanaian, who studied Biology at Harvard Medical School. Born and raised in London, she came to the U.S. to study Biology. Adowa first met Elias in a Cambridge café, when she was busily working away on her laptop, on the last chapter of her dissertation on "The Politics of the Body: A Theme for Biology." She did not like the way Elias intruded in her space, with his mild manners, and his learned inquiries about her work. He, himself, had finished the last chapters of his dissertation not long ago, so he knew exactly of how stimulate her interest by asking the right questions.

"So you are Ms. Biology," he said.

She was intrigued by the description.

"I have never been described that way, ever. What is even more, it is quite queer to call anybody that way Any way, may I ask who you are, now that you have decided to intrude into my space, just like that. Only in Cambridge, would this happen.

He laughed and said, "Which means, you are not from around here"

"No, I am not. I am from Ghana. Do you know where that is?"

He smiled again, and said, "Oh, yes. My geography and history are quite good. You will be surprised if I told you that I have read most of Nkrumah's writings. Do you know who Nkrumah is?"

"You got me," she said. "Now that we know you are familiar with Ghanaian history we can move on to other topics," she said.

She sensed that he was surveying her body. He began with her large black eyes, moved to her long and thin neck, descended further to her thin waist line, opened his eyes even more when he arrived on her abundant hips and shapely ass, and almost melted when he discovered her perfect legs. His eyes struggled to detect imperfection, and there were none, at that hour. Adowa was not sure if she enjoyed this attention in this transparent way, so different from the way other subtler men check a woman out, she said to herself. He released himself from the hold of her body, and returned to where they left off.

He inquired further about how and when she chose Biology, and she informed him that as an African, born to a continent savaged by diseases that date back to some of the ancient African empires, and further exasperated by the colonial experience, which lasted over seventy years, she has chosen the study of the African body as an ethical obligation.

"You see, for me studying the black body is an obligation, since the body is ultimately the foundation of an African future. Africans have to control their bodies and images. I chose to control the body by studying it."

Elias said, "You are so political, although you hardly look it. With the polish and much else, you send a different image"

"What image do I project?" Adowa asked him defensively.

Before he answered, something distracted his attention. Adowa turned her attention to her laptop. By the time Elias was ready to speak, she had occupied herself with her dissertation, and they exchanged phone numbers for a future meeting.

Elias confused women with his excessive attention, sparked interest in young boys and older men alike with his penetrating eyes. He made everybody nervous, uneasy, or simply annoyed. He did manage to command their attention, however.

Elias hopped in from one place to another, always on a lookout, as if he was intent on getting something, and not succeeding. His eyes focused on a woman's leg, a man's muscles, and a teenager's feisty walk. All of them attracted his attention, equally intensely, as if they all meant the same thing, or connoted the same meaning, or even weighed the same. His shifty eyes were not analytic. "They don't seem to be discriminating," was what Conrad said about him to Neil.

He surely looked "different." That was what many people said about him. Neither purely white; nor purely black. He was literally in between. His sexuality was also another object of curiosity.

So one day, Elias went to a party. There he met people of all nationalities, which is a mark of those Cambridge days. At any given day, one came across hundreds of people with accents. The moment Elias walked in, his eyes locked with a young graduate student in his late twenties. Short, dark hair, copper skin, green eyes, flat nose, he walked towards Elias and introduced himself as Turkish, studying Fine Arts at Harvard. He called himself Salim, and extended his small hands to Elias' big hands. For a moment his hands disappeared in Elias grip. He had difficulty recovering from Elias powerful touch.

"So you say you are a grad student, eh?"

"Yes. I am and getting pretty tired of it. The professors and their demands," answered Salim.

"I know what you mean. I have been there myself."

"So you know the ways of grad schools. That is where I am at now. And you, Elias?"

"I work for MIT as a consultant to effective teaching. I am some kind of teacher."

"It sounds as if you are a God send. I need help in that area."

"You got it. We'll set up time for a drink, and discuss it then," said Elias. Salim readily consented. Elias' eyes looked triumphant, as if he had won a trophy. He laughed and winked at Salim, and got close to his eyes, so close that Salim had to move back a little to avoid the penetrating stare. First the hands and now my eyes, Salim said to himself. But he was clearly touched by all the moves.

The moment Elias arrived home, he received a message from Adowa, this Ghanaian girl that he was crazed about, sending confusing signs to her. A number of times, she had caught him flirting with men, a habit she never understood. Because of him, she had checked out a number of books on bisexuality. She suspected that he might be "in the closet." When she called that night, she said to him, "Which guy did you hit on tonight? Don't deny it anymore. Just come out and free me." She left this message on the voice machine. He had known her for three years, and she had never been that direct with him. This was truly the first time, and probably the last, since she sounded quite upset with him. He characteristically received the shock calmly. Calmness in the face of adversity is an organizing

166

moral principle which he swears by. He has a way with anger. He contains it with a smile. To the hot tempered, this habit could be quite annoying. Many have asked themselves, why he does not get angry? A few have concluded that it is because he does not care enough to get angry about anything. Others thought that it was because he is endowed with patience. Many others do not know why, but are rather envious.

Elias' abrupt leave-taking seemed like a strategy aimed at confusing Salim. Surely, Salim looked confused but extremely eager to reconnect with Elias. Salim remembered Elias' smile long after that eventful encounter. Elias' hand shake had also left an impression on his body, a kind of ache settled in his heart. He actually wondered if he may be falling in love with this total stranger, given his fondness for the love of men.

When Elias smiled, which is rare, he projected an elegant feminine tone. His metallic handshake, on the other hand, connoted a brutal masculinity. His oscillation contributed to his enigma. His loud laughter, when excited, was neither male nor female, but a mixture of both.

Elias arrived on time to meet with Salim. Salim had been there waiting for Elias, much earlier. Anxiety seemed to have worked on him. They hugged each other, spoke about their jobs for a few minutes and then moved on to the serious matter about dreams. Elias told Salim that he dreamt that he had two organs, a penis and a vagina, and that he did not know what this symbol signified. Salim intently listened and was wondering what to say.

Born to a Jewish father and a West Indian mother, he had come to call himself a hybrid. In high school he was described as mixed; in college, people would jokingly say he could "pass" for white. His life was situated at the interstices of the lucid and the ambiguous, literally in-between, sometimes everywhere, and always nowhere. While Elias was still sitting in the same space in which Neil and I had been sitting a few moments ago, a male and female couple entered. The woman indifferently shot a quick glance at him. He froze on her, and she immediately averted her eyes away from him. The man, curious about whom she had just checked out, checked

Elias out too. He too glanced swiftly; so fleeting was his glance that others would have ignored it as insignificant. She wondered why he even looked at her, if not interested. She felt as if asking him that question. She did not quite understand what the object of the glance was. At first, she thought it was merely a fleeting chance, and she ignored it. Once he lingered with that focused glance, she decided to return it, thinking that there was a romantic touch to it. Obviously, she changed her mind, once she realized that, he was already looking elsewhere, particularly when she caught him, taken in by a young man who just walked in. All this took place in less than ten minutes

His mood was changing with the declination of the day. He managed to throw back a huge smile at the man. The man must have regretted what he did. Elias would not take his eyes off the guy. The guy finally had to signal his girl that they must leave. He could not tolerate the colonization of the ambiguous gaze.

After the couple left, missing the visual joy of the lingering smile, he pulled out a book that he must have read three times, called Difference and the Language of Desire. He read:

"Before her rose those ugly scarifying quarrels which even at this far-off time caused an uncontrollable shudder, her own childish self-effacement, the savage unkindness of her stepbrothers and sisters, and the jealous, malicious, hatred of her mother's husband. Summers, winters, years passing in one long, changeless, stretch of aching misery of soul. Her mother's death when Helga was fifteen. Her rescue by uncle Peter, who had sent her to school, a school for Negroes, where for the first time she could breathe freely, where she discovered that because one was dark, one was not necessarily loathsome, and could therefore, consider oneself without repulsion."

He read it again and then said to himself, repeating the last lines; "I am not loathsome either, just because I am different, a little different from most people."

He stopped thinking, paid his bill, and went roaming the streets of Cambridge. Restlessness pushed him on. He moved from one coffee shop to the other, entering shopping stores and visiting bookstores in between. His hungry eyes navigated spaces from the corners of his eyes, a gift reserved mostly for women. His eyes always diddled on males. Females were acknowledged only in passing. In

168

one of the cafés a young man was sitting alone, obviously waiting for someone. Elias encountered him at the entrance. He almost stumbled at his feet when he was looking straight down, but was then interrupted by the boy's presence. The young boy did not even bother to acknowledge the startled man. His woman friend came. With that Elias was completely taken away. Nothing else mattered. Elias's glasses fell on the floor while he focused on the boy. The young girl giggled a bit.

Elias entered and exited at least ten places in a single afternoon. No catch. At the last café that he visited, two men, an older one and a young companion, were sitting together. At first they sat looking at one another, as if they had just met. After a while, however, the older man stretched his hand to the younger man and began to stroke his face. He discreetly touched his smooth pinkish arms, moved toward his neck, and up to his scalp. After lingering there he moved his hands down to his forehead, around his entire face, and down to his finger tips.

Elias saw it all. He was eaten up by jealousy, for he too was looking for someone to do that to him. For months his body has not crossed path with any other body. Dying to be touched, he roamed the city, day in and day out, early in the morning and late at night, until the bars closed. He went home without love; empty handed, with hungry eyes, and a body congested with desire. Only he knew the depth of his longing, the seriousness of his loneliness.

Nothingness in the form of dread would visit him at night, in the middle of sleepless nights, he would dream that that he was being touched, kissed and loved. He woke up violently to discover that there was no one there, just a phantom, a wish, a longing, an aimless search.

On numerous nights, he would wet his bed with semen and tears at the same time. This pattern went on for days and nights, and Elias did not know how to break away from it. He decided to change his mood, put on his nice evening jacket and walked to Harvard Square and landed in one of his favorite bars, The Harvest. Everybody knows him there. They know his fancy jackets, his delicate sweaters, and his perfect shoes. They point at his elegance when he sets his foot in, wondering about which jacket, which sweater and which shoes he was going to dash in in.

Thus this evening he chose a corner and the moment he sat, he was spotted by a young man who must have eyed him when he came in. The young man was tall, red-headed, stubby nosed, freckled and kind of frazzled and drugged looking. There was an aura about him, which turned Elias on. Obnoxious type, and yet interesting. These were the apparent features which attracted Elias. They made him to want to know this total stranger, who invited himself to Elias' corner. Elias did not know whether he should be happy or not, but he accepted his fate and went with the flow.

They exchanged their names, and the stranger called himself, Matthew. Matthew was an upper Manhattanite and was currently a Fellow at Harvard Business School. Matthew gesticulated wildly while he spoke, gave the impression that the hands could express thoughts more than words ever could, in contrast to Elias, who only moved his lips, and had total control over his body when he spoke. The contrast was hilarious. Elias spoke like a monk with hands folded and Matthew spoke with his hands and lips, both at the same time.

Silence.

A few minutes later Matthew engaged Elias in a conversation of identity politics, and Elias was hesitant to enter into it, so abruptly he told Matthew that he did not know much about the subject, and in fact has never really thought about it. Matthew was surprised that a Harvard man did not know much about identity politics, since the city is steeped in it. He instinctively sensed that Elias was hiding something, and Matthew was intent on opening Elias up. Elias held his ground, and was thinking how different this man's approach was to Adowa's when they first met. He opened up to her so easily, whereas he was closing up with Matthew. The more Matthew pursued, the more he closed up. This by itself is a subject on identity politics, he said to Elias himself. Elias kept his thoughts to himself. All of a sudden, he tapped on his ties, a couple of times. Elias moved his legs subtly and smiled at Matthew. Matthew kept on talking about his publications, his travels all over the world, his shopping habits, and a couple of times, his love affairs with two boys, whom he described as black Arabs. Again, Elias' lips were tight liked a sealed bottle of red wine. Nothing came out of his mouth. He himself did not know why he was so guarded, so paranoid. He knew this is very unlike him.

Again Elias kept his thoughts to himself. Matthew kept on chatting away on his travels, publications, his shopping habits, his love of art, and a couple of times threw in his sexual conquest of dark Arabs in the Middle East, while he was teaching there. While chatting away, he hit over every male who walked in to the Harvest. He raped them all with his eyes, his hands, and even his legs, if they were close by. A few would stare in embarrassment, fewer still smiled back reluctantly.

This obnoxious behavior did not endear him to Elias. In fact, Elias regretted having invited him to his corner. Elias managed however, to ignore his behavior, and let him be himself. It was getting late, and Matthew kept on drinking and talking, without giving Elias a chance to do the same, at least to talk, since Elias is not much of a drinker.

The longer Matthew exposed himself, the more unlikable he became. It appeared as if Elias simply did not care what others thought of him. What mattered was his own happiness, not that of others. This has been made clear already. Elias kept hoping that Matthew would come to his senses. He did not. The situation got worse, to the point that Matthew could not stop touching Elias here and there, without reason. Elias wondered if this is a test of some kind. Perhaps, Matthew was unsure about Elias's sexuality, since Elias held on to his identity intimately, without deploying it. Whereas Matthew was deploying it everywhere with abandon and recklessness. The night rolled on. The city of Cambridge was graced with stars in the sky. A perfectly dark blue sky was illuminating the city. People were strolling late into the evening. The Harvest was teeming with crowd. Wine, beer, scotches were entertaining the loud crowd. People were in a festive mood. Televisions were on. The Celtics were winning on one channel, and the Patriots loosing in another channel, with Brazil winning in international soccer on another.

Elias and Matthew were still sitting there with Matthew talking away and Elias bored to death. They lingered on. Finally, Matthew asked Elias, if he would like to visit his home, a block away from The Harvest, after the bars closed. Elias did not see any harm in complying since it was Friday evening and he did not have to work the next day.

He said he would be happy to. By now Matthew had calmed down, and was a different kind of person, with manners and ways that he did not display for the first half of the evening. Again, Elias did not know what to do with this change of mood. He followed Matthew to his apartment on Troy street, at the heart of the Square. It was a one-bedroom apartment, nicely decorated, with relaxing colors of light green and black in the living room, light blue in the bedroom, a bright yellow dining room, and a tiny dark red study with a laptop and a beautiful lamp.

Matthew approached him aggressively and touched his buttocks. Elias removed his hands and told him to calm down, that it is too soon for anything intimate. Matthew told him that he was a chicken, and Elias calmly told him that he could say anything he wanted, but he should be careful with his words. Matthew raised his voice, the more he drank has he had more to drink since they arrived at the apartment. He forgot about entertaining Elias. He only had one thing in mind, and he was determined to pursue it no matter what. Elias pleaded with him to stop touching him. At one point Matthew came very close to tearing his pants, but Elias defended himself master-fully. The atmosphere in the room was getting dangerous. This time Elias himself could not bear it, and he was ready for anything. Apparently Matthew was into marshal arts and very conscious of his prowess. Elias was not intimidated by that and he stood his ground. He refused to do anything intimate and got up to leave. In ten minutes, with Matthew raving and screaming, he managed to escape the ordeal of the night. It was four o'clock in the morning when he left Matthew's apartment. This event was one of too many in Elias' night life, and he was getting tired of it.

As soon as he returned home, he sat down and wrote a long letter, with tears dropping on the writing desk. It took two full hours of intense concentration to finish the letter. The letter was addressed to Adowa inside, on the outside to the care of his mother, Rosa.

He had been contemplating suicide lately, and his eyes seem to have readied themselves to move towards death. He closed his eyes that night, perhaps for the last time. There was a glass of water, which had turned pink, and he drank from it, turned the light of and went to bed. It was seven o'clock in the morning when Elias fell asleep.

On a gorgeous day, Conrad and Kim met amid the breathtaking view of Harvard' business school. They sat on a bench overlooking Charles River surrounded by tulips and daisies. He came very close to wrapping Kim with his big and lanky hands, known for their firmness. Rightly, he decided against it. They sat very close to each other instead. It was so quiet that he could hear her heart murmur.

Kim stole many secret looks at Conrad. She liked what she saw, his passionate eyes, the thick black hair, and his thin and elegant legs, his sinewy ties slightly exposed under his khaki shorts, his biscuit skin color, and long hairy arms. What she liked the most was his eloquence, his way with language, and his elegant tone on the phone. For her these are windows to his soul. She hoped that the inside would live up to the enticing outside.

She averted her eyes from his body, and was distracted by the beauty of the yellow tulips. She had always preferred the yellow ones to the bloody red ones.

Conrad discovered that Kim actually wrote poetry for herself and on occasions for her friends. About them she said,

"They give me company. They are my concrete anchors to the world." He begged her to read just one, only one for his soul. He held her hands softly, looked at her in the eye, and asked her to read him one, only one. She insisted that she simply is not good. She was hesitant. She kept on telling him that she is not good, that she wrote them for herself, that they are a sort of therapeutic, but nothing to share with the world. They are too mediocre for that, she said.

He insisted nevertheless. Finally she gave in. "I will read only one."

There under the beautiful moon
The evening winds kissing me
Late at night
Those visiting hours of despair
Come angels on wings of desire

They blow wind of comfort deep into my ears
I laugh.
I cry.
I laugh and cry
Sometimes I don't know which
Hands of love stroke my face
Then I wake up to the same world
So much better was the world last night.

She was so bashful that she covered her face after the reading
was over. Her head fell on his shoulder, with her face still covered.
He said, "Extraordinary. To my ears."
She told him that was it. No adjectives. No analysis.
"Promise Conrad, never to discuss my poetry."

She threw a smile at him. The cool wind blew her short hair and jostled his like an old ship caught in a storm. After staying for a while
he took her home. She did not invite him in, for she had to leave for
Japan very early in the next morning. She bade him farewell and
said, "I will drop you a card from Japan. Be well in the meantime."

Neil

The annual Walk-a-Thon that Neil had been organizing for A New
Hope attracted a large number of participants. Among the crowd of
people, two young women yakked away about art, boys and much
else. One made a point to let the world know that she was an artist. She was dressed in total black, from head to toe, pierced everywhere—her ears, her nose, her belly button and her lips. She was
telling her friend that her pencil sketches and her watercolors were
going well, but that her oil paints and portraits were mediocre. They
frustrated her.

"I love doing portraits", she sadly told her friend, "but I just
don't get it right. It's like love, you know. You don't always get the
one you really love."

Her friend nodded in agreement.

The talk and the appearance of the painter took in Neil, who
was standing nearby. Because her situation struck chord with his,

he was eager to talk to her. He too found doing portraits frustrating, although he knew that portraits sell. People are so vain, he thought.

The female painter was twenty years old, extremely tall, around six feet, naturally thin, boyish looking, with a washed face, high cheek bones, huge round eyes, tanned olive skin, and very long dirty blonde hair, artificially colored and running loose over her narrow shoulders. After a while, she accidentally looked in Neil's direction. He was quietly leaning on a street lamp .She looked once, twice and a third time. Neil's eyes met hers, but in order not to embarrass her, he looked down.

His eyes must have yearned for her, for she made a point to return his interest immediately. Neil had not been with a woman since Heidi rejected him, almost two years ago. For the past two years he had been nursing the disappointment patiently. The pain was subsiding now. He moved towards the two women, and shot a question at the tall woman,

"So you're a painter, I overheard."

"Yes. I am Nirit, by the way. And you?

"Neil."

"You must have been eavesdropping on our silly conversation, then, on painting and stuff."

"Oh, yes. Hardly silly. I would say the opposite. Engrossing, in fact."

"You're nice. Maybe only to those who are vaguely interested in painting."

"I know what you mean. All those judgments. People laughing at those who are not the greats. Feeling sorry for the delusion, that one day we, too, can be greats."

Her friend readied herself to leave. They kissed and she split. Nirit excused herself and came back to the conversation.

"Are you a painter also?" She asked politely.

"I wish I could confidently, like you, say that I am. I do paint. If that alone makes one a painter, then I definitely am one."

"You do paint then," she repeated.

"Yes. Always. Sometimes I cannot stop it. It's so addictive."

"The same here," she said. "What is your preferred medium?" she asked him softly.

"It depends on my mood. But my first love is abstract painting and most often I use oils. I've tried portraits, but I do them so poorly that I gave up."

She laughed. His experience was exactly like hers. She too had tried and failed, he had heard her say when she first attracted his attention. They talked with abandon. She spoke miles. He listened attentively. For the first time in a long while, he felt something in his heart—a delightful, soft, light, good feeling. His face had not radiated for a long time. For a while all his friends were worried that his grieving heart, crushed by Heidi would not open to take another soul, another love. Many other women had tried, where Nirit had succeeded in a single afternoon. He could feel his heart dilating with joy. His face said it all: I am not afraid. I am going go where love takes me. Let it be. Let it be.

She talked about her plans, her dreams. She wanted to be a painter that matters. If she were to make it, she wanted to open an art school for women. Nirit enjoyed her youth, her confidence, and her absolute openness to the world as a beautiful place where one can be anything one wants to be. Neil embraced the youth, vitality and hope, that Nirit exuded during that hot summer day.

...

Sooner than he thought, their friendship mushroomed into a full-bloom relationship. On her first visit to his house, she was awestruck by the abstract paintings on the wall. She was one of the only people, besides his roommates, to see pieces from his series on "Birth."

"Wow," she said when his oil paintings glared at her. "You're damn good, Neil. You should have said so," she added.

"Thanks. I'm glad you like them," he replied.

"You're kidding. I love them," she emphasized.

They sat down to a light lunch accompanied with a bottle of pungent *Cotes du Rhone*. They were getting along so well that anybody who saw them for the first time would think that they were a settled couple enjoying the flow of time. This was a month into their relationship. Two months later, he drove her to the Berkshire Mountains. There they checked into a modest hotel, and went out into the resort town for some fine dining and jazz music.

There, under the luminous full moon, Neil slowly reached his pocket, took out a gold ring. Nirit was utterly surprised. She did not anticipate that the proposition was coming so soon, so suddenly and so eventfully. She took a sketch of the night in her head.he married her in Cambridge the next morning.

...

Married life had begun. Breakfast in the morning. Lunch and dinner became their shared times. This went on for a little over a year. Then things began changing. Habits overcame love. Neil began disappearing on her. Most mornings, he would get up before her, kiss her on the forehead and disappear to his café to hang out with me and wallow in self-inflicted sorrow.

Meanwhile, Nirit became pregnant. Anticipating their added expenses, she took on a waitressing job which she held on to well into her eighth month. They moved to a bigger place located between rows of old brick houses with a grocery store in the corner, a gas station directly overlooking the living room, and Dunkin' Donuts behind their bedroom.

Two aspiring painters, one getting old, the other young, a child on the way, waitressing and fund raising to make a living was their way of being in this world. Neil's parents came to visit once and stayed for two days. They had wanted Neil to have a wedding, and they were shocked by Nirit's radiant appearance. They never returned again. It was not long before Neil turned forty and Nirit celebrated her twenty-second birthday, but looked much older. Between his expensive habits at the café, the birth of Chad, an adorable boy with red hair and pure white skin, life changed forever. They did things together less and less. Most of the burden rested on the mother. Neil did not chip in much. Nirit soon realized that his painting was going nowhere. She herself had essentially given up the brush. She could not afford the supplies or the time, and felt guilty to take away anything from Chad. Her love was total, and consuming. She hoped that the birth of Chad would change Neil, but it did not.

I once came to visit with them and told him that Nirit looked unhappy and that I was worried. Two weeks after that she surprised Neil by leaving and taking Chad. A month later she asked for a divorce. After she left, Neil picked up drinking. At forty, Neil had three-part time jobs, which began to slowly kill him. He had no insurance. He gave up painting. Once he told me that all that he ever wished for was a peaceful death. He did not live for this world.

Conrad

After two weeks in Japan, where she had the time of her life, Kim returned to Cambridge. Conrad must have missed her greatly, because after her return, they spent every single day together for about a month. This period was probably the best that Conrad had ever had in his adult life. She too plunged into their romance without hesitation.

Both of them wanted to know each other well before thinking of something lasting. The idea of marriage, as frightening as it was to the divorcees, was not ruled out. It was certainly present in Conrad's mind, for it was he who cannot live alone, a fact that he effectively hid from Kim. It was one of his noble lies. Like all his other women, she was eventually taken in by his exuberance. She had no way of knowing the truth.

They did everything together. There was a clear division of labor. He was the main breadwinner and the financial manager. He drove, washed the car, and shopped. She was the cook, the cleaner, and the home economist. On Sundays they walked to the river. He carried a camera and she her writing tools. At the time, she was heavily involved in poetry, and he was experimenting with photography and the occasional painting of portraits.

Eventually, they married and her adoptive parents contributed generously to the lavish wedding with a party in a huge hall at the Marriot. They had rented the place for the entire night, including rooms for out-of-state guests. The buffet had thirty dishes in it, with an open bar for the whole night. The party lasted till dawn. Some people passed out on the dance floor. Others crashed in the bathroom and the kitchen area. Those who woke up sober the next day found themselves at a fabulous breakfast buffet.

...

Conrad came home every day to a clean home and an aromatic dinner waiting for him. They always began with soup, vegetables, lentils, sweet and sour soup, squid, and spinach soup. The meal was always complemented by a vegetable dish and two meat dishes.

Conrad came in each day and crashed on the living room sofa

178

with his shoes on. He kept on his smelly day clothes, and brought them into the spotless dining room. Kim came from an upper-class American family and was raised with detailed attention to table manners. Conrad was raised in a dysfunctional family who sat around the same table only twice a year at Christmas and Thanksgiving. Table manners did not mean much to Conrad and he brought this indifference to his marriage. But, kissing her on the cheek as he came in, looking at her eyes discreetly, asking her about her day made her enormously happy—that he was good at.

He was not always that way. He was that way with her because she was the first one that he really loved. If you asked him what love was, he would not define it for you with words. He would simply point his finger at Kim.

Conrad and Kim often lounged in the Coffee Connection, where they would see Neil by himself, or Neil and Nirit, or sometimes Neil and me. After staying two full hours, they would walk to the river hand in hand. She would have under her elbows her notebook to compose poetry and he always carried two chairs and a Canvas with paint and brush. They always sat at the Harvard Business School. From there Conrad gazed at the river while Kim composed poetry, which she would read for him.

Neil had once been sitting nearby and sketched them in the midst of their love. He used that sketch for a painting that he titled "Conrad and Kim by the River." He gave it to them a while later when he saw them in the café. They hung the painting so that it was the first thing that one saw when visiting their residence.

This period of their lives lasted for two years. He was loyal to her. She worked only a few hours and he had a fabulous full time job. At the end of the second year, they both agreed to buy a home. His mood, however, began to change shortly after they moved in. It began with financial worries. He went wild with decorating the house. Against her best judgment, he went for antiques, although she wanted simple, tasteful, light and modest modern furniture. She did not want a new car. He went ahead and bought a Saab. On her birthday he surprised her with a brand new piano, for which she had no use. He spent more than his salary allowed. Collection agencies wanted their money. He skipped payments. At one point he could not pay the mortgage and the bank threatened to take the house. Kim hated the furniture. She got tired of picking his underwear from the bathroom, his shoes from the living room, his repulsive table manners, his wrinkled clothes, and his late sleeping.

She began observing changes in his mood. He woke up late, shaved his beard only once a week, and had not approached her in bed for three months. Their outings became less frequent. The kisses, the poetry that they shared, the beautiful photographs that he took and developed in his own dark room came to a sudden stop.

Conrad became sullen and lost his interest in physical exercise. His appearance began to embarrass her. He finally got laid off. With that, the movement toward the deep end began. Nothing could stop it.

In order not to loose the house she took on a full time job. A friendship with her boss became deeper and deeper. There, in two months she began a fatal affair with her boss, which she could not stop. Her boss possessed a stability of character that she could not find in Conrad. Like Ana and Kwang, she too had failed to discern Conrad's condition. Completely ignorant of his mental state, she mistook his disease for foreplay. Although Conrad's intellect was exceptional, she continued to miss certain things in her new relationship. The sex was lousy. So, she endured the relationship only because it had class similar to her own. Even as Conrad's sickness got progressively out of control, Kim could not bring herself to see it. The change, the deterioration was so sudden, so fast, and so painful to accept. Yet she loved him. How could he forget? No one who was well knew how to live as Conrad did. How many times did she plan to leave? And how many times did she lack the courage to carry it out? She wanted this man so badly. She loved him so. Every time they fought she would discreetly put their best pictures in place, which he could not miss.

But she was not able to handle his depression, the total loss of self, and the erasure of the golden dignity she loved. Conrad was long gone; the diseases seeped deep in his soul, ate his body, and afflicted the fibers of his being. All that she saw every morning was a broken man who could not get out of bed, could not laugh, and could not make love. He had become nothing. He cried profusely.

180

He begged her not to leave him. He threatened to kill himself if she were to leave him. She took him seriously. The lion had become a kitten.

...

One day, Conrad went on his own to the café while Kim was at work. There as usual, Neil and I sat having a good time, to everybody's envy. Conrad had been discreetly observing us for quite some time. He came in with flair as he usually did, although he was now a changed man. He had gained a noticeable amount of weight. His cheeks were puffy and red. Conrad had rarely spoken to Neil or me although all three of us had been constant fixtures in the café for years. This time he surged towards us. He did not hesitate. It was as if he knew that his days were numbered and that he wanted to make contact with two interesting fellows. He knew that it was too late to turn himself inside out with two total strangers, and he resolved not to. On the other hand he wanted to talk about himself with someone, and he somehow intuited that these two fellows looked interesting, the types who would lend him their ears.

He approached us and asked us if he could join us.

"By all means," we said.

Neil pulled out a chair. Conrad thanked us and joined the group. A waitress took his order. I noticed that the tall, thin, handsome man had changed drastically. Even more shocking, he was alone for the first time.

For years he had associated him with Asian women. A happy-go-lucky kind of guy, probably Irish, moneyed, from an Ivy League school. And we were not wrong about half of him.

Neil almost asked, "Where are the chicks? Are you using us because you cannot stand to be alone?" but decided against it. We all had difficulty starting an actual conversation.

Conrad spoke first. "So you guys are academics, or what?

"Speaking for myself," Neil answered. "I am not. I double in painting and fund-raising."

I followed,

"I guess I am. An abused one, though."

This phrase picked Conrad's interest. "We were just talking about relationships, in case you would like to join in," Neil informed

Conrad. We broke him into our world quite nicely.

"Oh yes, relationships. The story of my life."

Neil looked at me. I did not betray a reaction. He remained quiet as he checked Conrad out.

Conrad continued:

"I have had had quite a few relationships but not a single one has been fulfilling, due to personal reasons. Relationships are quite tiring, and yet they are necessary for one's health."

That point rang a bell in Neil's head, but he did not say anything.

"My work has always dealt with Asian Cultures, which brought me into contact with Asian women, through whom I learned a lot about human relationships. Although contrary to many claims, all humans are, for me, fundamentally the same. Of course we eat, love, fornicate and worship differently. Our inner core, however, is the same. So much has been written about the mystery of the East, particularly its mystical women. There is no mystery there. They differ from all other women in only one way; they project appealing appearances to men. They pretend they are quiet, submissive, and self-sacrificing. I fell victim to this mystique multiple times and each manipulated me. I hungered for them and they were served to me in huge quantities. They were fine for a while, but then they got to me. I got easily bored, and moved on to another one again and again, I fell for appearances. I repeated a pattern in each relationship: at first, things would go smoothly, but I would quickly begin to fall apart and move away. I was not innocent either. I too feigned appearances. I gave a confident show, but always ended up being someone different than the person they fell in love with. So each of them split on me. I went through many loves and three marriages like that.

Please allow me to apologize for being so forthcoming on our first meeting."

Conrad had needed to confess to someone and thanked them for listening. Neil and I were preparing in our heads numerous questions to ask him. Conrad had confessed a lot, as if an unbearable pain was burdening him. It seemed that he simply needed to flesh out sorrow, so he could live. The depression, in fact, had pressured him to speak.

After thanking them, Conrad checked his watch and got up to

182

leave. That was the last time that Neil and I saw Conrad. When he went back directly to his home, Kim was not present. Kim never married again. She flung here and there, wrote lots of poetry and remained her old self. A secretive recluse, she flourished as a poet, prolifically producing powerful poems that many of her friends encouraged her to publish. "Sorrow," "Broken Dreams," "At Night," and "In the Silver Meadow" were her best long prose poems. Eventually they were published and translated into hundreds of languages.

Conrad spent his last years confined to a wheel chair in a mental institution. At forty-five, he appeared to be eighty. He aged very badly. Dejected and profoundly sad, his depression stopped swinging back to episodes of joy and his mood settled on a permanent sadness. A fellow traveler at the clinic remembered him as always staring at the wall straining to remember. His companions were many. He was closest to three fellows: a body builder who wasted his life on drugs after dropping out of college and turned his life into a living hell; a sixty year old manic-depressant who thought that he had killed his penis with compulsive masturbation and a failed scientist who constantly threatened to kill himself, but could not. Conrad spent hours in conversation with these souls with whom he shared much.

During the two years before his death, he resumed painting, leaving behind a few masterpieces. His last works of high quality recently appeared in an exhibition.

Through his paintings, Conrad attempted to portray our interiors lives onto canvas. Pain, intimacy, disappointment, betrayal, madness, and Eros weave through his paintings in intricate lines. Conrad had attempted to enter the human soul by penetrating his imagination and capturing it with lines, colors, and movements. All those who studied the paintings marveled at the depth of the scrutiny, and were overwhelmed by the stamina of the dying painter, willfully mastering the last shreds of his energy to paint the interiors of human lives. They also discovered that Conrad had left behind a few poems, including love poems, addressed to all the women he had encountered. A few were chosen for publication. People were captured by one particular poem titled "Intimate Identities." Others were attracted to a few poems that addressed the inability to know the self and the privacy of suffering. In almost all the poems, one could discern Conrad struggling to know himself. Behind the apparent shallowness and reckless sexuality, one could sense a mind at work, a mind struggling to answer the ultimate questions: Who am I? And what do I want?

One particular poem about love recounts his first love, the American Gabriela. It appears that he was burned by that love, by a love that he did not get. That puppy love seems to have had scarred him and he never came to terms with it. That memory compounded by the alcoholism and the manic-depression seems to have had led him to engage in compulsive sex with numerous Asian women, one after the other. All the poems struggle to plumb the depth of his needs. They examine the nature of desire and the structure of morality. They play the early Conrad against the later one. One critic wrote, "There were those who thought he succeeded and those who argued that he failed - because what he was trying to do cannot be done by any human being. Only the Being who created us knows what is there. The effort was note worthy. His life justified it. Perhaps, he was trying to see his own self. "

Perhaps. Many years later, some of his relatives collected his childhood paintings, and showed them to a publisher, who immediately published them. Again, a critic wrote: "Some lives are rewarded after death. Others are rewarded here and punished later."

...

Neil's condition saddened me. For months his life had become frozen. Death was contagious. He too had been getting up late, violating his routine of going to bed early and rising early. The world had become topsy-turvy. Friends were dying left and right—some, like my own father, at the ripe age of ninety; Makau, my best friend at the prime of his life, when his work turned for the best. The death of Conrad, however, hit him the hardest because he had thought that Conrad looked so carefree, so fulfilled by the gorgeous women who had always flocked to him. His sister, also seemingly carefree, killed herself by her own hands, right when she too had turned corners as a major poet.

That morning, I got up much earlier than had been lately and wondered what to do. I thought of going to the Coffee Connection, but changed my mind very quickly. The idea of sitting there without Neil turned my stomach. So I thought more of what I could do. I remembered those seamless conversations with Neil, which were always passionate, because we agreed on very few things. We did not see eye to eye on the causes of poverty, racism, why there are poor people, on creating a better world. Although we disagreed, I cherished Neil's honesty, his refusal to succumb to hypocrisy and political correction. I remembered the late parties at fund raising events that Neil sponsored; the poetry jams at café's, the painting exhibitions, the walks, the talks about love. But his life was not going anywhere.

I remembered them all. I was simply missing my friend, who had completely disappeared from the Café' scene. He had stopped contact with me.

The café was attractive when Neil was in it, part of its topography. When people saw us together, some froze, others stared, and a few ignored us.

A journalist who frequently visited the café described the scene in one of his columns for The *Boston Globe*: "Scene of Cambridge, the hub of liberalism. Two males. Black and White. Visible, for a change. Rarely with women in the background. Bright looking. Shamelessly arguing. That was the scene. Only in Cambridge can one see that."

I had not reconciled with myself about what to do that day. I got up, walked to the kitchen, peaked through the window. It was a downcast day. I went back to bed and tried to sleep a little more, but I could not. I turned on the radio and listened to the BBC. The news with the elegant tone of the reporters playing with English, however, failed to capture my imagination. I reached for The *Boston Globe*.

An article on massacre in Shettila in Lebanon attracted my attention. I read that an Israeli army entered a Palestinian camp and devastated it. Children as young as three, their parents and grandparents who were born there and had lived there for years, under the grip of pestilence and horrifying poverty were accused of terrorism and bombarded. Their bodies were scattered on the ground of the camp like a swarm of flies burned in oil. Their bodies were quartered into pieces of shattered metal - heads rocking from corner to corner; a pile of thighs and legs accumulated in the corner; hands in the far end corner; hands and fingers being eaten by cats and dogs. I closed my eyes in terror, and was overcome by a mild chest pain. The description of the scene was so horrible, that I threw the paper away the moment I finished it. I struggled to expunge the image from my memory. I got up, this time determined to plan the day. I brewed fresh coffee, reached the cupboard, opened a fresh bottle of cherry jam, pulled out cheese cream with my other hand, and served myself. Between reading the morning papers from the first page to the last, and occasionally sipping my coffee, two full hours passed. I got up, did quick push ups and sit ups, short stretches in between, took a hot bath, and read a short story in between, dried myself thoroughly, put on a T-shirt, a light rain coat, my elegant black sneakers, grabbed a paperback edition of *Rabbit Run*, and readied myself for a long walk. I read a short story about Amerindian islanders who did not believe in marriage without necessary infidelities. From the story I learned that only a very few individuals in this culture are fated to remain married. The lucky ones have no need to go out and commit infidelities. They somehow confine desire to a single partner whom they love until they die. For most individuals, marriage is quite boring, stifling, and at times unbearably oppressive. So they had developed a technique for handling this problem that contributed to the deterioration of community. They tolerate those who need other partners, provided they not hurt any of the partners. They believe that both the wife and the husband should know that each of them was sleeping with others. The marriage remains intact and the partners know that the others serve a purely sexual function. They meet when they can and they still remain married. Amazingly, they believe that the heart divides itself neatly into love and sex. The two are not confused. They see to it that those whom they enjoy sexually may not be lovable, and those that they love may not be sexually enjoyable. Nor do they confuse desire with love. They separate the two, and choose partners who fit into neat boxes.

It was an elaborate story that I had to discontinue reading after a while because I wanted to sit in the sun outside. When I stepped outside, the sky was dark blue, with round, square, and triangular mountains of clouds on the dark edges of the fading sun. Doom and

gloom hovered over my head. The day reminded me of typical winter days in my native village in the Rift Valley. A few hardy souls
walked through the irritating drizzle outside. Most of them walked in
couples, huddled under huge umbrellas, resembling miserable bodies caught in a storm. But there was no storm. Nor were the walkers
caught. Like me, they chose the outside to the comfortable inside,
the rain to the TV, movement to rest.

These were hard times for me. At forty-five, without a clear career, I had been wondering for sometime about what to do, what to
settle for before time caught up with me. I said to myself, I must
either work for my legacy, or accumulate wealth.

Lately, I had been thinking of marriage, children perhaps. The
free time that the walking had created made it possible for me to
examine my inside, to talk to my inner self. I slowed down to think.
The huge trees moved softly, responding to the gentle touch of the
wind and the steady light rain. An accident occurred on Mass Ave,
Cambridge's main thorough-fare, as I crossed to the river, and the
screeching sirens of a racy ambulance disturbed my thinking. The
avenue became suddenly crowded with people under soaked rain-
coats.

From the milling-about crowd I heard that a middle-aged man
had just dropped on the ground of a massive heart attack. The medics
had failed to resuscitate him and he had to be rushed to Cambridge
Hospital. People meandered in and out around the scene of the accident. Some were frozen with sadness. Some did not care. Others
were more concerned about traffic delays than they were about the
scene of the accident. A few did not make anything of it at all. I saw
a couple heartily kissing inside a car nearby and went about my way.
The rain stopped. The sun came out of hiding. The rain had left spar-
kling water on the leaves and the streets glittered with clean black
color with the sun's swords cutting through. The squirrels were hopping from tree to tree. A few ducks and ducklings emerged on the
banks of the Charles. Cyclists zoomed by sprinkling light water on
those strolling down the sidewalk. The Charles gradually filled with
tons of people. They had come out of hiding and flooded the bike
paths, the benches of the river.

I was heartbroken for the man and prayed for him in my heart. I read in the paper the next day that the man had died upon his arrival at the premises of the clinic. He was a university professor and the father of three children—by all accounts an exceptional person.

Endings

The city was radiant again. I thought of Neil. I imagined him breaking up with Nirit. I was not surprised. I had seen it coming when they were together. I had told Neil that she was too young for him, that she had too many expectations of youth that Neil may not fulfill, that she had impulsively concluded that Neil was going to be this famous universal painter, which may or may not have happened, that her absolute faith in Neil's future bothered me.

It turned out that, indeed, I was right. At the time Neil told me that I was jealous. In desperation I said, "Why am I fooling myself to advise a white man? White men know it all. They cannot be advised by a black man."

I stormed out of the café after making that comment. Neil followed me, grabbed me by the shirt, called me names, and asked me how I dared to walk out on him. Of course we reconciled after that. I did not change my mind about Nirit. I nodded my head, frowned a bit after remembering all that and related it to Neil's fate.

I thought about how I could help both of them. Of late I had been thinking about Africa, about home. The sweet smell of Africa had been visiting me late at night. I had been seriously thinking about founding a school in one of the villages I grew up in. What I needed was a lot of money. But my seasonal part time positions were not going anywhere.

Going back home, before it is too late is the answer. The angels at night have been advising me to go home, to die in Tanzania, to leave a legacy, an example for those who would come after me. I had never been religious. But I had always been a mystic. The mysticism of Elkhart had always appealed to me in college. My master's thesis was on African mysticism.

Lately, time had been taking me to this mystical past. I had been taking my dreams seriously. The voices that I heard at night reminded me about the voices of Africa. The cries of the crow which woke me in the morning; the howling of the fox which forewarned

188

my ancestors of an imminent danger; the church bells and chanting of village priests that invited my folks to prayer; the hospitality and generosity who would slaughter their sheep for an esteemed visitor; the subtle Eros of the village women, had been summoning me to come home, to embrace Africa, to teach its youth, to work the stones, the concrete, the fertile land, which was going fallow.

"Come home and serve the people" became an everyday chant visiting my willing ears. "Take Neil with you. Take him. Save a soul. Save yourself and another soul, who loves Africa," spoke another voice, which stunned me. The summoning became too serious to ignore. The walk that afternoon had brought things to the fore. I could not ignore them anymore. The voices kept speaking to my ears, nagging me; sudden apparitions of travel, destiny, vocation, and the voices of the poor saddled me.

Africa spoke to me. Home called me to return and help. Meanwhile, my walks sharpened my sensitivity to things. On a bicycle heading to school, I had noticed a tree from the other day that had grown five inches taller from the last time I saw it, almost a year ago. A nice family corner store owned by an old lady had vanished. It appeared that the lady had died. A new ugly gas station had replaced it. The location could not have been better, but it disturbed the quiet beauty of the corner. A young puppy, which jumped around the hedges of a brown house, had become a barking dog and almost tore off my native shirt with oblong ivory colors. My favorite bookstore had moved to Davis Square because the owner, hit by the quiet recession, could not any longer afford the rent.

Everything has changed, I thought. Africa is going to save my life. It was during that walk that I resolved to change my life once and for all. That is also when I decided to make money for the next two years by any means necessary. I was thinking of legitimate means, of course. The question now was what kind of jobs? What are the conditions that a teacher was willing to accept?

I developed a strategy. First, I resolved that the teaching would have to rest for now. I would have a lot of explaining to do to all those who called me "professor." They would have to get used to the idea of calling me Nyerere again. I had missed that light and informal way of interacting with people. I had always felt uncomfortable with the formality. So I returned to the old days, when people called each other by their real names. Then too, I had to get used to the idea of liking work, respecting work, rediscovering the dignity of labor, any labor. For years I had been afraid of work, thought that work was wearing a tie, driving a car, covering oneself with newspaper, snubbing cleaners, cashiers, waitresses and parking lot attendants for making a living through what is available, without bothering anybody, but going about the cycle called life, marrying, raising children, sending them to school, aging and dying, always in dignity, bestowed by labor.

So my mind went through a list of things that I could do to make money quickly. Selling books and magazines came to mind. I had always thought of business, clean business, as I called it. My way with words, my ability to deal with people both in person and on the phone I thought should help in the venture. I could always back it up by waiting on tablesn during the weekends.

That was one of the plans, but there were others as well. I thought of working at a bank as a teller and moving up fast to a well paying job. As planned, I diligently worked at three places: telephone sales at night; cashier at a parking lot during the day; and waiting on tables on the weekend. I worked eighty hours a week and made $4000 a month. In three years I managed to save over $100,000 and was ready for the move. My dream was in place.

In the meantime, I aged. Wrinkles invaded my face. My hair turned silver gray, which added to my character. I lost an enormous amount of weight. The thinness gave me . The school could not have been built on a better location. Nearby sat a convent and a church, convenient for the moral education of kids who chose the religious path. The school's mission, inscribed on the entrance gate, read:

"The best value must be chosen."

Within a month of having saved enough money, I packed and left. I resolved never to look back to my Cambridge days. That period was sealed in the envelope of memory. I only looked forward, like the movement of time. Time moves only forward, as should human beings. They have no choice anyway; I once lectured to my students. Before I left I managed to secure Neil's address. I had decided to formally invite him to teach at the new school within a year of its opening.

I arrived at my hometown one beautiful spring afternoon. The airplane glided into the African landscape through a sky saturated with clouds of all forms and colors, square, rectangular, oblong, round, mountainous, in dark, dark blue, snow white, pure white colors. They moved slowly through the horizon with the African sun in the background, gently making way for the arrival of the silent moon, shortly. The day was turning to the evening. The cattle were returning home by way of the airport.

The plane landed graciously. Hundreds of people waited at the terminal for the arrival of an African boy. They had all heard that the boy was returning home to build a new school. I could not remember either the names or the figures of all those who came to greet me. Most of my friends had been recalled by death. Those who were alive, like me, had been changed by time. A few had lost their eyes or legs to numerous wars and tribal conflicts in my country. Most of them could not attest to living in peace for more than a year in their lives. The blind carried by the deaf and the deaf aided by those who could hear, as well as the elders on their sturdy canes walking with immense pride flooded the airport.

They hugged, kissed and wrapped me with love. The elders welcomed the man with the Bible in their hands. The priests blessed me with their crosses. They all knew that I had come home to build a school for a thousand kids that would hire a hundred teachers. I planned to fully fund the school by appealing to the charity of good people, whose mission, like mine, was to help those who would help others.

Local journalists came with their cameras. My arrival and my mission received full coverage from all the papers. Titles read: "An African Son returns Home "; "A New Dawn"; "An Example for the Nation"; and " Nyerere Comes Back."

I gave radio interviews, met with the President, and gave speeches around the country. Within one week I settled into the hard business of overseeing the construction of the place. Architects, engineers and philanthropists gave me their free services. I was overwhelmed by human kindness. I spent very little money on the construction. I invested my savings in various sectors of the economy.

Within a year I had enough money to run the school comfortably for at least ten years. Some of the money accumulated massive interest. The other investments yielded huge profit. It was hard to believe. A few of the Architects and Engineers offered to give free courses at the school for nominal fees. My expenses were cut down even more. I gave myself a very modest salary.

The school was called "Self-Reliance." After a year, I contacted Neil, formally offered him a job, and brought him to Tanzania as an Art and English teacher. To this day, we both claim that Africa saved us. The school continues to prosper and our lives have changed only for the good.

Home Again

When I arrived home, I needed fresh eyes to take in the village. The Cambridge ways began to surrender to the village's ways. The urbanite always has to adopt different manners of being. The first month was spent visiting my past. I went all the way back to my first ten years. I wanted to revisit everything I could remember. I began by going back to an area of town where my wealthy grandmother owned property and in which I spent the first ten years of my life. I went back to a little closed house, used for storage, with descending steep stairs leading to a lush area with a brook that ran by. There a group of little kids would meet to see the sun set, then the arrival of the moon, and would huddle there until midnight, if there was no school. It was there that I learned the art of telling stories. That was where each kid would carve out of the rich imagination horrifying and romantic stories. Nobody was permitted to leave until he created stories. All the kids were boys. Two of them are now accomplished African writers. The house is still there. Old and ransacked, the stairs are cracked, the brook is dark brown, spoiled by dead poisonous leaves, and the smell is unbearable. The kids are now middle-aged, and a few of them are dead. My grandmother is buried in the compound. I paid my respects. My mother lives there now. Her gestures, in the process of getting old, reminded me of her mother, and my grandmother.

I remembered next a high school love. There was this girl that I was so crazy for. She admired my intelligence but not much else. Her interests lay elsewhere, with this rich boy that everybody thought was a loser. She liked him nevertheless. I went back to see the roads that she took, and which I secretly followed. The roads were still there. Famished, dustier than ever before. The trees that were there were old and ugly. The tin shacks that were there were now tall and rotting buildings.

Sometimes when I followed her she would be alone, the way I wanted it, and at other times she would be with that loser, fondling him, kissing him. I remembered them all, those heart breaking moments, which brought me to tears. That thin line of gray between envy and jealousy used to torture me in my younger days, while my family and I and lived in the smallest house in the block made invisibile by huge mansions, tall buildings, and villas with gardens. At one time, the bratty children who lived in these huge spaces were my classmates. Some of them drove expensive cars to school; their elders in their gliding European cars chauffeured others; their parents in Mercedes Benz and Citroens dropped off a few; and a few rode their motorcycles and bicycles to school. I and three others walked to school on our callused heels to my gorgeous high school at the foot of a mountain through which ran a powerful river.

My eyes were infused with memory as I thought of those days, those trying times for youth. I was today walking around the school with Neil. The high school has not changed much. The mountain is there. The river is there too. The huge tree under which I ate my lunch has grown older and firmer with time. It still grows leaves. A few fell on my balding head that day. The spoiled school children are there also; there are more of them now.

I was sad to learn learn that the girl I loved died recently.

I remembered too, the parties to which I was never invited, the show offs and their girlfriends, the boring Sundays, the boasting along with those mansions that I wanted to live in.

I had walked to my school from a far away place, for four full years, summers included.

I suffered silently. I was never given to complaints. Disappointment was always buried in my heart, but I believed in overcoming my condition through achievement. That is why I went to the U.S. on scholarship when I was chosen as the best student in my entire high school. I had dreamt that I would turn my life around in America. Sadly, that did not happen.

...

The mark of race, the badge of insult, the scripted identity stood in my way. The struggle continued even in Cambridge. One night, Neil and I slept on our hammocks looking at the black sky. Neil had never witnessed a starry night. There were millions of them in the Milky Way. We treated ourselves to cognac and reminisced about our Cambridge days. We talked about our friends. Neil thought of Elias, that "man in between," that "enigmatic figure." I thought of Conrad and his Asian women.

Lately Neil and I had been thinking about our social lives. Marriage and children were of grave concern for Neil; I remained obsessed with my legacy and my contribution to the "dark" continent. Neil thought of Michele, that young lady who unconditionally liked him at first sight but to whom he had not reciprocated. It was she who had invited him for a lovely Christmas dinner one cold winter evening, having met him only once at a café after her son Todd ran into him by accident. She had been charmed by Neil when he ruffled Todd's hair, pinched his purple cheeks, and engaged him in baby talk, so she invited him over for Christmas dinner the next day. Neil remembered how hungry she was that very night for love, for sex. Neil, however, was not available for either Todd or Michelle. He never saw them after that. Love terrified him, as his mother always suspected. In contrast to Michelle's unconditional love at first sight, Heidi's cruelty and Neil's obsession with her may have driven him to a mental institution had it not been for my constant counseling. Heidi had told him that love and marriage were political matters in her life. As a black person, she expected to marry within the race. Flings and affairs were frowned upon. Marriage to a white man was absolutely condemned, as evidenced by the titanic anger that erupted when the rare interracial marriage occurred. She had simply not been the type who would ever cross the racial line. Neil remembered her words while frenzied by the view of the Red Sea.

He looked at the jumping waves, sipped from his cold green tea, and took a deep smoke of a Lucky Strike. His eyes accidentally landed on a young girl passing by. Her thin waist, her plump ass, her long and skinny legs, and her deep brown eyes consumed his being. His eyes ate her deep brown eyes, his hands squeezed her perfectly round and surly ass, his fingers ravished her breasts, his lips sucked hers, his hands scuffled her short hair. He imagined that he entered her gently and wanted to stay there forever, to devour her whole. She too threw a quick glance to his corner, and it traveled right to his heart, exhilarating him, flattering him, taunting him with desire. As she walked, her heels tapped like raindrops tapping on glass. He heard them. The music tortured him even more.

Neil was in the mood for love.

I sensed Neil's loneliness as I secretly observed Neil's interaction with the woman passing by. I could tell that Neil was dying to get laid. Neil disengaged himself from the girl after she disappeared into the landscape, and turned to ask me, "How about you, Ny. What do you remember about our little Cambridge?"

I collected my thoughts as I strained to remember things. "Although you disagreed with me vehemently, Neil, for me it is the novel encounter with racism that I remember the most. I just could not get it out of my system. There were a lot of cruel people in that city. I remember all those who fingered me on the streets for no reason other than the fact that they would see me walking with a white girl, or simply that I was there crossing a street; my colleagues who would make captious talk about me, my looks, my smell, my accent, my writing, my values, right in front of me by pretending to be talking about a woman. I always knew that they were discussing me in the guise of another. Tears were wetting my eyes as I was remembering these events.

I stopped. The air was breezy outside. Cool air came steadily in to the living room where we sat, moving the velvet curtains as Neil admired the material. I could see birds flying. I could hear them chirping. Neil and I listened to the temperate quiet of mid-day in the African forest. Far away we could see children playing soccer and the crowd cheering them.

Both of us could smell Africa—its vegetation, its famished children, the garbage cans, the odor of the peasant vendors, the AIDS infected bodies, the corpses that have just died during tribal wars in neighboring countries coming home to be buried, the sweltering heat during the day, and the bitter cold nights.

I resumed the conversation. "Yes. Those days at the University where I lectured without a promotion for ten years on meager income that condemned me to live in the poorest quarters of town. I could not tolerate those swings of judgment from excessive 254 One day, praise. The next day, contempt and derision. One day, kindness. The next day, cruelty. And blacks are supposed to go in and out on white people, swinging from forgiveness to resentment, from love to hate."

As I said these words, I was filled with bitter thoughts, which I tried to brush off with smiles for Neil's sake.

"Hmm," said, Neil.

On the other hand," said I, "Some of the kindest people I have ever met lived in Cambridge. Americans are good at surmounting class distinctions. All Americans, when mood inclines them, can eat at the same place, shop at the same place, thanks to the equalizing power of the credit card.

What I miss the most is the convenience of everyday life, given the way Americans have perfected technology—setting my coffee maker to brew coffee for just after lazily waking up in the morning; the luxury of being able to find steaming hot water at all times that took care of my tired body every single morning; when I craved food, waffle and pancake makers took care of me; when my body yearned for a massage, a Jacuzzi took care of that. Stimulated by the Jacuzzi, I could start my day on a treadmill, while watching the morning news. That was available only in America. There, everything worked."

Nothing worked in Africa, in the huge continent with millions of people and a wealth of resources—diamonds in the south, oil in the east, and copper in the south and north. The place has green fields and lush land, but life is convoluted. When people wake up in the morning, they are told that there is no water, hot or cold; ninety percent of the population bathes and drinks from contaminated lakes and rivers; if one dares to stroll on the narrow streets, one hundred people obstruct the way, begging for anything. People find themselves giving them what they did not need—pennies, nickels, cigarette butts, and tattered cloth. You go to work with people who have been drinking their pains away the night before. Some sleep on the job. Others spread themselves on dirty grass in the back. Some are caught vomiting in the bathroom. Most are filled with despair, but it is difficult to help them.

They tell stories about their daughters who are mothers and grandmothers at sixteen. Some desire to save some of those kids, but do not know how. Only God can save Africa.

"I must stop," said I.

Neil cut in and said, "I see what you see; and I hear what you hear. Look at the bright side. Our school is trying to make a difference. It is a drop in the bucket, but it is a big drop. We are building for the future. One school now. Hundreds a few years from now. Come on. Let's go the Beach."

So we did. The blazing tropical sun was in full bloom. The earth filled the landscape like fire. Everything felt and looked hot. There sat hundreds of bodies, black and white. Neil and I were the latest arrivals. One was white. The other black. We two lay in the sun, contemplating the heavens, imagining the generosity and perfect in-telligence who created all those things around them, the birds that flew over our heads; the sharks who appeared and disappeared from the surface of the ocean to check the space above them; the myriad forms of beings on the ocean floor, the waves, the blue water that stirred our eyes.

I put on my straw hat and fell asleep. Neil was tanning his skin, which was rapidly turning into red brick. He faced the sun from all directions. First he faced it directly, and then he turned to the left, and then to the right, back up again, to face it squarely. He rolled his body and the sun gently baked it. He was colored everywhere, his hands, his legs, his chest, his shoulders, down to his fingernails. He became black, burned by the sun.

"this is how one becomes black," Neil mused.

I was invaded with dreams while baking there with hundreds of sun-burnt bodies. I saw a young African boy, in his early twenties walking alone in a wooded area. I was listening to the forest singing, to a fast flowing river making thunderous sounds, to the collec-

197

tive sound of thousands of birds crying, screeching, as if they were famished, and there was nothing to feed on. I stood in the middle of the forest looking everywhere, searching for an answer to a question that I had carried on my chest for years. I had come to this corner of Africa hoping to find an answer to my condition, wondering whether I was a man in a woman's form or a woman in a man's form. I looked up, as if responding to a call; I looked down searching for something that I had lost; I turned back answering a call; I turned to the left and stretched my hands to grasp a being that had swiftly run by. I stopped to collect myself. I was briefly lost, and I knew it too.

The boy was tall, thin like a feather, without an ounce of fat, with narrow slanted eyes and a small but powerful-looking head. He was by African standards what they call handsome. The animals in the forest observed him, wondering why he was there, alone, without any apparent purpose. They knew that he was not a hunter, for he had no guns, knives, or deadly sticks. He was bare, naked, without protection. But he looked protected. There was no fear in his face, only questions. He had come to the forest to think, to find a solution to his loneliness. He was not married. He had never had a woman friend. He was married to a dream, to an ideal. He wanted to be the champion of the poor. He had founded a school for them and wanted to live as long as it would take to make it the best school in Africa, to set an example for those who would come after him.

I woke up from my dream. Neil noticed that I had just woken up. He told me that a couple of times he saw me smiling in my sleep, and that he had never seen me so peaceful, so happy, like a baby. I said,

"Oh yes. I just saw myself in a dream, a beautiful dream"

We collected our things and headed towards home, for both of us had to teach the next day. Each went his own way, towards home. I walked towards the east and Neil towards the west. It was early evening. A constellation of stars brightened our path as we walked the mile from the beach to town. There was a full moon competing with the billions of stars, which were clamoring for human attention. We walked past huts, tin houses, and the meandering dwellings of prostitutes, presenting themselves for a quarter a night. We thanked them all. We passed through the full spread of the town and saw the black and white quarters, as they were then called. Mist and fog hemmed in the little houses in the black quarter. We were both a bit warm because of the gin we shared. The black quarter was dark without street lamps. We were literally walking in the dark. The gin had helped us both to be distracted from the dangerous condition. We could hear prostitutes screaming, elders reminiscing in front of their plastic houses. We could only hear without seeing. The black town was either mourning the dead or burying them in the middle of the night, with candles in their hands. There, human life was cheap. No one knew when people were born or how, why and when they died.

Soon we arrived in the white quarter. There we could see but not hear. The residents were inside their mansions. Only a few sat on porches smoking cigars with drinks between their white hands. The white town was rich, rich in light, in food and drinks, rich in lush and green fields. The houses were inside huge gates, which one can enter only if one is white. Street lamps light the paved streets. Chauffeurs, gardeners, butlers, cooks, and doormen welcomed the residents as they came and left the mansions.

The cooks prepared the food, the butler served the drinks, and the gardener tended to the garden for the master's pleasure. They worked and the master managed. The white town was always celebrating life—the birth of a child, a birthday party, a wedding, a ball. Life was celebrated.

The first year anniversary of the school was celebrated at the country's most expensive hotel. The black town was always mourning. Women in black dress. Men with black ties. Funeral services on the streets. Wailing, crying, black men and women walked all day long in the blazing sum.

Every dignitary in town and even the President came. Entrance to this event, a benefit party for the school was $1,000. There were 1,000 people who came to see and be seen. Neil could not believe his eyes, the sight of the wealth, the show-offs, the opulence, the dresses and the suits, the dinner itself; the conversations, he told me, "blew my mind."

This was the wealthy smell of Africa. At the door, doormen also dressed in silk, welcomed guests who emerged from limousines. The ladies were escorted by attendants to the very table reserved for them. Five hundred women were welcomed by men who sat them on velvet sofas. Inside the men flaunted their $3000 suits, their silk neckties, their leather shoes, their cuff links, and wool socks; the women wore designer clothes, attempting to outwit and outsmart one other. The older wives hated the appearance of the younger ones; the younger resented the youngest. Their husbands played the women against each other with their eyes. The womens' eyes traveled with the womanizing eyes of their husbands. The young ones harassed the older ones by staring at their husbands. The waiters came to every table and took orders. Some of the guests discreetly gave the waiters their private keys to their special bars, where they had some of the oldest drinks in the world, from which they ordered. They would only accept drinks from them. Everything else was snubbed. The others concocted accents with which to order their drinks. They tried to outdo the French and the English, with matchless accents. Those who waited on them were amused. Some laughed when they went back to pick up the drinks. They laughed their lungs out at the behavior of the "native elite," each and everyone of whom was raised in the native quarters, and were then hand-picked by the settlers to move to the settlers' quarters.

The fact that they so quickly forgot their roots did not sit well with Neil. I, a student of Frantz Fanon, already knew of this phenomenon and found myself simply witnessing what I had read about in his *The Wretched of the Earth*, the definitive text on colonialism.

Dinner consisted of fifty local dishes. The dishes were divided into hot, very hot and moderate; they were also separated into meat, poultry, and fish. The vegetable dishes were by themselves. Raw meat and fish were also lined up on a different table, as appetizers. The dinner lasted four hours, with the chats and breaks in between. The constant flow of drinks prolonged the dinner even more. Nobody complained. Not even one person bothered to look at a watch. African time is the absence of the consciousness of time. That evening the African world was disburdened of time. The African world was destabilized, as if it had been drugged.

A few of the guests were visibly drunk; both husbands and wives were a little off. Some were misbehaving, to Neil's utter shock. I was aware of it. In spite of, or perhaps because of, their conditions, a few of the repugnant types began engaging in political conversation. They began attacking the President and his African Socialism. Luckily, the President has already come and gone.

One drunken man was arguing with another man about human nature, contending that socialism is against human nature, that the compassion and kindness that it preaches is against the natural inclination of man, that man is essentially a power-seeking beast with a modicum of reason, and that no socialism is going to change his inclination. He insisted that man was guided by instincts and was a bundle of emotion. His wife, a little embarrassed by his attitude, gently tapped him. He screamed at her and ordered her to "shut up and learn." Neil and I, who sat at the next table, were shaken. Neil wondered if he should get in to the talk, but I discouraged it. The man was apparently a super wealthy donor to many foundations. I decided to play it safe that evening for the sake of the school.

A professor of philosophy lectured at their table on the nature of power. He was telling the table that Malraux, the internationally acclaimed French writer, had declared in *Man's Fate* that the essence of man is anguish. He was wrong, said the philosopher, that his view was too generous to man, that man does not deserve it. Man, for this philosopher, did not suffer. He enjoyed inflicting suffering on others. Man, according to him, willfully raped, attacked, lynched, and burned other human beings. He reminded the people at the table that the character, Chen, in the opening pages of *Man's Fate*, was in full control of himself as he watched a sleeping man, a helpless man, when he pierced him with a knife that passed through the mosquito netting. He did it to please the gods of his choice. It was a calculated move. He had thought about it for years, and then chose the right moment, the night hour, when the man was asleep. He killed a man who could not even defend himself; he caught him in sleep, and then killed him. "Where is the anguish in that?" he asked the group. This time, Neil the philosophy major took him on.

Neil told the professor that the theory of power that he upheld was really a folly. There was no way by which one could tell whether or not killers like Chen regretted their actions, or experienced anguish as Malraux, correctly hisview, argued. Surely, there were certain types, like Chen, who fit that model of deliberative killers.

"For me," said Neil, "Chen is atypical. He does not belong to the general human fold. Even a character like Chen could be educated to restrain that killer instinct. All of us have these killer instincts in us. Freud called it *Thanatos*, the death instinct," informed Neil. "Chen does not surprise me, as he seems to do to you. The professor put his hands around his mouth. My eyes were intensely focusing. He listened to every word carefully, so did I, and the entire group of academic types who congregated around that table. After a long silence, the professor said,

"You are an optimist Mr. Neil. You have faith in the human condition. You see, as a student of history, world events such as slavery, colonialism, and the holocaust, ethnic cleansing in Yugoslavia and Rwanda, have shattered my hope, and I have come to the conclusion that the essence of man is power, more power, and not anguish."

He looked at his watch. It was three o'clock in the morning. He wiped his face, and announced to the group that he was going to leave. He took Neil's number and promised to visit with him at the new school, to continue the discussion. He suggested to him before he left that he read Nietzsche, and Neil said that he had, but that he would follow his suggestion, and re-read him.

People began leaving at five in the morning. Very few were walking normally. Many were leaning on their wives' shoulders, using them as canes. The sober ones were leading the ones blinded by alcohol. Sober men were literally carrying their wives. Only Neil and I, the hosts of the party managed to stay sober. Luckily, we had reserved two rooms at the hotel and did not have to leave the place. We stayed over, and slept until mid-day the next day.

We woke up to a bright day. The sun flooded our rooms. The trees danced, and sent their happy messages to ourrooms. The bees were buzzing, and bustling from flower to flower. The birds were chirping in the middle of a beautiful day.

The unpaved streets were sprawling with people. Everyone in sight had something to sell. Some were nursing sickly onions and overripe tomatoes and sitting on strategic corners. Little children were holding their famished chicken for sale. Young boys were offering shoestrings for pennies. Mothers were advertising their daughters as maids; and fathers were offering their boys as drivers, doormen and gardeners for ten dollars a month. The sights consumed Neil. Often he was repulsed. I, on the other hand, was acclimatized. I was born here. I left for twenty years but felt as if I had never left. I discovered new things wherever I went. I was in the background, socializing Neil to the scene.

...

The next day, Neil decided to sit home and chill out. He sat with a glass of the local beer and his favorite Cuban cigar. Memory hit him. He was taken back to Cambridge, first to Harvard Square, to those sprawling streets where he spent twenty years of his life. He thought of the Café to which he went every single morning, in which he sat alone, absorbed in deep worry in the form of thought. He went there in search of people, having spent the night alone, without anybody to wake up with, to look at, to share his first words with; right next to him he would hear the whispers of love and the joys of love making, when he was alone in that empty room, longing for love, dreaming about sex. All his evenings were spent on painting; this went on for years, without stop. Of course, there were a few women in his life. Nothing ever materialized. (He did not like those who liked him). The only one he really liked, Heidi was in a universe of her own; he could not reach her. She had her own dreams, her own plans. Their paths crossed without intersecting.

He thought of his job, the daunting task of fund-raising for the homeless. How tiring it was to develop those long lists of donors that he had to call, considering his fear of people, his shyness, the endless follow-up calls, and the betrayals at the end. He was not a successful fund-raiser. It was the independence that he liked, the prospect of working alone. That he got from the job. But he could not live on that alone. Frustration ensued. He simply did not know what to do next. He stopped painting. He lost interest. People did not like what he produced, or at least they did not say that they were enthralled by the work. They would die on his paintings. He tried not to care. But he did care about what people thought. Neil longed for recognition. The public did not give it to him. The more he yearned for it, the more cruelly it was denied is how he put it once to me.

Those nights of tears, of sadness, of disappointment visited him this morning. He wondered why he was suddenly afflicted by the mood of sadness. The new setting in his lovely small villa in the out-skirts of the city, where he is sitting, provoked another mood swing; he was put in-the mood of gratitude for a new life, a new beginning, and the dawn of a personal era. The African setting displaced the first dire mood.

The Kangaroos were visiting him, circling around his feet, his legs, and his personal belongings. They so much reminded him of the ducks that he fed along with Heidi on the banks of the Charles in Cambridge. That is when he took his siesta, which he had just learned from the Africans here.

His new home was at the bottom of a valley, a mile away from the school where he taught English and Art, and several miles away from the Dodoma, the capital city. He shook his head to free himself from memory, and his attention was drawn to the sound of the river, the chirping of the birds, the sight of a small snake who zoomed by him, the fox that was chasing cattle, the shepherd that was running after the fox, the fox that was running for its life. As he rocked himself on a hammock that he tied to two huge trees, he took himself to Cambridge and back to his hometown. All of his habits had changed.

Here he wakes up to a flood of light that enters his bedroom every single morning. There are two seasons: a rainy winter with sunny days for three months, and nine months of sunshine. The weather is neither cold nor hot. It could simply be described as warm, comfortably warm. His house is modest in size. Two bedrooms, one for himself, the second for guests, a huge living room that had futons in the corners for guests, a sizable dinning room for six, a large modern kitchen and two full bathrooms. The servant's quarters are situated at the back of the house. The gardener, the maid, the chauffeur each has a bedroom. All three share a kitchen and a bathroom.

My backyard is very large. There I have a hammock, which directly overlooks a river and thickets of huge trees and dense green vege-tation. When I wake up, I open the shutters. That is how the maid knows I am up. I take my morning shower, then go to the dining room, where my breakfast waits for me. To my side are five local papers that I glance at every morning. I spend about an hour on breakfast, planning the day and reading the papers. It is exactly seven o'clock by then. I dress very modestly but neatly in ten minutes. The chauffeur waits for me at the door, and off I go to school. By nine o'clock my working day starts. The first person I meet at the Faculty Club is Neil, full of smiles. We embrace each other everyday, as if we have never met before. We briefly exchange notes about our plans for the day. We then go our separate ways. I administer as the director of the school. Neil goes off to teach the whole day., but we meet again for lunch. We go to different places. We preferr local restaurants where they serve actual home-cooked food. Most of the time others join us. Rarely dowe eat alone. Neil loves it when women join us. I am indifferent. He interacts with both sexes with great ease, and always at arm's length. He knows that he has to keep it that way, and he does it just right. No body has ever complained about my aloofness. In fact, people seem to admire me for it. I always say that I learned my sense of professional sense of restraint from my training in western universities, andI never fail to voice my gratitude to those from whom I learned and whom I observed during my long stay in America. Credit should be given to whomever it is due, is what I tell my colleagues, when they discuss the importance of professional behavior.

Even at lunch, Neil observed, I am a professional. When he goes, he is transformed. He laughs with abandon, drinks excessively, lets himself go, and never discusses school matters. He even manages to avoid that topic when he is a bit drunk. "Work takes place at work, and play takes place outside of the work place" is an ethic of his. He follows that self-originated philosophy of work like the Bible.

Neil and I have two totally different philosophies of work. For Neil work itself is play; for me work is not play. This topic came up once for discussion at lunch in the company of other colleagues. Neil was in a rare mood to talk on a Friday afternoon, when the group was relaxing in the tropical sun, after school was dismissed early in the afternoon. Neil said,

"In the West, where I grew up, Time dictates our existence. People are slaves of time, measured by that clock out there. Our existence on this planet is marked by time. Our age determines our prospects. Our careers are decided by what we wish to be at a particular time. We have marked responsibilities for people all the way from the age of one to forty. Kids are expected to perform and get awards for them all the way from Kindergarten to old age. If you do not land a job by the age of forty, you are doomed. You will be put on welfare, or you will end up cleaning peoples' homes. You see, it's rough out there. There is time for everything. You cannot leave things to chance and prayer. "

The Africans in the group were puzzled. They could not believe what they heard.

I broke in reluctantly. I do not like "essentializing" cultures, but I felt compelled as a student of culture to speak for Africans. I said,

"For native Africans, particularly for the people of the land, existence dictates time. It is the direct opposite of the western view.

"Life is here is like a lottery. Those who should not be rich are rich, and those who should not be poor are poor. The poor resign to their condition, and the rich get richer, and the rich think that the poor deserve their poverty. The rich go to church, they pray. One wonders what they pray for. Surely, they never say that they do not deserve what they have. Most of them did not get rich through hard work. They simply inherit what was not properly theirs. The poor have nothing to inherit. For them time is a curse. They live for the day, and they are not afraid of death. For the rich, time is a luxury. They live it thoughtlessly. They do not go beyond planning for their kins. The nation is a burden for them. Corruption and greed are ways of life. Planning for the future is foreign to them."

Neil was intensley focusing at the other Africans. He was dying to hear their views. None of them opened their mouths. The discussion was strictly between Neil and me.

Neil was going to say something, before he could; I was called to the phone. I was told that there was a family tragedy in the village, so I had to leave. I told Neil, and Neil insisted on going with me. My aunt had passed away the night before, and hundreds of people were gathered inside and outside the compound to pay their respects. Some relatives had come on foot from far away places. They had walked between thirty and fifty miles in a blazing heat. The close relatives have brought sheep, goats and cows with them, which they slaughtered on the premises to feed the guests. Many families cooked meat, lentil and a variety of vegetable dishes at home and

206

brought them sizzling hot to be served to the guests. Others brought beer, whisky, local wine and a plethora of soft drinks on their backs or on the shoulders and the tired hands of their maids. The poets prepared speeches remembering the deceased. They addressed her kindness, her love of the poor, her religiosity, and her courage in truth telling. They sang her praises, and told stories about her. A common theme was that she was a genuine friend of the poor, that she shared her wealth with her relatives, and whomever was brought to her house. Whoever came to the house was fed three times a day, and when necessary, the person would be given food to take home to feed an entire family. The very needy would leave with cash to pay their debts; the homeless ones would be encouraged to stay in the house until better days came. She took pride in helping the poor and enormously enjoyed listening to their stories, humbled by their courage to live to the bitter end.

The poets and soothsayers were beside themselves. Their stories brought tears to everybody's eyes. Food was served. Drinks were provided. Music flowed the whole night. At the end of the day, many stayed over and slept in the tents. There too the deceased was a subject of remembrance. This mourning lasted for the entire month.

On our way home Neil told me that if he must die, he preferred to die here, where his life on Earth would mean something for people. He told me that he did not want to die in Cambridge, and that he wanted to remain here to the very end, that he wanted to share his life with his students, with those for whom the little that he can offer means much more than he ever imagined.

***

One day Neil felt the need to paint. He had not felt that way for the past five years. The mood struck him during one of his visits to the villages when he saw a woman in a black tattered dress nursing an anxious baby inside a dimly little shack. Her thin upper body rested on a long neck, sickly thin, bulging eyes; she was struggling to feed a baby with her soggy, drooping, malnourished breasts unsuccessfully. The wrinkles on her face gave her the body of a sixty-year-old; the presence of a few old months old baby could only put her in the category of a childbearing woman aged-twenty and above. No one could have guessed her age, not even Neil who studied every detail of her presence, for the sake of the painting.

There she sat with a sad expression, looking down past the head of the baby, squeezing her dry breasts. The baby was screaming, and pain-racked to suck milk. There was none. All that one could see was a hungry baby, scratching his mother's breasts in despair. The mother did not know what to do. She had nothing to give.

Without her noticing, Neil took a quick but concentrated sketch of her with the baby. He gave the background a dark green field full of famished trees, without leaves, and brittle stems on the verge of collapsing. The tall black woman with a long face, tears flowing down her cheeks, past her neck, and spread on her breasts, was telling the baby that both of them will have to die; there was no food for either.

Neil called the piece "African Pain."

A few days later, he went to the richer part of town, and caught young girls playing on the grass with total abandon. He asked one of them to pose for him. The painting depicted an effervescent fourteen-year old gazing at the tropical sun and looking far into the horizon, as if she is seeing her bright future. Wearing braids in blue, yellow and green tied to snail shells at the end, her large round eyes, her small mouth with snow-white teeth smiled at the world, expressing pride and gratitude in her Africanness.

Both of us were entranced. I told Neil that what was remarkable about "African Pain" was the unadulterated effort by which he captured the depth of the mother's sadness and the despair of the hungry baby, who must have starved to death. At the other extreme was the joy and hope in the young African girl, which he appropriately called "African Hope."

I noted that I liked the juxtapositions of pain and hope in the African world. "African Pain" and "African Hope" were exhibited all over the continent. They were finally given a home in a national museum. They are a part of a modern African treasure.

I woke very early one morning and invited Neil to meet me at the house, to experience an African morning. We met and walked on a meandering country road.

The wind blew gently across our light bodies. The village was

208

Teodros Kiros

deeply asleep. Silence engulfed the scene. Raindrops had left their marks on the trees. A few raindrops fell on our noses and ears. The church bell rang softly, leaving echoes that lasted for several minutes; Muslims were being invited to prayer; cattle were being shepherded to grasslands; beautiful butterflies rested on Neil and Nyrere's bodies, shoulders, their arms, and their ears as morning strollers carried them far away.

A few times, Neil was uncharacteristically overcome by joy and stood in the middle of the road to inhale the cool breeze and ended up taking his shirt off and wrapping himself with the gentle wind. I did the same.

After a while, I said, "This is the beauty of Africa, the birth place of our human ancestors."

Neil put his arm around me , and profusely thanked me for bringing him to this land, in which he wished to age and die. He made sure to let me know that this was the place where he would like to be buried.

As the weather became progressively warmer, we decided to head to the beach.

Marriage of Dreams

The great day had arrived. The conference on Emerging African's schools was in full swing. Ethiopia in 1990. The African sun was in Ethiopia that day. It was forecast that Addis was going to witness one full month of extraordinary days. Of course, amid famines and poverty, the Almighty had given Ethiopians the most extraordinary weather. Almost every single day is beautiful in Ethiopia. Sunny days, and when the rains come, the whole city is covered by lush, green, with roses and tulips on the side streets, and hundreds of items for sale on the roads and streets of the great Addis.

As expected, the conference attracted Africa's greatest educators in the Humanities and the Sciences, with novelists, painters and artists leading the way. Among the dignitaries were the founders of a major school, on its way of blending with a new university in Tanzania. Of course I was there with the American, Neil, who describes himself as "American by birth and Tanzanian by choice. "

To my great pride, and through the efforts of a friend, the African

209

world was also introduced to Adowa, the emerging leading African expert on the Biological Self. There were fifty papers. Among them the three panelists chosen were Neil and Adowa and I, who were introduced to the audience as the emerging voices of the continent. I was the first to speak on the necessity of educating the African mind.

I said that education is the nerve center of being. Moral education in particular is a task, an indispensable task for the liberation of the continent. The major thinkers of the world, chief among them the Egyptian priests, who in turn educated the Greek mind emphasized the necessity of organizing the self through the mediation of thought. Thought, these major thinkers argued, is the organizer of the moral self; it is the organizing principle of life itself. The uneducated self could be rich, courageous, and lucky and much else, but that which contributes to its moral organization is thought, critical, undiscriminating and disciplined thought.

The organization of the self cannot happen without an organizing power, self-sufficient and humble enough to submit to guidance by the Transcendent, the origin of origins, the horizon of horizons, the perspective of perspectives, the whole that is a part and the part which is a whole. A vigilant openness towards Being is the beginning of education, and the fulfillment of the commands of Being is the end of education. Being commands and beings obey, not blindly but intelligently, not slavishly but freely, not sluggishly but with moral alertness.

The Heart is the seat of thinking, particularly, moral thinking. It is in the heart that great decisions percolate. When the blood flows to the body, so does thought, in the form of thought impulses, which flow with the blood. Movement is what propels thought, what makes the blood flow. The heart is the moral educator of the self. We must therefore listen to the heart, before and after we act, before, because thoughts wants to originate, and after, because thought has originated, and a choice has to be made.

The Egyptians, and following them the master thinker Aristotle, made the Heart the seat of thinking, because they knew that nothing great is accomplished without the heart's task, the task of teaching the citizen dreamer, to transform the world by engaging our moral

210

reasoning, our duty. It is the task of the African entrepreneur in particular to make the dream of founding new schools and new universities in the heart of the continent a reality.

Our ancestries left for us the alphabet, the pyramids, the churches and obelisk, which continue to be the wonders of the world, and we modern Africans should cease to be beggars. We must strive to give to the world. Our ancestors were not beggars. They were inventors and fighters. We must rejuvenate that culture of originating, that culture of inventing souls and hearts.

I appeal to the wealthy and powerful to give so that the model school that I and Neil constructed from nothing could be reproduced elsewhere in the continent.

As I finished, I saw the first row Adowa, next to Neil, and they could not stop clapping, moved by the Tanzanian who wore a simple white shirt and dark pants, and brought the audience to its feet with his "brilliance and his simplicity," wrote a reporter the next day.

In the meantime, the city of Addis was celebrating St. Michaels's day. The cattle were grazing, and Ethiopians were dancing with abandon, eating and praying on the narrow streets and the wide Bole Avenue, Addis' choicest avenue. It was decided that lunch would be served at the majestic Hilton, a few blocks away from the *African Union*. Adowa, Neil and I sat at the same table with Ali the host of the event. The Hilton dished out its choicest offerings on a lavish buffet, consisting of thirty kinds of Ethiopian cooking, from the hottest, through the mildest, and coldest dishes. Ali introduced the guests. Characteristically shy, except on the podium, I rose from my chair to greet Adowa. From the very second my eyes rested on hers, for the second time, having not seen her for the last three months, something changed in my body, and I shook my body, as if to free it from the invasion of Eros. I had not been with a woman for two years, married to my ideal. My companions have been books and speeches across the continent, with many eyes falling in love, and I struggling to cleanse myself of the power of Eros. Eros, I once told a friend, is a curse, except for the blessed few, for the rest, including myself, it is a source of suffering, because it does not last long, and when it is gone, you have memory to fight against.

I told the friend that I am now happily married to an ideal, a project, a life-time work, that will be finished in the grave, and perhaps beyond it, at the Creators table, where I can finally rejoice for a work well done while on Earth, guided by ideals, seeking to transform reality, the reality of the African condition. I was thinking of Adowa while I was visited by the hands of Eros, when this beautiful mind from Ghana sat across from me, examining my soul, and she herself, fighting memory, the memory of the other man, inside her, containing, her mood for a new love, the love of a mind this time, the love of an ideal. She took many secret looks at me, through lonely eyes, eyes fighting against love, by a new love. She looked outside. Then looked at this tall Tanzanian man, thin like a feather, wiry body, born for fearless thought. She nervously looked outside, but not for long. Eros would pressure her to look at the man in front of her, looking at the ceiling. Neil caught us both looking at each other, and he smiled.

I did the same. I wanted to remain a virgin, free from Eros. Eros was about to win, but lucky for both of us, the lunch was over, and we returned to the conference hall, and Neil ascended to the podium, and spoke on African Art.

He was introduced by Ali as "an American by birth and a Tanzanian by choice." He wore a colorful dashiki, a local trouser and a leather sandal, which matched his skin color perfectly. It was a scene to remember. And he felt it too. The African audience was respectful and anxious to hear his words. He was not an "other" in their eyes, but an intimate analyst of the African condition, as an observer and a humble participant in African pain and African joy. He had already painted those two contending realities that are now part of African visual pleasure. But this time he has come to speak on an African matter, the duty of the African Artist, of whom he is one.

"African Art," he said,

"is a unique art, a uniqueness imposed on it by the tragedies and triumphs of the African situation."

The moment he said that Wole Soyinka, Chinua Achebe and Ama Aidoo, who were the guests of honor, together, rose and clapped, and the audience roared.

"Yes," he repeated, "African art is indeed unique. The African artist does not simply write, because she could; the African playwright does not write because he is gifted; the African story teller does not tell brilliant stories because she is skilled; no the African Artist must write because she must educate the African public about its own treasures buried in African reality, the reality of pain and joy, hope and hopelessness, wealth and poverty. It is the juxtapositions of these realities which impose on the artist, the duty of writing, painting and singing. The African condition has politicized African sensibilities. African art is destined to be socially relevant and politically vigilant. African art is not autonomous and cannot remain indifferent to the African condition. African Art must speak truth to power. " He paused. The audience roared again. Neil was sweating and said.

"The African artist writes with purpose and characteristic lucidity and accessibility. The African artist must perform her task to be understood and to be followed by the generations to come. Art, in the African situation, is an educator, a transformer, and a reporter. The artist must report what is, and imagine what could be. The African artist cannot afford to be neither irrelevant or irresponsible. She must be relevant, lucid, responsible and visionary."

It was a short but powerful piece accompanied by slides of African art that is being produced in the continent as an illustration of the present, and a projection for the future. The audience consumed the slides with great interest and much appreciation. Several panels examined many other educational themes.

Shortly before dinner, it was Adowa's turn to come to the podium. Shy and self-contained, she impressed the audience with her youth and beauty. After several seconds of preparation, she opened her mouth and gave a tantalizing image of the African body and the future African Science. There was a remarkable marriage of ideal between her paper and mine. The papers sounded as if they were precise distillations of ideas that these two minds have worked on for years. Of course that was not the case. These two souls met on African soil for the first time. There was a gap of twenty years between them. One in her thirties and the other one pushing sixty. But the two of them met at that tangent where reality encounters truth, and truth cuts through age, time and space, and speaks justice to truth and truth to justice.

Adowa addressed herself to the situation of the human body,

with a particular focus of the African body, men and women, young and old. She argued that the African body suffers because African men and women are not being taught to know their bodies, so as to take care of them, to the best of their ability, with the aid of the African Scientist. It is imperative, she contended, that Africans are given free education in the Sciences at all levels of their existence. And drawing on my paper and Neil's paper, she concluded, literacy and African Art will blend in a perfect harmony to complete the education of the African mind.

The knowledge of the Biological self is a project that is bound to last for centuries, if the ground work of the production of the African Scientific Mind is done in this generation. The applause for the paper was even louder that the first two. The talk lasted for one hour, with illustrative tails of pain. She spoke at length about Aster, the Ethiopian whom she met there two years ago, who died at the hands of an abusive ex-husband. She brought the audience to tears with this tale of sorrow and the defeat of the African woman in the hands of African male ignorance and insensitivity. She told the tale coolly and dispassionately, and many in the audience could not help but listen to an African woman speaking about the rights and abuses of her sisters across the continent.

Thus, the conference was closed with her paper. I invited her that evening for dinner at a local bar, after I knew that she was departing in just one week, and may not have time for me beyond that evening. And I was gravely mistaken about that. After that evening, we met every day and every evening for the entire week. It was as if we wanted to stretch that week by using every second of it to one year and more, so that our hearts could justify what I had planned to do.

Upon meeting her for the second time in less than a year, I had already made up my mind to lock my hands with hers, through an engagement ring, which I dreamt, she would accept. She said yes, and accepted my ring on a Saturday evening, on her way to the U.S. to wrap up her dissertation at Harvard, and to return to Tanzania a year later.

When she returned home and opened her mail box, she found a letter from Elias' mother Rosa. She opened it immediately, and two

214

lines later, she read that Elias had killed himself, and declared his love for her, with painstaking details of the ambiguity of his life, and his bitterness about his forty years on this earth.

Her trip of joy was juxtaposed with the visit of pain, which is a theme of the human situation, and the seriousness of existence. She immediately wrote her first letter to me and told me, among other things, about what she encountered on arriving home.

She did not leave her apartment for one whole week. She devoted that time to grief, to the memory of her only encounter with a sensitive soul, who died without knowing who he was and what he wanted from life.